Heart, Be at Peace

www.penguin.co.uk

Heart, Be at Peace

DONAL RYAN

doubleday

TRANSWORLD PUBLISHERS
Penguin Random House, One Embassy Gardens,
8 Viaduct Gardens, London SW11 7BW
www.penguin.co.uk

Transworld is part of the Penguin Random House group of companies
whose addresses can be found at global.penguinrandomhouse.com

Penguin
Random House
UK

First published in Great Britain in 2024 by Doubleday
an imprint of Transworld Publishers

A CIP catalogue record for this book
is available from the British Library.

ISBNs
9780857525239 (hb)
9781529940138 (tpb)

Typeset in 11/15.5pt Electra LT Std by Jouve (UK), Milton Keynes
Printed and bound in Great Britain by Clays Ltd, Elcograf S.p.A.

The authorized representative in the EEA is Penguin Random House Ireland,
Morrison Chambers, 32 Nassau Street, Dublin D02 YH68.

Penguin Random House is committed to a sustainable
future for our business, our readers and our planet. This book
is made from Forest Stewardship Council® certified paper.

To Lucy Ryan, with love, infinite.
Oh, the places you'll go.

We make no wonder of the rising and the setting of the sun which we see every day; and yet there is nothing in the universe more beautiful or more worthy of wonder.

Gerald of Wales, *The History and Topography of Ireland*

Bobby

I SIT AWHILE some evenings by my mother-in-law's bed, and I watch her sleep. Triona doesn't know I come here to the hospice on my own. It's on my way home from the sites in Limerick, though, and I can't pass without tipping in for a few minutes just. It'd feel wrong to drive past, even though I know that she'll have Triona later in the evening and a parade of neighbours in from the parish. There's something soothing about this place in a strange kind of way.

Now and again Marjorie wakes for a few seconds and she always smiles at me and says, Hello, Bobby. I feel a foolish kind of happiness that she always knows me. They have her on heavy drugs in here and she hardly even knows Triona sometimes, but my name she always gets right. Her brother was here a few days ago, and every time he spoke she looked at him and asked, Who have I in it? And he started to get upset, and nearly a bit panicky for a finish, saying, It's me, Marjorie, it's Liam, how don't you know me? Then he started sniffing a bit and making things uncomfortable so I told him to go on away and get a cup of tea for himself. He knew by me not to argue. Triona gave me a funny look but she said nothing.

There was a yahoo here last week in a stripy tracksuit causing awful trouble for the nurses downstairs. He was coming in to see his mother-in-law, too. I heard him down outside below Marjorie's window roaring in at his wife, Tell your mother I love her. The security guards were standing near him and one of them was saying, We told you, Willy, you can't be coming around here pissed and upsetting people, and still you keep doing it. The other security guard had a foreign accent, Slavic I'd say. He reminded me an awful lot of a fella I knew one time.

Willy Boy was still below when I was leaving. He had the sliding doorway blocked and there was a man behind him wanting to get in and an old couple inside waiting to get out but Willy was having none of it. He was holding tough in the doorway, squaring up. That fuzzing started in my head at the sight and the sound of him, and at the look of fear on the faces of the people around him, those good people, just being decent, carrying their sadness around quietly; that feeling like my ears and eyes were being strained by something in my brain, being pushed out against the edges of themselves. That's been happening me a lot lately. When things go wrong on a job or when Seanie Shaper is mouthing, or dropping sly hints about what happened on his brother's stag, or when my lad Rob is playing a match and the ref acts the prick. I don't know if that's always happened me and I just didn't notice. I'm way more aware these days of the things my body is doing.

I walked out past the security guards and one of them made shapes to get me to wait but he thought better of it and just stood watching. Willy dropped his hands and stepped back out of my way at the sliding doors and he was all manners and apologies, *sorry, sir, sorry, sorry*. He never for a second expected my left elbow to meet his throat the way it did. I don't know if he even knew what was after hitting him when he was lying on the concrete between the ambulance bay and the step of the door with his two hands up under his chin and a raspy kind of a wail coming out of him. I got him right on the windpipe. A sneaky shot, in fairness. All he deserved.

I took one look back on the way to my van and I could see the security guards looking down at Willy and Willy still flailing for air in a puddle on the ground and the people who had been trapped by Willy's tantrum were walking out past him, giving him a wide berth, holding on to one another for comfort. I hate to see old people frightened like that, and for no reason beyond a gobshite not being able to conduct himself like a man is supposed to. As if the world isn't hard enough a place for them already.

The old boy looked at me as I drove past. He had one hand on his wife's back, guiding her gently along the path, and he raised his other hand to me, and he nodded and sort of smiled, a sad kind of knowing smile it was, and I winked at him. The peace I felt driving home, you wouldn't believe. I'm not like my father was. I'm not.

THERE'S THIS THING that happens me now nearly every day. It feels like a stab of something in my middle, not pain exactly, just a kind of a force that takes the air out of me so that I have to stop what I'm doing for a few seconds until it passes. It only comes on me when I let my thoughts drift. It feels like all the things I'm worried about come together in one ball and the ball fires itself at me and hits me right in the centre of myself. Someone putting their hand on Erin. A car pulling up alongside her and her being dragged into it. Rob getting bullied. Or showing off the way boys do, climbing something, falling. Getting dropped off his team. Triona getting sick. And the dealers never leave my mind. It's nearly two years since I started seeing them. Penrose, Pitts, Braden, Dowel. They're always, always on my mind. Triona is obsessed with them and every time I see Augie Penrose's blacked-out Audi little bursts of light flash at the edges of my vision and something prickles and itches on my skin.

I got a good trick from the internet. This four-seven-eight breathing thing. It actually kind of works. I breathe in for four beats, hold it for seven, and exhale for eight. I feel things settling on the exhale, slowing and regularizing, my heart calming.

AS IF THE list wasn't long enough. I don't know in the fuck why I went on Seanie Shaper's brother's stag. I thought I had to, I suppose. Colum is a good skin, and I thought the lads would think I was a dry balls if I didn't go, and I suppose I am Seanie's oldest friend, and he was best man, organizing everything. I used to escape to their house years ago when my father was on the warpath, and I was always welcome there, and Seanie never once mentioned the shite my auld lad had our house in, smashing the place to bits when his bad temper came on him and that rage overtook him.

Seanie only ever opened the door to me with no questions asked, only How ya, Bobby, and he always made room for me beside him at their dinner table, the whole wild clan of them in a raggedy circle, all shouting and laughing and fighting over food, and his auld lad seemed like a kind of a king to me, smiling around at them, proud of all his handiwork, of his lovely red-faced queen of a wife, of his brimming table and the noisy fruit of their years of love. It's a wonder how Seanie is such a sneaky low-down rat bastard with all the love he was given.

I still can't believe how slow I was about the whole thing, how long it took me to cop what was going on. Seanie was like a dog with me when I left the WhatsApp group for the stag. I left the Sunday night that we got back and the next day was the May bank holiday and when I met him the Tuesday morning he had a puss on him. You left the group, did you? I said I did, why wouldn't I? The stag was over. He said he thought we'd all stay in it until after the wedding at least. I told him then that was a quare idea. Weddings are women's business, I told him. There was no need for men to be discussing them high up or low down. And anyway, I said, I couldn't listen to the fucking thing dinging non-stop, morning, noon and night, and only ever shite on it when I looked at it. He was bulling all that day; he hardly once looked at me, except to throw the odd sly dig here and there, always being careful not to go too far. Seanie is tasty enough in fairness, but still he's nervous of me. He knows never to get too smart.

Mobile phones are the greatest curse that was ever

visited on man. I'll never forget the feeling I got when I turned mine on a few days after I left the group and saw that I had a text from Seanie, and I opened the text with Triona sitting across from me and Rob sitting beside me eating his cereal and my lovely Erin walking behind me searching for something in her schoolbag. I sat there looking down at myself stepping out through that big heavy black-framed door with the one in the picture window beside me, blowing a kiss from her hand towards me, and only her black knickers on her and that tiny black see-through bra. And a smile on my face like a schoolboy after coming from the castle field at lunchtime. There was one word with the text, in capitals. GOAT. I thought at first of a billy goat, a puck, a ram, a creature bred to reproduce. Then I remembered that Rob and his pals were always referring to lads that did well at things as goats. Greatest Of All Time. That's what Seanie was calling me. Out of one side of his mouth he was calling me that, and out of the other he was showing me that he had power over me now. He was threatening me.

I remembered the rest of it then. It came back in a boiling flood. I think I said, Oh, Jesus! out loud. Triona asked what was wrong and Rob looked over and I don't know how much he saw of what was on the screen of my phone but he said fuck-all. I was dizzy from the force of the sudden remembering. The drags I took from one of those little dark tight-rolled joints that Rory Slattery bought in the café. The small glasses of sweet clear liquor we threw back, two, three, four in a row. The feeling of being outside myself, watching myself acting the yahoo around the streets, roaring out of me, singing along with the boys, all sorts of stupid songs mixed together and we only really knowing the choruses,

LAST NIGHT AS I LAY DREEEAMING, IN THE VAAALLEEEY OF SLIEEEEVE NA MOOON, SOME SAY THE DIVIL IS DEAD AND BURIED IN KILLARNEY, MORE SAY HE ROSE AGAIN AND JOINED THE BRITISH ARMY, and tangling here and there with groups of English lads who threw some shapes but backed off again fairly quick, and feeling like I could do anything, like I could take on anyone, and slapping all the lads on the back and telling them they were great lads, that I loved them, and buying round after round, insisting in every bar on paying for every round, the boss man, the Big I Am. And then getting to the row of streets where girls stood nearly naked in windows, smiling, beckoning, and Seanie pushing me in the door of one of them, saying, My treat, Bob, my treat, and the boys all shouting, Go on, Bobby, hahaha, aboy Bob, and sitting inside the square room on the edge of a low hard bed with a dark-haired girl who smiled at me and called me baby, and kissed my ear and went to open my

Jesus.

I drove over to his house. Réaltín was coming out the driveway as I turned in. She smiled up at me from the driver's seat of her little Mazda, the two-seater that torments Seanie so much. He doesn't trust her in it, he says. She turns into someone else when she drives it. I smiled back at her and she told me he was just left, he mustn't have known I was collecting him. I wasn't meant to be, I said. But we're going the same way today and I thought I'd save him the diesel. She winked at me before she drove off. I didn't like that wink. There was something conspiratorial about it. I knew then that she knew. Seanie as sure as God had shown her the photo and he had her told what I did in Amsterdam.

I don't know how I didn't write off the van and myself with it on the road out to Monsea that morning, but I met Seanie as he was going in the door of the house we were doing and I dragged him by the back of his shirt out along the yard and I pushed him in between the side of his own van and the high straight hedge that divided the house from the house next door and I held him up against the van with my forearm against his throat and he was fucking smiling at me. I'll kill you, Seanie, I said, over and over again. I'll fucking kill you. And he just kept smiling at me, and then I heard a voice saying, Dad, what's going on?

And Dylan was there, the poor boy, looking in at us from the corner of his father's van. I'd forgotten he was doing a few days a week with Seanie, just carrying bits, painting skirting boards, sweeping and tightening up, collecting cuts and that. He's a lovely boy. He's a small bit younger than my Rob but they're great pals. They both hurl under-fourteen because we're short of players and Dylan is tall and tough like his old man, no bother to him to mix it with the older lads. Seanie started laughing then and telling Dylan we were only messing and I did my level best to dampen down the madness in myself and to laugh along.

Dylan didn't believe a bit of it. He's smart like his mother. Later on that day I met him in the yard on the way to the back of Seanie's van carrying a sander. I reached to take it out of his hands just to have a reason to stand him up for a minute and I said to him, You know, son, me and your father are friends since we were children, the very same as you and Rob, and he's the closest thing I have to a brother. And brothers fight, even when they're very close. Maybe even more so when they're close.

Poor Dylan looked embarrassed. He scratched the ground with the toe of his boot and he looked to the left and the right of me and up into the sky and anywhere but straight at me, and I saw Seanie then in the doorway, lurking like always, the creeping Jesus, and he nodded at me, and I nodded back.

That evening as we were packing up he said to me, in a low voice, kind of flat and serious, I have that picture deleted. And I never sent it to anyone, only you. And I just nodded again because I couldn't trust myself to talk.

IMAGINE IF TRIONA knew what I'd done. If only I could find the words and the way to tell her the truth of what happened. This then would all be over and I'd be one worry lighter. I know well that rat bastard Shaper still has that photo. But whatever about that, there's a lie now between me and her. If I could just tell her. That I lost the run of myself in drink and whatever else. That I was acting the big man, trying to impress the lads, that I was as high as a kite, that Seanie must have slipped me something, that Seanie was slagging me, egging me on, that it was all Seanie, that I only sat on the girl's bed awhile, that she put her hand on me but I stopped her, that she left her hand then on top of my hand and said words I could hardly hear over the roar of blood in my ears. How could I explain why I went into that room and why I came out pretending I was after doing something I didn't do at all? How could I explain to her how it felt when I saw the look in Rory Slattery's eyes, and young Brian Walsh's eyes, and in Colum Shanahan's eyes, behind the laughter and the cheering, that strange look almost of weariness, that I was just another disappointment to them after all, that I was just like any other dirty auld bastard with two balls and half a brain?

I WAS SURE I was dying a couple of years ago. I went to the toilet and there was a smear of blood on the tissue. I looked into the bowl then and there were streaks all through it. I took a photo the way I could look up the internet and compare. I was convinced within a minute that I was for the high road. I was worried and relieved in equal measure. I had to think awhile about the relief, why I felt it. Things would be settled. The mortgage would be paid; Triona would have a good lump sum from the life insurance; I could maybe even see it out for a few years so Rob and Erin would be nearly reared and they wouldn't miss me too much. And it'd all be over. What'd be over? I didn't know then and I still don't know.

The day the doctor stuck his finger into me and had a good old root around and told me I had piles, to eat more fibre, I was afraid to speak. I could feel my eyes filling with tears. He's not the most demonstrative of men. He doesn't seem to like sick people. I only went to him because he's not a talker or a shaper and he always sorted the children when they were babies, white and pukey and as hot as hell with those bastard bugs that all kids get. I remember him looking at me and his face all red, scratching his jowls in embarrassment. Maybe you should talk to somebody, Bobby, he said. Things well up in men. You wouldn't believe the difference it can make. Just to let someone know, you know, how you feel.

He gave me a card and I took it and I sat in the van looking at it for ages with my phone in my hand before I tore it up.

TRIONA GETS UPSET sometimes at the thought of Rob and Erin being out on their own. Inside in town with their pals, or even just down in the village, hanging around the pump or the yellow bridge. She frets and holds her phone in her hand, looking down at it every second they're out of the house. They're dealing right there on the street inside in Nenagh, she says. They're out here in the village, too. You can order drugs by text and they'll deliver to your door. There's children being sold drugs. Everyone knows who's doing it, too. She gets breathless talking about it. What if Erin or Rob were ever stupid enough to take something? There's no knowing what goes on in their closed-off private lives, on their phones and in their little tight groups, out at the yellow bridge or inside in town when they go in on a Saturday on the bus. There's nothing to do in town except hang around the streets. We used to have the arcade at least but that's a gambling den now, full of foreigners losing their wages. There no pool tables or video games any more. She works herself into a state and it's all I can do to keep her from driving into town looking for Augie Penrose and his sidekicks, and God only knows what she thinks she'd do.

I OFTEN FIND myself, at the oddest of times, just before I fall asleep, maybe, or sitting by Marjorie's bedside, lost in close and quiet consideration of terminal violence. It brings me a strange but welcome peace. I used to do the very same thing with my auld lad years ago. I used to sit there in the cottage looking at him, and imagine myself killing him, God forgive me. I imagined it so vividly and so often that when Jim Gildea asked me straight out did I kill him I answered that I didn't know. I don't know, Jim. And I didn't, at the time.

I only know one murderer and he committed his solitary crime nearly by accident. He's not really a murderer at all, in fairness. He got done for voluntary manslaughter. He pleaded guilty. He nodded, he said the word, and he hung his head, and I nearly shouted out to him, Don't fuckin worry about it. He killed my father all right, much the same way I'd considered doing the job myself. I visited him in prison a few times and I've put some of our overflow work his way since he got out a few years ago and we'd be friends if it wasn't for the awkward thing between us. I couldn't exactly ask him how it feels to kill someone.

I pull up sometimes beside Augie Penrose's black Audi when he's parked near the cinema in Summerhill with his partner Pitts beside him and his two little archangels Braden and Dowel in the back and I look down at him and he looks back at me from under the peak of his Chicago Bulls cap and I imagine myself pulling him out of the Audi right there and beating him to death in the middle of the street. Or resting the sawn-off barrels of a side-by-side on my left forearm and letting the four of them have it. One round for the front and one for the back, a heavy lead pellet, good spread. I could do the time. It'd be an ease.

Whenever I need to calm myself I breathe in for four beats of my heart, and I hold it for seven, and I breathe out

for eight, and I imagine myself standing over Augie Penrose's body while his blood pools around my feet and flows
in a stream to the waters of the lake. I imagine Triona standing at the shore, watching, the wind lifting her hair gently.
In my imagination, she smiles. She's happy with me, her
man. I've done right by her, by my family.

I'm not the same as my father was at all. I'm way, way
worse than him.

Josie

I WAS STANDING here at this window the very same way as I am now the day my son Pokey walked into the yard the bones of three years ago. He was after getting a bus from Shannon Airport. He was halfway across from the gate before I recognized him. His hair was longer and he was tanned brown and he had a big bag up on his back like a hill-walker or one of those adventurous tourists. In the first moment of recognizing him I felt relief, plain and simple. He was back and he was safe and I could talk to him again, try again to make amends, and to get him to make things right somehow for all the people he'd wronged. Then in the second moment that old crossness came back. Before the poor boy even made it as far as the front door I had him forgiven and unforgiven, welcomed and unwelcomed; before a word passed between us I was giving off to him, roaring at him silently, Where were you, you ungrateful lying bastard, you broke your mother's heart, where were you when she was dying, where were you when she died, where were you?

But I said none of that when finally he landed in the door and stood with his hands hanging, looking at me, his auld man. I leaned heavy on my stick and I reached one hand out to steady myself on the edge of the dining table. I could see him looking at the stick in my right hand and the shake in my left hand, and I could hear the whirs and clicks inside his brain, the gleeful whisper. The auld fella is banjaxed. He's on the way out. I'll fall in for the house now, or a share of it at least. I had him judged like that, imagine, before he had even one word spoken.

I got back the use of myself after the shock of his appearance and I stepped in closer to get a proper look at him. He was hunched in the shadow of the archway of the kitchen, dressed like a schoolchild, in a running suit. Still he hadn't spoken and nor had I, and the clock struck one in the hallway and I said, Lunchtime. Just that. Then I said, Are you hungry, son? And he nodded and I could see then how tired he looked, and that he had tears in his eyes, and they were threatening to spill out onto his face, and he said, Thanks, Dad. And the seven years of absence seemed like nothing all at once, like a dream that faded with the morning light.

He asked me all about his mother, my Eileen. If she'd suffered much. I told him no, she went gently enough. By the time they found the shadows on her lungs at the end of that summer four years ago it was too late and she knew if she gave battle it would be in vain. I remembered that he loved mustard, and that he preferred white bread, and that he only ever had a bare skim of butter on one slice and none on the other. I had good ham in the fridge and fresh bread, like always. I gave him sugar in his tea, two spoons of it, the way he always had it years ago. I used always to give out to him over it, telling him it was a woman's way of drinking tea, white with milk and poisoned with sugar.

He was hungry. He hardly left a crumb, God help us. I brought him over a cut of tart then. This was bought in a shop, I told him. It won't be anything like your mother's. He frightened the life out of me with the sound he made all of a sudden, a long high moan that cut through the air and seemed to shake everything; my eyes blurred at the sound of it and the walls of my ears vibrated. And he shook and he shook and shook with the sobs and I sat looking at him and I could easily have reached my hand across to him. I could have stood up and gone to him and put my two arms around him. But I just sat there, looking, embarrassed, wishing he'd go away again and leave me be. God forgive me.

IT WAS FINE, though, for a good long while. We rubbed along grand. He's great fun sometimes. Watching television with him is very funny, especially the news. Some waffler will appear on the screen and he'll say, Watch this prick! Listen to the shite out of him! And he'll take off whoever it is then to a T, making up all sorts of rubbish. He's as good as your man they always have on *The Late Late Show* any day.

His brother Eamonn was pure delighted to see him home, of course. They were always great pals as children and they slipped with ease back into their old comradeship. Eamonn is a secondary-school principal now inside in Limerick. He's a great lad. He's a couple of years older than

Pokey but he was always stone mad about him, even when Pokey was acting out, and jealous of Eamonn, because I always favoured Eamonn and I couldn't hide it no matter how hard I tried.

Some evenings their sister Mags calls over with her wife, Ger, and Eamonn's wife and kids come in and we all have dinner and we talk about Eileen and what she might be saying about things in the news or the goings-on in the parish, and we roar laughing at the memory of the way she used to react to things, the way she could cut through the foolishness and fakery of people like a scorched blade, and Pokey imitates his mother, but in a gentle way, kind of reverent, and it's like having her back for a little while, back among us, making sure we're all okay, even and we breaking her heart over and over again with all our auld grudges and sourness and silence.

Pokey went down to Bobby Mahon shortly after he came home. He shook the man's hand and told him he was sorry about the way things had gone. Bobby was grand about it, he told me. Why wouldn't he be? There wasn't a fear in the world of Bobby Mahon. Once he had his father buried and that man from the city pleaded guilty to murdering poor old Frank, Lord rest him, Bobby started into retro-fitting and extensions and attic conversions and he wasn't a half-hour idle since. As far as Bobby Mahon was concerned Pokey was just a fella he used to work for who'd scarpered to the Costa, leaving him and the rest of his crew high and dry with a few weeks' wages unpaid and no social insurance paid in, but all those knots were long untangled and Bobby knew there was no point in refusing Pokey's apologies, fulsome, abject or otherwise.

SO EVERYTHING WAS grand. Pokey had a friend from Malta or one of those quare places who was living down near the lake, just back from the foreshore, in one of those big low houses that was built on a foundation of bribes and bullshit back in the eighties. You can see the long roof of it from my front yard. The Maltese lad was after starting up a language school inside in the city. He wanted Pokey to manage it for him. He explained it all to me one evening. It's a licence to print money, Dad, he said. He knows I hate that kind of auld foolish talk, the suggestion that a man can defy the balancing of the simple equation that has effort on the one side and reward on the other. That's what landed us in the shite the last time.

Anyway, I let him off because he looked so animated and so happy and what he was saying actually made sense. The country is crawling with foreigners, he said. And most of them have only a bare few words of English. They're all mad to learn English. And also, if someone from outside the EU wants to get a visa to work here they can get one no bother if they're enrolled as a student. So we do a lovely package deal. Four grand, all in. That's a year's tuition and a stamp on their visa and they can work twenty hours a week in term time and forty outside term time. They learn English, and we have courses in computers, bookkeeping, you name it.

He had it sold to me. Even Eamonn told me it all seemed sound. I went in one evening to see the place. Up above a shopping centre, nearly a whole floor. The classrooms were all empty but that was because classes were finished for the day, he said. The place was sparkling. Pokey had a dark suit on him and a man with a beard and a briefcase called him Mr Burke as he was passing and I saluted him back, presuming him to be addressing me. Pokey roared laughing. I'm the new Mr Burke, Dad, he said. And I felt a taste of the old resentment seeping back for a second. Little shit. But it was gone again just as quick.

MY DAUGHTER MAGS has a beautiful way of putting things. She's a civil engineer but she could have been anything. The mind she has, you wouldn't believe. And when she's telling you something she always makes it interesting. There's a kind of an ease to her knowingness, not like some people, who'll beat you on the brow with what they know or think they know, and they usually only having half a story, or something half-baked they saw on the computer or read off of their phone. She's not one bit afraid of anyone, either. Signs on I suppose, she had to fight for everything.

And she had to fight me the hardest, God forgive me. The disgust I felt at having a lesbian for a daughter, the shame of it. All the jokes we used to shout to each other across the muck of the building sites years ago were now on me. I was the butt of every yarn about bull dykes and strapped-on tackle and every filthy drunken story in the world about people's private things, their predilections, their natures. Anyway, I got past it. Eileen made me promise before she died. I was to leave my door open for Pokey no matter what, and I was to remind myself each day how much I loved my daughter, my Maggie, my beautiful little Margaret, who made a daisy chain so long one time that neighbours walked the road up to see it, stretched across from the haggard gate to the trunk of the second oak, a hundred yards and back again. I was to ask for her forgiveness and I was to earn it.

Name of God, Eileen, I said, you're not asking much. She looked hard at me then as weak as she was and she smacked the back of my hand sharply in warning and she said, I'm not asking you, Joseph Burke. I'm telling you what you have to do, what you have to have done before again we meet.

Anyway, as for my daughter's way of explaining the world, of directing me gently to the truth of myself: Phoebus was the god of light, she said, he was the sun, and his son was Phaeton. I interrupted her straight away. There's only one God, and He's the God of all things! She told me to shut up if I wanted to hear the story. It's about you and Pokey, Dad. It was written for ye two fools thousands of years ago. Go on, I said, and she sniffed at me and I sniffed back at her, but I settled myself all the same for the pleasure of listening to her that she has inculcated in me with the years, ever since she relaxed into the truth of herself, and I did too.

Every day Phoebus drove his chariot, drawn by a team of winged horses, from the stable by his palace into the skies, across the mid-heaven and down the far side. It was this daily journey that lit and warmed the universe and kept all things in balance. The horses were mighty and incalcitrant; they bucked sometimes and tested the limits of the god's strength, and it was all he could do to keep them on their proper arc across the firmament. Even Jupiter, the god of gods, couldn't tame the beasts that drew the sun across the sky.

Phaeton was the son of Phoebus but he had no trust in his father's love, or in his acceptance of his parenthood. He asked his father to grant him one wish to prove that he was the father he purported to be, and Phoebus swore by the Stygian marsh that he would, and such a vow could not be reneged upon. Phaeton's wish was to take the reins of his father's chariot, and to drive the winged horses across the vault of the heavens, rising the sun and setting it again.

Phoebus, hamstrung by his vow, begged his boy to reconsider his request. Anything but that, he said. Phoebus knew the son was incapable of the father's job. They were too different. And sure enough, bold Phaeton pushed ahead with his foolishness, eager to feel at his fingers the power of the god, to exercise control over the fabled horses, to be responsible for the dawn and the day and the setting sun. His father warned him of the dangers in the heavens, the scorpion and the bull and the crab, and the fiery mettle of his horses, their unwillingness to submit to any hand but his.

As Phoebus knew it would, it all went wrong. Phaeton lost control long before the zenith, and the horses bolted across the firmament, dropping so low that they dried the oceans and scorched the fertile earth to barrenness. Jupiter for a finish put paid to the chariot and its young driver with a thunderbolt, and the horses stampeded on until they had no breath left, and they came to rest on the charred, cracked, lifeless earth. Phaeton's mother Clymene searched until she found her poor son's bones, and Phoebus lashed his rage against his horses' sorry hides and against his fellow gods in congress. Failure doesn't merit destruction, he roared in the face of Jupiter, the god of gods who'd killed his son, the boy whose wishes had transcended his mortal limits.

By God, I said, when Mags finished her story. This was shortly after Pokey had landed back after his seven years in the wilderness. That's a good one. And I was a long time getting to sleep that night, only finally closing my eyes with the light of dawn behind the blinds.

I DON'T KNOW in the hell why I was so surprised when they came to the door. A man in shirtsleeves and a woman with dark hair. Pretty but cross-looking. One of those professional-type women I usually can't bear. They asked me was I Joseph Burke and I said I was; then they asked me was I a director of a company called something or other, trading as Elite Colleges, and I recognized the name. No, I said, but my son Pokey, I mean Seán Pól, works for that company, inside in Limerick. But I could feel a weakening in my voice and in my body as I spoke. I could feel the certainty rising up inside me, filling every part of me, gushing from my stomach to my lungs in a bitter acid wave. The two at the door looked worried about me. Sorry, sir, the man said. We should maybe go inside if that's okay? We won't take much of your time but we need to just ask you a few questions.

So they sat me down, those two, and I gave them nothing for the first few minutes. I kept my powder dry. I remembered the revenue men and the welfare inspectors the last time I tangled with them, ten years ago, and the way I used to bawl them out of it on every one of their many visits, accusing them of victimizing me, and telling them they were no-good parasites, sucking the taxpayer dry with their big government jobs and if it wasn't for the likes of business people like me who had built the country up from the bare soil they wouldn't have an arse in their trousers or a bean on their plate. Pokey left me to deal with it all those times but this time at least he was near by. I rang him and he said he'd be home straight away, and I believed him. The city is only a half an hour away. I gave the two a cup of tea each and told them that my son would be able to answer all their questions, but still they came at me all barrels blazing.

Why were there nearly two thousand students enrolled in a college that occupied a single premises with capacity for one hundred and ninety? Why, on any of the several occasions of their unannounced visits to the college, were there no classes in session? How did they come to enrol students exclusively from Bangladesh? Their list of questions went on in that way for a long time and I was able to give no answers except to say over and over that Pokey, I mean Seán Pól, would be able to answer when he got home. But they kept telling me that unfortunately that was no good, that I was listed with the Companies Registration Office as the company director, and they wouldn't be able to speak to anyone else about it unless that person was officially registered as my agent. They had a form that had to be filled out for that purpose. When eventually Pokey arrived, well over an hour after I rang him, he was all smiles. I barely looked at him but I told him he was to sign the form and answer the people's questions. I said nothing to him about why was I listed as director of his friend's company. I left him to it.

I swear, Dad, he kept saying afterwards. I swear to you we had this conversation. You were sitting right there and I said to you I needed a name of someone who had never been bankrupt to use for the paperwork for the college. And technically you were never bankrupt because you had the company signed over to me when it went bust. How can you not remember? He kept at it and at it and I was so bamboozled for a finish that I nearly believed him. I think I actually did believe him. What about his Maltese friend? Oh, he was just the money man, really, and he wasn't legally domiciled in Ireland so he couldn't be a director. It was only paperwork. Just to cut through the red tape. You know how it is, Dad.

I surprised myself then with the loudness of my shout. Where are all the Bangladeshis? Ah, Jesus, Dad, come on. You're in this world longer than me. The letter of the law is what counts, not the spirit. He explained then exactly how the whole thing worked. How his mate did all the recruiting abroad out foreign in Bangladesh. How the people he got over to Ireland on the stamp-two visas were being saved from the sweatshops and the paddy fields, from disease and starvation. How this work was the only thing he was ever proud of in his life. How he felt a duty to every man and woman who arrived into that college. How there were plenty of classes being run at any given time and the door was always open, and some of the classes were held remotely, and the jobs they were doing in their allotted weekly twenty hours were good jobs and necessary, but you couldn't get Irish people to do them, or even Eastern Europeans, these days. They all wanted forty grand minimum and never to have to exert themselves. I had to give him that, in fairness. He drove away again then in that brand-new BMW with the low burbly exhaust that sounds like the exhalations of eight cylinders at least but I was afraid to ask if it was or not. How in the name of God could anyone afford to buy and run a V8 car in this day and age?

I GOT THAT question answered for me just this minute. After I chose to believe him about his reasons for naming me as a director of the company, and to believe him about the pen-pushers' vendetta against him and against all the language schools that operated within the law but, okay, maybe up against the edges of it at times, and I resigned myself to the notion that I was responsible for the way he always flew by the seat of his pants because it was the way I'd always operated myself, truth be told, and here I am, after coming across a stack of brown boxes in the corner of the small shed while I was looking for shears to cut back a thorny branch from the trellis of my roses. Out of curiosity I lifted the loose seal from the top one and looked into it. And I looked and looked at the neatly packed bags of powder until I finally realized what I was seeing, what my boy's business really was. And I felt the same bolt of thunder that the sun god had felt when his wild son was hurled from the sky.

Lily

I WAS A witch by training and a whore by inclination. Bride Cranty was mistress of my long apprenticeship as a witch, though we never used the word. Nor did we ever see ourselves as such. The title was attached to us by people hereabouts for their own ease. The whoring I learned myself as I went along. Bride was from Travellers out of Galway, but she settled here and she loved this place. She caught roots, somehow, is how she put it to me. She married Jeremiah Cranty at a young age and he an old man but by God did she love him, and the son she bore him, Michael. Mickey Briars as he's known. I see Mickey passing down the Lake Road most days. He's fierce busy in himself these times, fierce occupied, whatever's going on. There's no knowing with that man. He's a hard read, even for me, and he's one of the few men in the world I have regard for. We go back a long way, Mickey and me, back to our childhoods.

The pain I used to be in is nearly fully gone. I did my damnedest to cure myself and I wasn't able. But Bride had me well told that that was how it would always be. You can't turn magic inwards, girl, she'd say. No matter how much you want to. But it'll find its way back around to you all the same. What you put into the universe you will have to take back, in some form or other. That's why it's so important always to be judicious, wise with it, and fair.

So my pain was taken away by the hand of a doctor. A lovely man out in Croom in County Limerick. My son Hughie took me out there shortly after we made up. He got me in through his own GP and he filled out rakes of forms for me to get a medical card and everything. Even the strap of a wife gave a hand. I suppose she was afraid I'd cost them anything. She has her eye on this cottage, of course. Why wouldn't she, I suppose. What about it.

The hospital out in Croom used to be a workhouse long ago. I could feel a creeping on my skin all the time I was there, and I could hear carried through the ether of the place distant whispers and cries, moans of anguish. I could hear them even when I was inside in the man's office and admiring his lovely silvery hair, the way he had it combed beautiful back from his forehead, and the fine strong line of his jaw. I could feel the cold waves of their suffering washing through time and breaking over me.

When the kind gentle man was finished examining me he held my two hands in his across his big wide desk and he said, in his lovely soft voice, giving care to every word, You know, Lily, there's no need for you to be in the pain you're in. And I started to get upset in spite of myself. I'm not sure was it his kindness, or the warmth of his hands, or the joy of his promise to take away my pain. I nearly told him about the bottle I have at home, way in at the back of my cupboard, with the preparation inside in it that Bride Cranty taught me to make if ever I need it, if ever I suffered a pain I couldn't bear. I've been drawn to that bottle before. I've held it in my hands and I've held it to my lips and I've breathed in its bitter fumes but I've always retightened the cap of it and hidden it away from my sight again.

WE MADE UP over my granddaughter, my son and his wife and me. Not that there was anything to make up, really, except time. Millicent, her name is. What a name they gave her. Lord, if you saw her. The long legs of her and the blue eyes and the shine off of her like the sun on the water of the lake. She started calling down here to me of her own accord, and she defied Hughie and the wife even though I gave her no encouragement, and I told her plain and straight that she wasn't to go against her mother and father on my account or for any reason. I could see so much of myself in her that it was frightening at first. I had to force myself to come around to living with the fear, that feeling of being overwhelmed by a terrible mixture of love and worry. The world is a more dangerous place now for a young girl than ever it was before, for all the so-called progress.

The parents followed her down here one day. They suspected her of some devilment, going off by herself, and wanted to satisfy themselves that she was safe. It was the first time in I don't know how many years that Hughie spoke a word to me. I don't even know rightly why he turned so sour against me in the first place. Even the day we buried his brother John-John he was only barely civil to me. And my heart smashed to smithereens. For all the hatred that John-John showed me, I loved him, God, I loved him. Maybe that's why Hughie was so sour. My poor John-John. To think of him lying dead on the floor of a dingy flat above a chip shop inside in Limerick city with his skin pulled tight across his precious bones and hardly a vein left in his body. And the law practice of his brother Gerald, my youngest lad, only three or four doors down from his foul resting place. Isn't it a fright to God all the same the way things work out?

That was when my Millicent came to know me, and she took a fierce shine to me. I think maybe it was a way of acting out at the start, a way of defying her mother and father, of spiting them. That's what young ones do once the madness starts coursing through them. It's a dangerous place in a person's life, that shadowy path between child-hood and adulthood, and it's pocked and hexed with all sorts of traps and trials. She's seventeen now, my Millicent, and she thinks she's a woman but she's not, except in her shape.

She began walking down here from the village on her own, or cycling some days. I don't know which frightened me more, the walking or the cycling. Any kind of an animal could grab a hold of her and she walking and carry her off in a car or the back of a van. And she could be killed stone dead off of a bicycle, the speed some of them do around here, especially the blow-ins with the big houses and the jeeps. The first day she came she stood smiling at that door there and I knew her straight away, though I'd only laid my eyes on her properly once before. She had in one of her hands a bunch of wildflowers and in the other she had a box of chocolates. Dairy Milk. They're my favourites, I told her. You're only saying that, she said, and I said I wasn't, and she laughed her sweet laugh and that was it, she had my heart. We made little of that box of chocolates between us and she talked and talked to me, the words flooded out of her, and I felt like I was in a dream, the kind of dream you never want to wake from.

She doesn't only talk, she listens, too. Not that I have much to say. Most of the things about me I couldn't well tell her. We walk the river callaghs some days looking for wild garlic and dock leaves and sorrel and we collect bramble leaves and wild strawberries and whatever else might be in season and in bloom and she asks me about my life, and what her father was like when he was small, and she really listens to my answers and sometimes when I lie she turns her face to me and I can see in the depths of the blue of her eyes that she knows well I'm lying, or changing things around or dressing them up for her benefit. Stop, Granny, she says, and she smiles, and I know then that she understands the truth of me better than anyone. Better than my own mother, or Bride Cranty my dear old friend, rest well, you blessed women.

I told Millicent she should learn to drive and we'll see about getting her a little car for herself. You'll need it next year if you go into the university in Limerick, I tell her. But she rolled her eyes at me and said, Granny, why would I need a car? Augie drops me everywhere! Augie. I couldn't sleep for a fortnight after that started up. He's a ratty-looking fucker. There's a coldness off of him. He drops her there at the end of the boreen and I saw him once or twice pulling her back into the car after her trying to get out and I couldn't make out then what was going on because he has the windows of his car all blacked out. I can't for the life of me figure out what draws her to him. But I can't talk, I suppose, when I think of the way I handed over my heart to Bernie McDermott, Lord have mercy on his tattered soul, the only man I ever loved, and he one half of a gorilla and one half of a bull and two ends of a bastard. Isn't it a curse the way it was that weakness was passed down from me to her, that malady that overtakes some women and not others, that strange blindness?

He's one of the Penroses from the bungalows out the Ashdown Road. I couldn't warn her off of him. I knew she'd choose him over me and I couldn't bear that. God forgive me, how was I such a coward? How was I so lax in my duty to the child of my child? The Penroses are the sorriest pack of mangy dogs that ever pissed against a tree. His uncle has only one leg because he had the other one shot off of him by Paddy Rourke years ago in revenge for a terrible beating he gave to Paddy's godson. Right there inside in the village at the pump. The poor godson was shot then by the guards only a few months later, and he a grown man but with the innocence of a babe. May the angels smile on him.

WHEN I SHOWED Millicent my money she was quiet for a good long while. Where did you get all that, Granny? I couldn't very well tell her the exact provenance of my riches, the men who called to me in desperate need, and the women who called to me in desperation also, wanting to know was there something they could eat or drink to take away the burden of their worry. But I gave her as close a story to the truth as I could, and she accepted it. I sold spells to people, I told her, and cures.

Spells? Her eyes were wide and her little nose twitched. Yes, I said. I used to give people spells for all sorts of things. For love and for babies and for luck with getting jobs and things like that. They worked too, but only because the people who came to me wanted them to work so badly. The spells were only little rhymes and pouches of dried leaves and sets of instructions for times and places to incant and cast them, and they were magical only in as far as the person believed they were, because belief itself is a kind of magic. You can do things that seem impossible if you believe truly and with your whole heart.

I kept my money in tidy bundles in a leather bag at the bottom of the same cupboard where I always kept the makings of my spells and cures. There was the best part of a hundred thousand euros in that bag. The trouble I had to go through the time years ago of the changeover from the old money you wouldn't believe. The way the smart ones sniffed at me inside in the bank in Limerick. I didn't want the Nenagh ones to see what I had. You never know the tongue that will betray you. But they made a fuss and a favour of it inside in the city, wanting to know would I not like to open an account and deposit the cash. I had to threaten them with that fella on the radio that people ring when they're wronged before they agreed to do it for me, but I had to wait for a week while they ordered the money, they said. A bank, having to order money, I ask you. And I had to go away on the Kavanagh's bus again, and carry home the worth of my life's work in an old leather bag.

I told my Millicent that every single euro in that bag was

for her if she wanted it. I told her I had it saved up for her uncle John-John in case he ever came good and needed a fresh start, and for her father in case he ever needed a dig-out, and for her other uncle in case his good weather ever broke, and for her aunties in England, if ever they got properly back in touch and were in need. But now they all seemed to have their lives worked out, even my daughters beyond, by all accounts, and John-John, my beautiful man, was at rest at last, and so the money was going to pass by default to my precious gift of a granddaughter, who had brought me a new life the day she arrived at my door.

Millicent started crying then, like a small child, and she leaned herself into my arms and I held her close against me and I smelt the sweetness of her skin and hair and felt the feather brush of her eyelashes against my cheek and the whole universe seemed in that moment not to exist, to have no form or function outside of my little sitting room, beyond the heat and the weight of her precious body next to mine.

I SHOULD HAVE known what would happen. Some months later she asked me could she have a spell that would fasten Augie to her for ever. No, I said. No, no, no. And she got wicked vexed and I couldn't believe the sounds that came out of her, the words she said to me. I forgave her, of course, even before she was finished her litany of abuses. She quietened a bit to draw her breath, and I explained to her again that the spells weren't real magic, that the power of them was already inside the people who wanted them, the spells just allowed them the use of it, that the magic was in their faith that the magic would work, and she screamed at me then, That's what I want, Granny, that's what I want, to have faith that he'll always love me, that he'll never leave me. I can't bear the thought of losing him, of some other bitch touching him. He's MINE, Granny, he's mine.

She was like a wild animal, like a vixen with her teeth and claws set to savage any predator that threatened her litter, and she was yowling and keening the very same as a creature of the night, and then she was down on the floor curled up into herself, sobbing. My heart broke but still I said, No. My magic is realer than I made out to her, but I couldn't leave this world knowing I'd bound my beautiful child to that dark boy.

I wasn't surprised when I came in from the forest and found my door open and the wood of it splintered and my leather bag gone from the back of the cupboard, and all my potions spilled and smashed across the flags of my floor. And the only bottle left unbroken is the one whose contents Bride Cranty instructed me so carefully in the making of, and my fingers I think will just about have the strength to loosen its cap after all these long and painful and wondrous years.

Vasya

THIS SUMMER IS clement and dry and the lake has kept its level but when the river raged last year the waters rose and I was forced to strike my camp and move back from the shore. Back, back across all of these fields to the road and across it and into the low hills. It was harder to find a sheltered place there and the rain was falling hard so I pitched my tent by a hawthorn tree in the corner of a field in long grass, and hoped not to be noticed. The foreshore of the lake is commonage and so is the land of the hills but I hadn't climbed high enough and early the next morning when I rose from my tent a man was standing there with a face of stone and a gun resting in the crook of his arm. It's many years since I saw a gun being held that way, cradled like a small child or newborn beast, and I watched and watched for movement, waiting for its muzzle to lift and its dark eye to find me.

The man spoke then. Are you going to cause me trouble? I shook my head. He stepped back, slowly, and I could see that he was old. He was stiff and deliberate in his movements, as though his joints were seized and painful. On the grass beside his feet was a plastic bag and it was full but I didn't know what it held. He nodded down at it and said, You can have that if it's any good to you. And he nodded then back downhill towards the long tiled roof of a house nestled in the valley that was hollowed from the earth of the hill we stood on and the one that opposed it, and said, That's my house and outhouses. Don't go near them. Do you understand? I said I did and he was gone.

The bag contained bread and slices of cooked meat wrapped in silver paper and apples and bananas and a cold carton of milk. I'd planned on walking to the village and buying food with the last of my summer fruit-picking money but now I was able to save it and live two days or maybe three on the stranger's generosity. Before the rations ran out he returned with another bag and this time he was unarmed. My wife feels terribly sorry for you, he said. There was a set to his features as he spoke and a light in his eyes that told me he was lying. About his wife's compassion or her very existence, I wasn't sure. I could tell by the shift in his features, his probing expression, that he was searching for the truth of me and concealing the truth of himself.

Three more rainy days went by and I sat mostly at the mouth of my small tent in stillness, looking down the hillside through the mist at the grey lake and the thin ribbons of white across its surface, wondering if my grove, my winter home, was still drowned. My fishing rods and tackle were bundled tight and wedged high between two branches of an oak tree. I prayed silently. Father oak, brother oak, my only family, protect them. Imagine if the torrent had washed through the soil and torn my oak tree from the earth! I felt for long moments a terrible fear before I remembered the uselessness of worry, the hollow that fear could open in a man's soul if he allowed it, and I settled myself back into the present moment, into a slowing of my breathing and my blood so that the fat of my body might be preserved.

A week or so of sameness. I had a book, though, a big one, full of stories of battles fought among tribes long dispersed, of heroes and villains and captured maidens and voyages to strange lands, that a man had given me in the train station in Limerick the season before. A man of Khakassia, of my own country. He told me he had translated the book himself from Turkish to Khakas and I had no reason to disbelieve him. This, my friend, is one of only one hundred copies of this book in the world.

A strange thing happened to me suddenly when he said this. I heard clear and ringing true in my head, as loud as if he were standing right beside me in that train station, the voice of a man I once knew called Seanie Shaper. And Seanie was laughing his deep, barrelling laugh and shouting in his sing-song voice, the way he always did when we toiled together all day each day on building sites, Ha ha! Signs on there's only a hundred copies, you, sir! It's SHITE! And in my mind's eye he was standing holding the book open at arm's length in front of himself, and he was saying, Jaysus, pal, there isn't even fuckin *pictures*!

I laughed at the sound of my old friend, the ghostly echo of him saying things he never said, and my countryman looked at me as though I were crazy, and I was crazy, in that moment, slipping a bit into some kind of dotage borne of the oppression of the dank city. I knew then that I had to return to the lake, to where my heart had nestled itself.

SOME MEN CAN lie with such ease that they quickly begin to believe themselves, and so in a way their lies become truth and their sin is expunged. I knew men from Belarus and Armenia and Azerbaijan who changed their nationality with the wind. One day they would be Russian, but in the presence of actual Russians they would become suddenly Slavic, or even Arabic if their complexions would support such a fraud. Or if they were presumed to be of a certain place they would play along with that presumption.

Some of them gained birth certificates, passports, driving licences, all sorts of legal documents that supported their new realities. I knew a chef once who had a wallet filled with identity cards, a dozen or more of them, and on each one he had a different name, a different hairstyle, a different birth date, a different nationality. I envy those men. I wish that I could lie. Honesty is my greatest failing and yet when I try to cast it aside it cleaves to me. This is why I have nothing to identify me, no piece of paper I could take to the office where men are given money to be idle, except one from years ago that has my name spelled wrong and my birth date incorrect, like someone who was too unbothered to ask me just made it up. When I open my mouth with a lie on my tongue I see my mother's eyes and I hear her gentle voice remonstrating. Never lie, my son.

I wonder if my dear mother is alive, and my father. I

wonder if they still roam with our herds across the plains, following the rains, searching always for the best grazing. My father could smell new growth from a hundred miles.

I came to know that I could live off the land and the water. Sometimes in the city when I visit my friends they laugh and call me Vasya the hobo. But I am proud of this intended insult. Why would I not be? There are no shackles on me, and I am beholden to no one. No law binds me but my own, and I have the power to decide and to impose my own morality and to live without sanction for my transgressions except for the punishments I inflict on my own self when I think about the ways I've failed, how I lost my brother, how I wasn't able to save him from himself, how I robbed my dear parents of their joy.

I have no name except the one given me by my father and I have no country except the country that stretches itself from river mouth to river mouth and from the water's edge to the fenced-off land where cattle graze in squares of green grass, the greenest grass in the world it seems, grass that would make my father whistle through his teeth in wonder and joyful expectation of bounty.

MY ODD NEIGHBOUR downhill brought me an old racing bicycle one day, and a pack for my back, and a thin but warm blanket. The bicycle was in good condition, and he gave me spare tubes for the tyres and a kit for repairing them if they burst. These were only lying around below, he said. They used to be my son's. He won't be using them again, I'd say. They might be of some use to you, if you're heading back down to the lake. Isn't that where you came from? And

I said it was. The lake is as good a place as any now to name as a provenance.

The river calmed itself, the lake waters fell, and the earth dried. I returned to the shore a richer man. I cycled downhill with my pack on my back, and my tent rolled tightly into it and my new blanket. It occurred to me then that I had never asked the man his name. All those weeks pitched above his home, benefiting from his strange grudging kindness, and I knew not even that about him, nor he that small thing about me. And I was glad. I felt less beholden to a man who had chosen to keep himself entirely secret from me.

As I wheeled through the sweet breeze down to my stake in this earth, to my fishing, my trapping, my foraging, my secret kingdom of grass and soil and giving waters, I felt a joy I hadn't known since the earliest part of my childhood, when I ran with my brothers and sisters and our dogs behind our mighty king of a father, across the flat plains that we thought were ours alone.

A strange thing happened then. I was reminded of how small this world is, how closed-in this country is, like a bowl containing berries that you can pick up and swirl so that each berry touches each other berry in the space of an instant. I heard a voice one evening coming from behind me, where I sat holding my small pan over the low flames of my campfire. He must have followed the line of my smoke or the smell of my sizzling trout and frying crab apples. Well, fuck me pink, the voice was saying. Fuck me fucking sideways. I stood and turned, and over the low dome of my tent I could see a man standing and pointing at my bicycle where it rested against the trunk of my dear oak. I could see in the evening light through a haze of flies that he was smiling. My fucking bike, he was saying. That is my fucking bike! Just as I began to explain how I came to own the bicycle, he laughed, a thin reedy laugh, like a drunken woman's laugh, or that of a boy on the verge of manhood, and the frequency and pitch of it were familiar to me. I'd heard that high wavering laugh before.

CHAPPY HARA. TOOTING Fuckin Kamoon. Whatever your name is. Long time no see, auld shtock! Vasya, I said. My name is Vasya Afanasiev. Long time no see to you too, Pokey Burke. And I was happy to see him, though I knew him not to be a man of honour or a man of any kind of word. But he had about him always a sense that he might at any moment begin to laugh, or to say something to make you laugh, something idiotic or scything or outrageous, about the shape or the virtue of a woman, or the worth of a man; there was a feeling of a kind of wild freedom about him, of not caring what any man thought of him or what he might do or say.

The parts of this small story began then to come together in my mind. Pokey was the son of the man whose house I had unwittingly camped close to, and whose generosity I had benefited so handsomely from. I had worked for Pokey years before, and for the last months of my labour I had been paid only in promises, and the promises had proven themselves to be of no value.

For all that, I have yielded to Pokey's request that I become a ferryman. He says I'm the only man he can really trust, and the only one with muscle enough for the daily crossings. He says he knows I won't put my hand in the till and that my books will always balance. By this he means that my inventory, taken on the far bank, will match my deposits on this side. While I am his go-between no collusion can take place, no embezzlement.

The shades have their eyes on the roads, he says. The Devil's tongue is sweet and coaxing. I can reconcile these sides of my reality quite easily. As impossible as it is for me to utter a lie, I can form them with abandon inside myself and offer them to myself as a balancing payment in exchange for certain undertakings.

I WILL NEVER open the bulkhead doors at either end of my little deck once I have inventoried my cargo as it's stowed, and committed the figures to memory. I repeat the figures as I row in time with my strokes. The men who work for Pokey on this side of the lake secure the doors anyway with a thick padlock, out of the sight of my eyes, and the shadowy men on the far shore have the other key. I will concern myself only with the safe and timely transport of the boat itself from my tiny crescent of stony bay to the opposing shore, where the bulkheads are opened and the stern and bow emptied and refilled, and I will not engage with the men who act as stevedores beyond the stark pleasantries required by manners. For all I know it could be bags of sugar I am ferrying to the far bank, or sticks of butter, or jewels or dust or the ashes of burned warriors.

When the weather is calm my work is easy, though my shoulders and chest ache sometimes and my feet sting where I push against the stanchion. I've learned more deeply than when I was a mere fisherman to read the moods and movements of the lake, the dip and rise of the clouds of winged creatures, the patterns of the birds that fatten themselves on the flies and crawling things, the abundance or otherwise of darting shoals of tiny fish, the thickness and the temperature of the air and the darkening water. I can sense now the caprices of the water, can tip my oar at its roguery; I can time my voyages to the second so that the dark-eyed men on the far bank have no cause to remonstrate with me or complain about the efficiency of my service.

And at night I can lie beneath my blanket warm and tired, a pleasant kind of tiredness, and listen for the electric buzz of the scooters on the distant towpath, the voices of the youths employed to come in darkness across the callaghs and the high parts of the marsh to the secret dock of the boat of which I am keeper and captain, and to carry its cargo on their backs to a car that I can hear idling in some secret redoubt somewhere along the lake shore. And I wonder if ever I'm captured whether I'll be able to keep myself from speaking the truth, to my captors or to myself, of the foul, thrilling things I'm party to, of the man I've allowed myself to become.

Réaltín

I CAN'T REMEMBER when Dylan stopped looking like Daddy and started to look like Seanie. I suppose there's no way of noticing such gradual change. It wasn't even change, really. He's just growing into himself and he's taking after his father in every way. Except he's nicer. He's a pure dote, so he is. He'd break your heart, the way he takes things on himself. When I roar at Seanie, Dylan reddens up to the tops of his ears and he goes all quiet. I keep telling him this is the way people are, people who live together in the same small space, day in day out for years. They fight and make up and fight again.

He was eight when me and Seanie got married five years ago. The night we got engaged he danced around the sitting room. He kept shouting, Let's go! Let's go! Get in! Yes! Yes! The same kind of celebrations as when Liverpool score a goal or Munster score a try except it went on and on for ages until we ended up just sitting here on the couch, me and Seanie, watching him, laughing, and Seanie was holding my hand and he kept kissing it, kissing the ring he'd just put on my finger.

I kind of can't believe still that he asked me in such an unimaginative way, in the middle of *Pirates of the Caribbean*, completely out of the blue, while I was sitting with my legs on his lap in my old pyjamas, eating a natural yoghurt with blueberries, and my Bridget Jones knickers on me, no bra, no makeup. I hadn't even showered. And all of a sudden he produces this big fuck-off ring inside in a box.

What d'you think of that? he says, holding the box open, and a big cheesy grin on his stupid face. What the fuck is it? I said. Dyl turned around then, and his eyes opened wide and there was no way I could say no. That's probably partly why Seanie didn't bother his arse to use his imagination about the proposal. He needed Dylan's little heart as leverage.

Thank God, though, that he looks so like Seanie. It was literally fifty–fifty whether he was Seanie's or Georgie's, my sleazebag of an old boss. Thank God, thank God. I kept meaning for ages to go to mass to say thanks or something, that my prayers were answered. But things are gone arseways now again so I have less to be thankful for at the moment. Although imagine how happy Daddy would be if I started going to mass with him!

He loves going to mass for some reason. I think he goes nearly every day. He actually lies about the extent of his mass-going, like it's an addiction. I suppose it is in a way, a psychological dependency, stemming from something that was drilled into him as a child, maybe, some fear he had of

damnation or of being out of favour with God, or of someone noticing that he wasn't there or God knows what.

We're all traumatized by our childhood, I think. We all
drag these invisible weights through our lives, some more
than others. Who knows why people do the things they
always do? If people stopped and asked themselves if they
really wanted to do the things they always did, or if there was
something else they actually wanted to do, or to be, the fear
of the truth of themselves would probably be too much. We
all spend half our lives in denial.

I WAS IN denial for a good long while about Seanie. About
his ways being changed. After the kidnapping he was like an
angel. For the two nights that Dylan was gone I was para-
lysed, but Seanie never stopped going: he searched every
field, every outhouse, every copse of trees; he waded along
the edge of the lake; he drove the roads up and down. Then
we got him back. Timmy Hanrahan the simpleton over-
heard two guys talking and told Jim Gildea the sergeant,
and Jim followed them and walked into their apartment and
lifted my baby into his arms and walked back out. One of
them worked in Dylan's crèche as a Montessori teacher. It
was a big story on the news for around a day and a half but
after that no one really gave a fuck. It never made any sense.
No one knew why those two took him or what they wanted.
Turns out the teacher was a fucking schizo, imagine.

Seanie wasn't mad over the two lunatics who took Dylan
or anything. He was just so determined that no harm would
ever come to him again that he turned into this perfect

father, responsible and rational and full of good ideas about how best to share the burden we had between us, and he was never a second late picking him up, and he brought him to matches and to shows and the cinema and pantomimes, and I was so scared by the whole kidnapping thing that I went nearly everywhere with them, and Seanie didn't annoy me one bit, and Daddy was all with the Oh, look how good he is, say nothing now while he's being so good, didn't I tell you that boy would come good? Imagine if he'd known at the time that I wasn't even sure if Seanie was the biological father!

The prick seduced me slowly, without even seeming to try. I started feeling so safe with him, and so respected. For a horny bastard he has a very subtle set of moves. He must really work on his game. Or he used to anyway. He'd nearly have you thinking it was your idea to go up to the bedroom at lunchtime on a Tuesday when you were in the middle of doing the tax returns for Unthanks Bakery. And afterwards he'd be so grateful, like a dog you'd just fed, nuzzling and licking and lying with his head in your lap. All of a sudden he was as good as living here, then he was fully living here, then Dylan was so happy and so used to him, and Daddy was so happy with the whole situation, and starting to say things like, Yerra, would ye not think about tying the auld knot now altogether seeing as ye're living as a family anyway, and I thought for a second he was going to say living in sin, and I was just about to take the face off him. Thank God I didn't. He'll be dead someday and I'll regret every unkind word I ever spoke to him. Imagine, I'll have to live in a world someday that hasn't Daddy in it.

I'D KNOW EXACTLY why Daddy was addicted to mass if I'd finished the psychology course by night in UL, and hadn't switched to accountancy. Or I'd be able to have a more informed stab at explaining it. And I'd be able to psychoanalyse Seanie and his fucking low-down dirty urges. Something to do with some struggle he had in the birth canal as his poor mother suffered to eject him from herself, or some issue around breastfeeding or toilet training or competition for affection or something Jungian or Freudian or Oedipal or something like that. I'd love to have finished that course. But it got too intense after a few months, I started to think too much about myself, about the reasons people do what they do. I nearly started to forgive the scumbags that snatched my baby. One of them wrote a letter to me and Seanie and it was nearly sweet. Seanie put it into the fire after he read it.

The accountancy was the better bet, I know. Daddy was able to help me with it. He still does, thank God. The thrill I feel every time I get a payment notification for a transfer into my account of my fee never wears away. And I love the way Seanie reacts when I get dressed up to meet a client in their business or at their house. I go all out, in fairness. I even put on stockings and suspenders sometimes just to torture him. Really slowly I put them on, really early in the morning, before he leaves. Even if it's hours until my meeting. To give him something to think about. Something to regret. A sweaty minute was all it took him to fuck our marriage up.

I wouldn't mind but your one had a face like a bulldog chewing a scorpion. She had a good body, I suppose. That's all he could fucking see, boobs and arse and opportunity. I can't even think about it. The second he sat back on the sun-lounger I knew there was something wrong. I could fucking smell it off him. The guilt, the acidy sweat of it. And lower down, below the cloud of stinking panicky phero-mones he was emitting, I could smell something rotten, something earthy and familiar and unexpected there, at the poolside of a four-star family hotel on the Costa. And when I looked at him closely I could see that his tongue was flick-ing at his lips, and his eyes were bulging a tiny little bit in their sockets.

That's the beauty and the horror of knowing someone better than they know themselves. I always know he's been up to no good when his face does that, watching porn on his phone or whatever dirty things they do in what they think is privacy. Can you imagine the danger he put me in? If I hadn't rumbled the bastard. They were after having a dirty quickie somewhere inside in the complex. By arrangement or by chance I still don't know, nor do I want to know. I know enough.

He could still have maybe got away with it if your one hadn't sashayed out onto the terrace about a minute after him looking like butter wouldn't melt. The bold bitch looked straight over at him. His stupid tongue flicked out again, like a demented fucking lizard, and he rolled over away from her view, away from his own view of his fuck-up, his unforgivable sin. He thought my eyes were closed behind my sunglasses, I'd say. I stayed still, I barely even breathed, like an animal I stalked him, let him walk himself to his doom.

They'd been flirting all week. I'd let it go. There was another woman there who kept saying stupid things to him at night during the shows when he was walking past their table, like, Oh, I'd cut rashers off of that arse and eat them raw, so I would, and she'd laugh this common shrieky laugh and her husband would smile, all embarrassed, and the other couples would laugh, because that's the way of these places, all the families kind of thrown in together, and everyone's kids swim and do the activities together and you're forced into this weird, intense, temporary friendship group of middle-aged dipso randomers, and so the one who was really flirting with him, silently, with actual intent, it turns out, just with her eyes and her witchy lips, thought she had cover, that no one would notice, but I fucking noticed. I never dreamed he'd do anything, though. Four years married and I actually fucking trusted him. I never dreamed he'd let me down. How stupid am I, knowing him the way I do?

I bluffed him so beautifully I'd have been proud of myself if I'd been able to think about or feel anything beyond the explosions going off inside in my brain. In a real even, normal voice, I said to Dylan to go into the shop and get a bottle of water, and when he was out of earshot I put a hand out and I grabbed Seanie's arm and I dug my nails right into his skin, and I said, I know what you're after doing, Seanie.

He said nothing. He didn't even flinch from the pain he must have been in. There were thin crescents of blood forming where my fingernails were piercing the soft skin of his forearm. You and that one from Dublin with the black hair. I know that you and her are after having it off inside in the hotel. Don't bother denying it, Seanie, it's as plain as the nose on your disgusting face and as true as the sky is blue.

Before he could get his stupid brain into gear to say something back I moved my hand down to the waist of his shorts and I pulled them out and I could see his miserable cheating prick still half stiff from its adventures and his foreskin not settled back in place. Seanie was as still as a statue and as silent. That told me all I needed to know. We were leaving the next day and I left an envelope in Reception just before we got into our taxi with a letter inside in it and an FAO on the front of it for the slapper's poor husband. Will you please put this with those people's passports, I told the girl, and make sure that it's handed to that man and nobody else? Fuck that. Why should my marriage be destroyed and not theirs?

Anyway, I have him told now that he has to leave, as soon as Dylan turns eighteen. He has to take his shit and his shovel and sling his hook. That gives him nearly six years of living here in the lap of luxury in my house. They'll be a hard six years for him, though. I allow him some slack in the rope I have around his neck now and again but as soon as he avails of it I pull back hard and nearly choke him to death. I let him think now and again that there's a chance I'll get over it and I let his hopes rise for a day or two before tearing him back down and stomping all over his spirit and his heart and his confidence.

I never say a word to him when Dylan is around, though. There's no way I'm going to let Seanie's bastard prick do damage to my Dylan's happiness. He worships Seanie, and Seanie adores him, and I can't risk my baby's happiness. I'll probably let Seanie stay after he's eighteen, in all honesty. I'm going to torture him until the day he dies, though. You can take that to the bank.

TRIONA MAHON WAS one of the first people to ring me after I finished my accountancy course and got my cert and put my ad in the *Nenagh Guardian*. I called myself AAA Bookkeeping Services. That way my ad was always first on the list. Great rates, my ad said. Small business/sole trader/limited companies. Tax Specialist. I had to take it out of the paper within a year, I was so full up with clients. I even thought about taking someone on, but who can you trust? Bridget even offered to give me a hand. Ugh. I rang Daddy after she hung up and said, Your girlfriend wants me to give her a job. And poor Daddy was all flustered, trying to pretend he hadn't put her up to it. I bought a lovely garden office that I saw advertised in the back of the *Sunday Times*. A really posh one. Seanie offered to put it up. Fuck off, I told him. Don't go next to or near it. The company will put it up. Don't even look at them while they're doing it. It's got nothing to do with you.

I always do the Mahons' accounts here in the garden office. I used to go over to their house to go through things with Triona, and she was always so good to me and so nice, even though there were all those filthy rumours years ago when I moved here first, about me and Bobby, because he called here a few times to do a few jobs that I wouldn't let Seanie do. She'd often pour us a glass of wine each when we were finished, and I loved being there with her, being kind of like her friend, because there's something so calming about her, the way she carries herself, really confidently but like she doesn't fully know how beautiful she is, with her high cheekbones and her full lips and sculpted chin and smooth forehead and blonde hair always so perfect.

But, of course, like always I felt myself getting sourer

and sourer with every visit to that house, to their kitchen the size of a soccer pitch, and the marble island in the middle of it that you could feed an army at, and the Aga and the chandeliers and the high ceilings and the perfectly chosen tiles and the two living rooms like something out of a magazine, and the exact suite I wanted but couldn't afford in a million years. And worst of all, worse than the feelings of emptiness and envy that their massive detached mansion on the hill gave me when I got back to our little three-bed semi in our estate half full of refugees and Limerick city rejects, is that I know how much money Bobby's business turns over, down to the last cent, and Seanie is there on the list of employees, and I'm their employee too in a way, and Triona Mahon just seems to have everything. Life for her seems so easy; everything about her smells so nice and feels so perfect and calm and right.

When Seanie told me last week he had something to show me, and I wasn't to tell anyone about it, and I was to swear I wouldn't say a word to anyone, especially Triona Mahon, I screamed at him to just fucking show me. He took his time taking out his phone, with that big shit-eating grin that he always has on his face when he thinks he's a great fella, and he showed me the photo on his phone of Bobby, the saint, the great saviour, the martyr, the hero, coming out of a whorehouse like the cat that got the cream, and the whore nearly naked, blowing kisses after him.

I felt such a surge of joy and relief that I nearly kissed Seanie on the lips, I nearly did. Maybe I did. Fuck it if I did. He might even have deserved it. What kind of a bitch am I?

Timmy

MICKEY BRIARS TELLS me the same few stories over and over again. I think sometimes that maybe he's going a small bit daft. They're good stories, though, in fairness to him. I often kind of half close my eyes while he's telling them and I imagine myself being in the stories, doing the things Mickey says he did on his seven years out foreign, or doing the things he says his father did during the war against the British long 'go.

He always arrives in the early morning out of the blue. I have a mobile phone and so has he. It wouldn't kill him to send me a text or give me a ring when he takes a notion to come visiting but he never does. I always buy biscuits in the shop and sweet cake with a long date for when he calls but then sometimes I forget myself and I have them all ate when he arrives. I don't think he gives a shite, though, about biscuits or sweet cake, or even the tea I make in the pot. He nearly always leaves a half a cup go cold, and if he picks up a biscuit or a slice of cake he always looks like he doesn't even know he's doing it, and he holds it in his hand for ages before he takes a bite.

He's some man to talk all the same. I wonder sometimes am I the only person he talks to, or one of a small few, because he seems sometimes like he's trying stories out on me, or like he's telling me the same stories to get them straight in his head, to keep them fresh in his memory, or to perfect them, kind of. I don't know in the hell. My brother Peadar says I'm a fuckin eejit to entertain him at all after what he done to me ten years ago. You're an innocent boy, he says, to give that fella any hop.

But I know that Mickey wasn't in his right mind that day years ago he came on to the site roaring about money he was owed by Pokey Burke for his builder's pension and all that, and lamped me with a shovel. It was kind of half my own fault for standing up looking at him instead of getting out of his way like all the other lads done.

Anyway, the past is the past, as the fella says. The past is done and dusted and there's fuck-all way to change it. After he has me asked how am I getting on working for Bobby Mahon doing the attics and the insulation and the extensions, he takes off into his reminiscences and it's an ease to me to be able to sit here and just listen.

Peadar says Nana came to him in a dream one time and gave out stink to him for trying to get me out of the house. He told my sister Noreen about the dream and she straight away knew she had a good way now of convincing him that I was to be left here in the cottage. I had the exact same dream, she said to him. She was lying, but it was a good lie, and it worked because we all know, Peadar as well as anyone, that Noreen never lies.

She said to Peadar, And in my dream Nana told me I was to make sure you were good to Timmy, that you were to be a good brother to him and to help him with the cottage, to make sure the roof had no leaks and all that. Peadar was convinced then beyond doubt that Nana had to be obeyed. He never gave me a hand with the roof but he was too afraid of going against Nana's apparition to keep on trying to take the cottage to sell it.

He had no right to it, anyway. I looked it all up in the library on the internet, and then when I got this particular make of phone I was able to look all the same stuff up here at this table. I have a rake of screenshots of the bits of the law that I'd need if Peadar ever took another one of his figaries about trying to get me out of the house so's he can sell it. The Succession Act, 1955. Between that and Nana's ghost arriving into Peadar's dreams there's no fear of me.

MICKEY KEEPS TELLING me lately about how he used to be a pirate. I love those stories. If he's making them up he must be some kind of a genius. He used to sail with a lad called Captain Vane, who turned out to be a right bad bastard. They had a real fast boat with a reinforced prow called a blockade runner, and they used to chase rich fuckers' yachts in the sixties down around Spain and Portugal and the top of Africa, and they'd board them like proper peg-leg pirates and rob them blind. Then they'd ram the yachts and split them in half. They were always careful to make sure the rich people and the crew from the yachts had a lifeboat or a raft or something the way they wouldn't drown or get ate by sharks. That's what Mickey says, anyway. Mickey has a nephew who's going to write a right good book about Mickey's life, by all accounts, so I won't give too much away. About what happened in the end with Captain Vane and all that.

Mickey's father was a captain, too, in the Irish Volunteers, the time of the war against the British. He carried two barrel bombs across these fields through Pallasbeg and Pallasmore and all along the lakeside of the Arra Mountains as far as Ballina and they ambushed a British convoy there on the road below the graveyard. One of the bombs failed to explode so Mickey's auld fella carried it home again.

Three volunteers were captured that day and they were executed on the bridge between Ballina and Killaloe. One of them was seventeen years old, born and reared not even the throw of a stone from the place they killed him, and his whole family were made to stand and watch with the rest of the parish at the point of the Black and Tan guns. His mother's screams carried across the mountains and the lake; they were heard at Coumparker on the Tipperary side and in the valley of Corragnoe on the Clare side, and they can be heard still sometimes, echoing around this countryside.

I believe that. I've heard those cries myself. The very same way as I smell Nana's powder and hear her footsteps now and again outside in the kitchen while I'm lying in bed on the edge of sleep.

MICKEY SAYS THAT the barrel bomb his father carried home from the ambush is still below in his house. Holding up his kitchen table, he says. He always roars laughing at that part of the story, and I don't know why he thinks it's so funny, but I laugh away along with him. I'm still a small bit wary of him all the same. He tells me then how he'd like to die when his end comes. I always say something like, Yerra you haven't to worry about that for a good long while yet. You've plenty of life left in you. Placating him and rising him at the one time. I have in my bollix, he always says back. I'm for the high jump off of the long plank, son, before there's snow on Keeper again. But Keeper has been white a good few times since he first said that to me.

He got fierce poetical about it the last time he was here, just there this morning. I was stacking turf up against the gable wall under the lean-to when he strolled in the yard. God, I love this place, he says, with no preamble. I thought for a second he meant my house but then I realized he meant the whole place, the fields and the hills and the lake and the sky above us; he swept his hand around like a lad on a stage in a play like one of the ones I went with Nana to see inside in the Scouts' hall, and he went on then, saying, If I could designate my end and exequy I'd choose to die at dawn in this shallow valley and lie in secret state among the rushes and the long grass of the riverbank and the birds could sing me across the sea of the dead to the shores of eternity and my body could melt back to the earth and water from where its atoms came.

I stood up looking at him, and he looked back at me, but I don't think he was really seeing me at all. He was like a man having a vision. Like your man from X-Men that sees things from the future. Then he said, But I don't deserve a good death. And I had no answer for him and nor do I think he expected one, and he started helping me stack the turf that Peadar brang me in his trailer and we made little of the job between us.

We were having our sup of tea then and currant cake with butter on it that Noreen left in for me and everything was grand and Mickey told me he was talking the other day to Jim Gildea. Jim is retired now from the guards but he still knows every single thing that goes on around here. Or as much as anyone can know of the goings-on of a place, anyway.

This country is divided up, Jim Gildea told Mickey, the very same way it used to be, into little kingdoms. Each kingdom is broken into earldoms, and all the little earls must pay their tribute in full. That's what Jim Gildea told me, Timmy. Do you know what that means, Timmy?

I hadn't a fucking clue but I nodded anyway, *mar dhea* I did, and that seemed to please Mickey. Of course you do, he said. You're not half as thick as they make out. I nodded again. He's right, I suppose.

HE WENT AWAY then but I was a kind of worried about him, the funny auld talk out of him, so I followed him a small bit down the lake road. Just in case, like. You never know what a man might be thinking of doing. Especially when he's talking a bit quare the way Mickey was, about his end and his exequy, whatever in the hell that is, and kings and earls and all that.

I shadowed him down as far as the cross near the *cillín* and I saw him then, standing up in the road talking in the window of a car. I thought I recognized the car. I've seen it around the roads at quare times of the day, early in the morning sometimes and once or twice in the middle of the night: I've been out in the kitchen when I can't sleep and I've seen it pass down the road towards the lake or back up from it. I'd been meaning to try and get a good look at who was driving it but the windows were tinted nearly black. The only way would be to face the car head on and get a look in through the windscreen to see who owns it. You never know when that kind of information might be useful. I was well known for noticing things once, like that time when them two quarehawks lifted that little lad and everybody was looking high and low for him. That kind of fame wears off fierce quick, though, thanks be to God.

I stayed standing where I was, in the thick of the far side of the ditch from where Mickey was, and I could see that it was Augie Penrose he was talking to, and your man of the Pitts from town was beside him, leaning out to get a better look at Mickey, and I knew that the two in the back would be Dowel and Braden. I know all about them, or as much as anyone can know. I heard they arrived up to a house the day after a young lad died out around Gurteenasallagh and they told the boy's parents he still owed them money for drugs, that his debt didn't die with him, and those poor people had to hand over thousands for fear of them.

I know that to be the gospel truth because Noreen told it me and Noreen is not able to tell a lie or to repeat something unless she knows for a fact the thing to be true. Except for the lie she told Peadar about her dream, I wouldn't say she ever once in her life committed a sin knowingly. And anyway Nana will have interceded for her and for all of us, you can be sure, the way our slates may all be clean and our accounts settled or at least not too far into the red when our time comes.

Mickey drew something from the pocket of his jacket and he threw it in the window of the car. Augie Penrose looked shocked for a second. Then he started smiling, then he winked up at Mickey and he said something and he drove away. He spun the wheels of his shitbox all the way up the road. Gow-lacting is all that is.

Mickey stood awhile looking after them and then he started towards his own cottage and I kept an eye on him until I seen him go in through his little rusty gate and up to his door and into the darkness of the house. And I feel a weirdness in the air ever since, a heaviness kind of – it's after settling around me and I can't find any ease no matter what I do.

Brian

EVERY TIME I went anywhere my whole life the mother
used to be boo-hooing and making a show of me and tor-
menting the auld fella with her carry-on. She'd be saying
novenas by the new time and drowning me in holy water,
filling my pockets and my wallet up with bits of relics and
things that were touched off of relics and slips of paper with
little one-liner prayers on them. I found a whole prayer
inside in my passport the last time I was in Shannon Airport,
cut out from a *Sacred Heart Messenger* or one of those luna-
tic magazines that give the mother and father such peace.
They give me peace too if I'm honest, just the sight of them
on an armchair with my father's reading glasses closed on
top of them, the absolute sameness of them after all these
years, the resoluteness of them, the same things being said
over and over again in slightly different ways.

The prayer was a plea for intercession to Saint Jude,

whom I presumed at the time to be the patron saint of travellers and adventurers, folded up and with my mother's handwriting on the top of it in blue biro, *Dear Brian, please just say this once in morn, once at night, love Mam x*, and I was only going to Amsterdam that time, for Colum Shanahan's stag weekend. I found out since that Jude is the patron saint of hopeless cases and desperate situations. No one knows you like your mother, no matter how you try to hide the truth of yourself.

Mam was always convinced for some reason I was going to be killed out foreign. I think maybe it's partly because the world to her was such a mystery. I don't think she ever went further than Galway. I used to think Galway was another world all of its own. The year we rented a house near Spiddal for a fortnight when I was maybe ten it felt like we were driving for a week to get there, but maybe that was because I was a bit carsick from sitting on the green couch in the back of a van the auld lad borrowed, with Granny and my sister with our backs to the engine, even though it was brilliant, sitting on the couch from our sitting room in a van, with Granny farting out of pure nerves every time the auld fella hit a bump and trying to blame Marian, and Marian and me nearly wetting ourselves laughing.

When we got there it was like we'd landed on the moon. That flat, rocky, treeless place, with the mountains blue and purple in the distance, and down the road from the rented cottage there was a little beach that was nearly all ours the whole time we were there. Granny and me and my sister and the parents swam there every single day, even in the rain. The rain feels warm on your body when you're in the ocean. I remember Granny laughing louder than I'd ever heard her laugh; she was like a child, and she was well able to swim. Mam and Dad brought us to a little pub in the village every night and all the people there spoke Irish. Myself and the sister hadn't one fight the whole week. I remember we were all nearly crying as we left to go home.

I've checked Google Maps and it's only 127 kilometres from our house to the house we rented that year. That'll show you how thick I was as a child, how I wasn't able even to measure time or the space around me. I could never judge things the way other people can. I always work off impressions, and my impressions, it turns out, are mostly shite.

MY TRAVELS ARE over now and still the mother is meeawing. I did a lot of it, in fairness. I dragged the arse out of it for a finish. Australia for a year, then New Zealand for another six months, then the whole of Vietnam, Cambodia, a Thailand trek, then across to America on a holiday visa that I outstayed by about four years so I probably can't ever go back there but no harm: I have enough of it done now.

The thing about the travelling, though, is you can keep everything else in abeyance while you're doing it; you can tell yourself you're going to settle into something when you're home, finish your course, maybe go back and do teaching as a mature student, apply for the cops, the civil service, the county council, the ESB, go farming with the auld fella, write a book, get married, have kids, build a house, live, live, die, die. Jaysus.

Signs on in fairness the mother won't stop worrying and

giving lectures and cutting prayers out of holy magazines. All the things I could have done, or had a good go at, at least, I have left undone, unattempted. I have rebuffed all possibility, declined all opportunity, rested on my peripatetic laurels, considered myself worldly by virtue of my time spent in various parts of the world, passing along tarmacadam or through the sky or drinking in bars or working on building sites or in pot washes at the back of steaming stinking kitchens, saying things I didn't mean, laughing at things I didn't think were funny. And all the world still a mystery to me, and all the people in it, myself especially.

I read an interview with your one Saoirse Aylward. She was born and reared not a mile from here and she still lives in the same house she's lived in her whole life. She was talking about the infinity of opportunity offered to us by the imagination, and the contradictions inherent in the unknowability of the true nature of anything outside of our own selves and the struggle, in which she is perennially engaged, to describe some kind of universal experience, some common state of being. Or some shite. What it boiled down to for me was that she was admitting she knows fuck-all. She's only guessing at things, like all of us. And she's on the fucking Leaving Cert! Six number-one bestsellers in a row. There's hope for me yet. There's hope for every cunt.

Although when I look back at the putrid shite I wrote in my journals while I was travelling, all the notes I made and all the ideas I was so careful to store for myself, thinking I'd someday make something out of them, something decent, I just feel embarrassment, and a kind of sick dread.

I WAS WAITING always I think for something to happen that would justify me to myself. And I know how narcissistic that sounds. But it's the opposite, really. There never seemed to be a reason for me. It's like a curse, that questioning, that inability to accept my passive role in the expedition of Fate, the seeming fact that I am just because I am and there's no explaining it so therefore there should be no questioning it.

I wish I could be like all the lads and just live in a happy stupor, only getting upset over the results of matches or horse races. Or marshal my thoughts properly into something creative, something worthwhile, something that comes from me and exists outside of me and might make a difference, however small, to someone else. Some other miserable fucker who thinks too much might read it or look at it and realize they're not the only one living in a prison of their own making, inside their own skull.

The first time I did coke was in New York, in the toilet of a bar in Queens, with a fella I barely knew whose brother was a cop in Harlem. I thought there was something so cool about that and I wasn't even sure why until a few days later I remembered that the words *cop in Harlem* reminded me of the lines from the Lou Reed song from his *New York* album, the first song, 'Romeo Had Juliette'. I was obsessed for a while with that album, and then thinking more I realized how subliminally influenced I was by the things I thought were cool, how I'd been looking for the seedy, filthy, broody, dangerous New York that Lou Reed described in that album. But it was gone, for the most part, and I wasn't brave enough to walk into the places where it might still be, down the alleys of the Bowery or around the warehouses and dive bars on the dark side of the waterfront.

The worst thing about the feeling I got when I took my first hit was that I knew what a cliché I was. I'm not thick enough not to know how sad it was to feel so suddenly happy, so euphoric, so full of confidence and purpose, to finally have a reason to exist. It was different to the yokes, somehow. It seemed realer or something, like it could maybe last, could transform me into something better.

ISN'T IT FUNNY how history repeats and repeats? Like an ouroboros eating itself over and over again, we come back upon ourselves doing the same things in different ways, different settings for the same old scenes. Like the way Bobby went off with a hooker on Colum's stag and now it's a big secret that everyone knows but no one's allowed to mention because Seanie Shaper and Bobby boxed the heads off each other already over it, and even the ratty little bollix I get my wraps off every Friday knows about it. I heard your man big Saint Bobby fucking Mahon was off riding hookers in Amsterdam, the dirty cunt, ha ha ha. Seanie sent the photo around everywhere.

It proves nothing, in fairness, but it looks fair bad. Bobby smiling, halfway through a step, and your one behind him in her knickers and black lacy bra, blowing a kiss at him. The only way it could be more incriminating would be if he was closing his fly as he went. Your one must have seen Seanie holding up his phone to take the picture. You're not even meant to be taking pictures on that street. There's a crew of massive fuckers in security outfits watching everything, policing the whole place, bouncing the pissheads and the perverts. Seanie pushed him in that door, though, and I remember him saying, This one's on me, Bob, and Bobby was out of his mind, in fairness, he'd been talking absolute shite in a bar just before we went down that street, and he was back out too quick to have done any damage. A man like Bobby, surely he'd be more than a one-minute wonder.

Something kind of closed itself off in me when I saw Bobby coming out that door though, which or whether. Something about the world and the people in it and the possibility of goodness, of integrity, of honour. Everything gets corrupted, everything. She was someone's baby one time, that girl in her underwear, blowing the kiss at Bobby; she was warm and soft and helpless against someone's breast; she was held and kissed and loved and all the potential in the world was vested in her little body; and now she's for sale in a window on a cobbled street. Even if Bobby didn't ride her that night some other fucker did. Someone's probably in there with her right now, behind that heavy curtain.

And then Seanie WhatsApped us all the photo. There was something so lousy about the way Seanie did that, so sneaky. He lets on to be Bobby's best pal, his right-hand man, and then he fucks him in the arse like that. Prick. I typed out a right tasty message to the group calling Seanie out for being such a bollix but then I deleted it instead of sending it. It's got fuck-all to do with me at the end of the day. Everyone did their nut ten years ago over Bobby riding Seanie's missus and then everyone had it that Bobby killed his own father and neither of those stories turned out to be true.

I heard another one that says Bobby is best friends with the fella that actually killed auld Frank Mahon, the builder lad from Limerick that was owed a rake of money by Pokey and he thought Bobby's auld lad was Pokey's auld lad or something. It was all a bit of a mash-up on the news at the time and everyone had bits of a story, and Bobby apparently used to go to the prison to visit your man and all. That sounds fucked-up on first hearing but you have to know a full story before you can get a feeling about a thing, and you can never judge anyone.

Anyway, fuck them. I have bigger worries than that prick Seanie or Bobby's weird life. I have nearly thirty thousand bigger worries now, according to Augie Penrose's fucked-up accounting system.

I ONLY EVER judge myself. I never come out well from the judging. When I drive into town on Friday evenings I judge myself the whole way in and the whole way home. When I lick the back of my hand and leave a thin line of powder along it so I can suck it like a fucking lollipop all the way back out to the village I judge myself. I start feeling better when I'm sitting at the bar in Ciss Brien's talking shite with the lads and everyone is roaring at each other and laughing and slagging and a few of the lads get shirty with each other and make up or the odd time it spills into bad temper and pushing and shoving starts and Ciss gets wicked and starts threatening to fuck lads out.

When I go into the jacks to count the cash for the wraps I passed around I judge myself and when I push the last wrap into the key pocket of my jeans I judge myself. When I think about how in the name of God I've ended up where I am I judge myself, two months' wages behind on my payments and in rapidly mounting hock to a drug dealer, a mile from the house I was reared in, a world away from the life I thought I'd live, from the man I thought I'd be. How will I judge myself when I do the *little job* that Augie keeps mentioning? I've a little job for you, Brian lad, it'll only take you a minute and your bill will be squared after it. Jason will owe you one after it. And he makes the shape of a gun with his hand and he laughs that soft mirthless laugh of his, and I see myself reflected, an empty silhouette in the flat blackness of his eyes.

Saint Jude, friend of Jesus, I commit myself to your care at this difficult time. Most holy Apostle, pray for me. Help me to remember that I need not face my troubles alone. Please join me in my need, asking God to send me consolation in my sorrow, courage in my fear, and healing in the midst of my suffering.

Trevor

IT'S NO COINCIDENCE that I was interned in the Dean
Swift ward. Jonathan and I share many commonalities. It's
quite possible, given my acute and heightened sensibilities,
and the cast of features peculiar to me and him, that I
descend from the great man, perhaps by some occluded sur-
reptitious heredity, an impregnated servant, perhaps, or
something less base: it may be that I am the descendant of
the love child of Swift and Esther Johnson. Whatever the
flesh-and-blood, tiresomely temporal truth of the matter,
the spiritual truth is quite clear: some cosmic force of wit
and intelligence such as abounds in the ether all about and
makes itself apparent only to a chosen few elected to deposit
me in that place at that particular point in my struggle. I
read widely in that place; I vastly expanded my knowledge
there; I immersed myself in learning. The world remains

mysterious but something of my true path, my singular purpose, was illuminated.

This delineation was most welcome. It allowed in me an initially curious (curious as in strange, not probing) but gradually more amenable facility for subterfuge and misdirection. I have been able to present myself as subjugated, docile, pliant, and deferential in my dealings with so-called people of medicine, people of learning, so that they see in my presentation a creature dampened of spirit, doused of flame; my belly is metaphorically presented to them as a beta dog will present itself, and none suspect that this dog has retained its ardour, its obstinacy, and its keen-edged perspicacity. I see more clearly now into the core of things, through the masks and makeups that adorn the creatures all about me.

Lloyd sends me messages almost daily, implanted in news stories he thinks I'll be interested in. I laughed so hard when I first heard our old code, coming through the television on the afternoon news! I gave Mother quite a start. She'd been dozing, as is her habit now for most of her afternoons and into the early evening, since she and I took up residence in this little gated community. I don't know how Lloyd achieves such wonders, but I'm never surprised. We worked out the key years ago and we both committed it to memory. Lloyd was always far more able than I to subsume himself into the masses. He is workmanlike, plebeian, in appearance; my elongated, patrician features are striking, memorable, even unsettling to some. He can attend sporting events and frequent hostelries, conveniences, entertainments, without arousing suspicion among the lower grades, the opiated. I must conceal myself as far as possible, sequester myself here in this strange arena, this *community* of the decrepit and the imminently expired. Mother is my cover and my front, and has been transmuted from my direst enemy to my dearest friend.

Her infirmities serve me well. The fellows who deposit their cargo here on a weekly schedule of two visits announced by a text message comprised of two numbers, the first indicating a day and the second an hour, would surely arouse suspicion in her, were she able to examine, appraise or interrogate them. As it is she believes them to be suppliers of oxygen and, indeed, such is their disguise: the livery of their van and their somewhat rudimentary symbol of a supine stick figure being administered to by a vertical stick figure and the company name in a half-halo around the figures suggest that they are homecare operatives and purveyors of medical supplies.

Maybe they are. I don't discuss business with them beyond the optimum time to make their deposits, predicated on the anticipated movements of Sonya, Mother's healthcare assistant, who is employed by the faceless management company of this so-called *sheltered village*, this centre of *assisted independent living*, and remunerated I presume from the proceeds of our hefty monthly fee.

MOTHER SOLD OUR house after the unpleasantness. She couldn't very well remain living so close to the child in the abduction of whom Lloyd convinced me to assist. Or was I the instigator? I was told that I was but that second-hand testimony does not tally with my recollection, with my knowledge of myself, or with my impressions of that fraught time.

Poor Mother. I suspected her for many years of being demonic, or at least of being inhabited by some kind of evil entity, but that conviction faded with the shock of my apprehension and incarceration and my sudden brutal disconnect from the comforts and the routines of my life, as compromised and straitened as it was. She was a perfect angel about it all. She wept in court as I was led away, comporting myself heroically. She drove behind the prison van as I was transported to the penal colony of Dundrum, and she arranged to stay with a friend in Dún Laoghaire for almost the entirety of my internment.

On my release she decided to undertake a leasehold for life on this apartment, because she could be anonymous here, she said, and she could look east from our balcony and see the Silvermines, and look west and see the Clare Hills, from where she rose, as she puts it, and when the prevailing conditions align themselves in a particular way, when the day takes a certain mood, she can taste on the breeze the salt of the ocean carried up the estuary and along the river to her dear tongue. Even now that she is confined almost entirely to her bed or, for short spells, the chair beside it, I can open the French doors to her balcony so that the east breeze can greet her, and she can glimpse from her confinement the hills in the near distance just above the balustrade.

SONYA AND I dance together regularly. I suspect she's deeply in love with me. Her *amour* was aroused by my piano playing, initially. I've been composing a libretto for some time now. My industry also soothes Mother. She asks me to replay certain phrases over and over again and makes suggestions for rearrangements now and then, some of them quite insightful. Her voice carries through from her bedroom to this light-flooded living room and my music makes the return journey to her vastly experienced ears and we have the pleasantest creative congress imaginable.

When Sonya and I dance, however, Mother often spoils it by raising her voice to enquire as to why I've got that awful pop music on, and I can't very well tell her that Sonya likes to dance to popular ballads, to the ephemeral melodies of youth. Sometimes I am so seduced by Sonya's blazing simplicity that it's all I can do not to rush from her arms to Mother's bedside and smother the old bat to death so that we may be left to our gyrations.

Sonya has no business in my bedroom, and that therefore is where I conduct my more nefarious business. I have been prevailed upon by a shady figure, invariably hooded, heavily bearded, and sonorously crude of voice, whom I presume to be an agent of Lloyd's, to accept certain deliveries, and to perform a series of procedures on said deliveries, diluting one component with another, decanting the mixed product into bags of various exact weights, marking each with a single figure denoting its particular weight, and repacking and resealing all of the boxes.

The brawny fellow who performs maintenance in this sleepy and gated little complex appears to be a sub-agent of the hooded chap, and a baser but integral part of the cartel that Lloyd has assembled. He wordlessly enters the apartment at regular intervals and removes the prepared boxes, loading them into his van, a conveyance of the same basic style as the oxygen purveyors', and similarly liveried. I have to say that the operation in its entirety, from delivery to collection and with my ministrations in between, is devilishly slick.

I'd expect no less from Lloyd. His is a particularly utilitarian genius; he has an uncommon flair for practical execution. I haven't received a detailed explanation yet, but I presume this thrilling yet squalid operation to be a means to some glorious end. I find myself lapsing into pleasant abstractions as I toil among the powders and the scales, daydreaming of a villa overlooking a steeply terraced and sunbathed vinery that sweeps to the shore of a placid lake, where Lloyd and I stand taking the air in evening dress, smoking fine cigars and drinking cognac from crystal snifters, decanted from a cut-glass carafe, as Sonya sways rhythmically in the background, always in my fantasy wearing a particularly sparse version of her uniform, dancing not to Taylor Swift but to Johann Strauss, because I'll have cultured her by then, muted her rougher impulses, refined her inclinations.

I'VE ONLY ENCOUNTERED Lloyd in the flesh, *in the wild*, so to speak, on a single occasion since I was released from the care of the central mental hospital. We were remanded in separate institutions, or at least I presumed such to be the case. We were two of the most notorious criminals in the state, after all, desperately feared and respected by fellow inmates, jailers, administrators, nursing staff, medics, occupational therapists, psychiatrists, psychologists, librarians, teachers, caterers, cleaners, and all branches and ranks of the army of mortals who were deployed to attempt to understand us, and in so doing to subdue us, with a view to decommissioning our internal arsenals, our latent, inbuilt powers.

Lloyd acted most peculiarly on the occasion of our solitary meeting. I played it well, stifling my surprise and delight at our chance encounter and sitting wordlessly beside him on the Castletroy bus from William Street. We are forbidden to meet and communicate on pain of immediate reinternment, but I knew that the chances of our being recognized, in spite of our notoriety, by any of the sweaty ham-hock peasants or acned youths on the bus were minimal to non-existent. Besides, I've grown quite a splendid beard in the intervening years, and Lloyd has taken to wearing proletarian baseball caps and sporting apparel where previously he always presented immaculately in collared shirts and jackets.

What in the fuck are you doing? he hissed at me. Get the fuck away from me! He struck me forcibly in my ribs with his elbow. Fuck off! he cried then, in the most plaintive tone imaginable. And he rose from his seat and rushed past me, pressing as he went the red button that alerts the driver to the desire of a passenger to alight. The bus stopped and he was gone, and I was left to writhe beneath the gaze of some kind of a working-class Medusa.

He waddent too happy to see yoo, love, she gummed at me from beneath her serpent's nest. Har har har! He was like a cunt with yoo! Har har har! And a small gaggle of her associates joined in the jocularity, and began discussing my situation as though I weren't present. Lovers' tiff, I'd say, one plebeian offered. Prolly fuckin called him the wrong pronouns, another ventured, and they laughed their grating common laughs while I sat and stewed in a broil of mortification.

I realized shortly afterwards, naturally, the quickness of Lloyd's wit. Of course we must be disassociated one from the other. His abrupt and voluble departure from my company was calculated to create between our physical selves a barrier, and to establish in the eyes of any potential witnesses our innocence, and our upholding of the terms of our parole.

If questioned I might proffer the explanation that I took the seat beside him unwittingly, and his angry reaction to my presence was born of fear at being found to have contravened the proscription. The driver of the bus could easily be located and called upon to corroborate the story if necessary, as could perhaps one or two of the passengers. They had about them the grimy patina and world-weariness of regular bus travellers.

IT'S ALL MUCH of a muchness now, though. Until a moment ago, my life was pleasant, and fulfilling, and containing at its core a gradually accreting dark mass of potential. But there was a bang outside just now, so loud that I knocked my scales and its cargo of powder onto my bedroom floor. And on my security app I can see that there are uniformed policemen swarming up the stairs. They're hammering now and shouting at the door. I can hear Mother wailing through their clamour. My only means of egress is the window onto the balcony, but we're three floors up. My sphincter has loosened, as has my bladder, but otherwise I am acquitting myself well in the midst of this foul contingency. I do find myself rather deprived of breath, though. As I repeat the word *oxygen*, by way of pre-emptive explanation, by way of practice for the interrogations to come, *oxygen*, *oxygen*, it was only supposed to be Mother's *oxygen*, I feel my breath leaving my body. How appositely Swiftian the irony.

Bridie

MAYBE I LOOK like a madwoman going around the place these days. I don't know. I do my best now to take care of myself but a body is like a lawn or a garden of flowers: you have to constantly cultivate and trim and pluck out the creeping imposters or it all goes to ruin on you.

A man asked me would I go with him to the horse races in Galway not too long ago, all the same. He was a fine cut of a man, too, not one of your average desperadoes looking for a servant, or a handmaiden, or a fumble in his car parked up on the side of the road somewhere. I've heard about that kind of a thing.

He had a lovely accent. I told him I was married. He frowned at me then. We were standing in the corridor of the hotel and I was wearing my housekeeping uniform and he was wearing lovely beige trousers and a dark jacket, and his shirt was ironed beautifully and his shoes gleamed. I'd say he was in the army one time or something, and I was very tempted to say, Yes, yes, I will go with you to the Galway Races, but I couldn't renege on the promise I made, whatever about Michael, my ex-husband. I don't go to mass: I'm not on good terms with God since the sea took my little boy Peter from me thirty years ago, but still I can't renege on the promise I made in His house.

I'd say that man had been egged on by Marek in the bar or Violet in the dining room. They're forever trying to set me up. I keep telling them that I still consider myself to be married and they only laugh at me and shake their heads. Bridie, Marek says, you are a fine-looking woman. You are a queen. You deserve to be treated like royalty. He's as bold as brass, that Marek. Sometimes I sit in the staff canteen with him and Violet and a few more of the bar staff and the kitchen staff and the aping out of him, the lepping and singing and slagging, and everyone roaring laughing at him, and their laughter only making him higher and higher. Lord save us he's a pure solid tonic.

He lives me with me in my house now but he doesn't be as boisterous at home with only me to show off to. We're *roommates* as they'd say in *Friends*. Ever since the thing. But I'm able some days for hours at a stretch to forget all that, to forget myself, to rise above the flooding rush, to stay clear of the dark waters.

I LIVE NOW in a little house on the street in Nenagh. I bought it for half nothing after we sold the *home house*, as my children insist on calling it. It needed a lot of things done to it but my son is very handy, thank God, and my husband, or my ex-husband as he likes to be known, especially when he's in earshot of that little madam he's shacked up with, even gave him a hand a few days so it cost me only the price of the materials and my son got them cheaply for me at a discount below in Chadwick's and above in McLoughlin's hardware shop.

My daughter still makes a song and dance about the house, especially when she brings her children to see me, which isn't too often. Jesus, Mam, she says. Like, it's *tiny*, and there's no *garden*, like, I always imagined my kids running around our big huge garden at home in the *home house*. I'm always tempted then to shout at her, Go ask your father why the house was sold, why he insisted on selling my Peter's home, why he pulled that rug out from under us, ask your father and the little bit of fluff he's dipping his wick into.

But I never would. I say nothing back because her little fella reminds me so much of my Peter that I'm terrified she'll stop coming if I fight with her. And anyway, I kind of abandoned the house, I suppose, when I took that live-in job out on the west coast of Clare. But I'm back here now, in the town I was born and reared in, living a stone's throw away from the door of the hotel I work in now, in a house on the street my father was reared on, and I'll die here in this house.

I don't even tell my daughter how much like Peter I think her little fella is. I don't know does she see it herself, or does she even look at the old photographs from years ago to compare. Maybe she spares herself that. She told me there not too long ago that she practises *mindfulness*, that she *lives in the present moment*. Well for you, I said, and she started to get a bit sniffy and so I said no more.

I know she thought I was making little of what she was saying but I was actually envious of her. I'd love to be able to do that. Imagine being able to shuck off the weight of the past, the burden of all your sorrows, and walk the earth free, light-footed, sure of your step, not worried that you might buckle and fall at any moment, lose the breath from your body in a moment of remembrance, of realization, of sudden stabbing grief.

TWO MEN CAME in here one night. They came in the door of my bedroom while I was still waking up so I thought I was dreaming and I only lay there watching as they moved the few steps across to my bed. I figured out afterwards that they'd opened the kitchen window by prising it with a flathead screwdriver. The same one the taller fella had in his hand when they came into my bedroom, I'd say. The smaller chap had a knife with a jagged blade and holes for his fingers. He had a hammer, too. He produced it with a kind of flourish, like a magician, from where he pulled it I don't know, and he held it out like he was awful proud of himself, or of the hammer, or both maybe. I had a mad impulse for a second to clap my hands at his little performance. All I could see behind the black mask he had on was his eyes, and there was a bright watery light in them. The taller fella sat onto the bed and leaned himself down over me and he spoke in a whisper, Don't make any noise. Tell me where your bank card is, and tell me your pin number.

I sound brave now telling the story but I didn't feel it then. I'm not afraid of dying but I didn't want that jagged blade cutting into my flesh; nor did I want that hammer smashing me to pieces. I could feel a bloom of warmth between my legs and I couldn't find the use of my voice or of my limbs. The tall lad was leaning too close into me anyway for me to be able to move very much. My mouth was as dry as dust and my heart was hammering so hard in my chest I was sure it was going to burst. The lad behind was talking then, in a louder voice, calling me a manky auld bitch and all sorts. I snapped into myself then. Look who's talking, I said. The fine boy who's in an old woman's bedroom in the dead of night threatening her with a hammer and a knife.

The short one hit me then with the hammer on my leg, right on my shin through my blanket and sheet, and the pain of it shrieked up through me. The other lad pressed his hand down over my mouth and I bit him hard through his glove. I wouldn't say they expected me even to have teeth. The lad yelped and he jumped up so fast he nearly knocked into his comrade and he slapped me then with the full force of his arm across my cheek and that was the first time in my sixty-three years of life that I was ever designedly hit on my face. Even in the deepest depths of his rages Michael never put a hand on me roughly. The shock of it robbed me of all my faculties for a long moment. I knew I was done for if I put up any more of a fight.

They found my handbag anyway, down between my locker and my bed, and my purse was inside in it and they took what bit of cash I had. Two fifty-euro notes I'd taken out of the cash machine, one for my granddaughter's communion card and one for my son's thirty-second birthday. The tall lad was leaning back over me again and he asked me again for my pin number. And if it's wrong, he said, I'm going to come back here and cut you open.

I nearly couldn't think of the blessed number, but eventually it came to me. He left his pal minding me and I knew by instinct to say nothing to him, and not to move a muscle. I got a feeling he was itching to hit me again with his hammer. He put my rings and my necklaces and bracelets into his pockets and then his phone dinged. He looked at it for a second and he shook his head like he was annoyed and he told me to get out of bed and I said I wasn't able, my legs were too weak.

Get out of the fucking bed, he said, or I'll kill you. I managed somehow to get up, and when I put weight on the leg he'd hammered I felt tears come in spite of myself but he walked me across the room and told me to go into the bathroom and he asked where was the key for the door and I said there wasn't one, there was only a bolt on the inside and he said, Ah, fuck, fuck, and he picked up a bottle of hand soap from the sink and he pelted it across the bathroom in a temper, then he pulled the belt off of my dressing-gown that was hanging on a peg on the bathroom door and he tied it tight around my wrists and he knotted the other end around the handle of the window so that my arms were up over my head. Then he was gone.

I SAT A good while gathering back the use of myself and the sun was streaming in the high window before I had the strength to stand up and turn myself around so I could work the belt away from the window handle and off of my wrists. I said to myself then, Well, they have my phone taken. I'll have to walk to the barracks. Or call in to a neighbour. But there was no one in any of the houses along the street I knew very well. Nearly all the old neighbours were gone, replaced by younger people, strangers, and anyone left that I knew I couldn't bear the thought of me arriving beaten and bedraggled at their door.

I felt suddenly a wave of shame and fear like I never felt before in all my days. Even in the deepest part of my sorrows I held on to something defiant in myself; some bit of fight always stayed sparking and flaming in me, but now all my strength was gone, I felt like a husk, like I could crumble to dust at the touch of a fingertip against my skin.

After a long while I washed myself, and I put on my clothes, and I went down my narrow stairs to the sitting room and I felt a strange relief at the sight of the place. They hadn't made too much of a mess. And then I remembered Peter's watch. My son Peter's watch. The black Casio watch I bought him for his seventh birthday and he took a tiny little brush and he painted two white hearts on it, one above the time and one below, and he said, Look, Mam, one heart is me and one heart is you. And he minded that watch and he only wore it for special occasions as he called them. His cousin's wedding, his sister's confirmation. I kept it all these years and every now and then I'd take it out and I'd hold it to my lips and I'd brush my fingertips over the little white painted hearts, one above the empty screen where the digital display used to be before the batteries ran down, and one below.

My lungs burned and my heart beat ragged in my chest. I could hardly bring myself to look in the drawer. When I saw that it was gone I screamed, I think, or maybe it was just air rushing from me silently, and I collapsed to the kitchen floor and I stayed there for a long time.

I DON'T KNOW why I never told anyone. The shame, maybe, the fear of the lad making good on his threat, the embarrassment of being so frightened, after all I've been through in my life. The thought of my brother Jim, and he not long retired from the guards, breaking his heart over me, and his heart already broken beyond any repair.

I stayed in a room in the hotel for a few nights, lying to the manager that my floors were all pulled up because they had rot in them. She asked me was I okay. My face was still a small bit swollen from the tall lad's slap, and I think I saw her looking at it kind of funny. I told her I was fine, that there was no fear of me, and I was careful not to slack off any bit in my work, and after a few nights of using the room privilege I told my daughter I might stay with her for a few nights and she wasn't too happy but she sighed and said, Grand.

Then Marek announced that he needed new digs because his landlord was after upping his rent to nearly as much as his wages, and I nearly jumped for joy. I nearly shouted it across the canteen at him. You can stay with me! I won't even charge you! But he pays me anyway, he insists on it. I have it all kept for him, though, in an account in the post office.

I WAS KIND of settled in myself again then. Marek is the best of company. He's quieter at home, and as clean as a monk. I got a monitored alarm and a big lock for my bedroom door. I always turn the key quietly in case Marek thinks I'm locking it against a fear of him. I settled back into a bit of a rhythm. My daughter wrinkled her nose up at Marek the first time she came visiting and he was there but he soon won her around.

Then one day in the Centra shop I saw a child wearing Peter's watch. He was in the queue in front of me and he had his hand up reaching for a bag of sweets and he was saying something to the little lad who was with him. He was small, the watch looked big on him and it was loose on his wrist. I could see that the bottom one of Peter's little painted hearts was scratched nearly fully off but the top one was still there, tiny and white and perfect. Someone had replaced the batteries because the screen had the time on it in big digital numbers: 13.07. That was the time on my Peter's watch when I saw it on that child's wrist. That was the time it was when I reached out my hand and grabbed that child by the arm and started to scream, That's my son's watch, that's my Peter's watch, you dirty little thief, that's not yours, that's not yours, that's not yours.

And then there was shouting and people had their hands on me and on the child and the child was wide-eyed and bawling but I wouldn't let go. Someone hit me hard on my shoulder, by design or accident I don't know, and still I wouldn't let go. I was holding the child's arm with one hand and with the other I was trying to open the strap of the watch, and I couldn't, so I tried then to pull it down over his hand, and I couldn't do that either, and then someone, the friend I think, pushed me so hard I fell onto my back on the floor and the young lad was free of my grip and he roared,

MY UNCLE GIMME THIS WATCH YOU GOWL FUCK OFF YOU MAD BITCH, as he and his pal ran away out the door.

A young girl helped me up and walked me gently out to the footpath, and she whispered to me that the child was one of the Dowels, and I knew that name, and I knew why she was saying it in a whisper, with fear in her voice, and why she looked around her before she told me.

I walked up towards Summerhill to where I knew Augie Penrose often parked his car. I've known that lad since he was small. I know the carry-on of him and his gang. I remember one night last year seeing him getting booted out the door of the hotel by Pat Donnellan, for what transgression I don't know, but I'd put my money on there being drugs involved. I stood up at the driver's side window until he opened it. I looked in past him to the back seat. Penrose hadn't spoken and I didn't look at him.

Is one of ye Dowel? I said. Who wants to fuckin know? one of them said from the shadows. I just want the black Casio watch back, I said. I don't care about anything else. I saw Penrose then looking back at his two disciples in the rear-view mirror. The lad beside him was smiling, pulling slowly on a fag, looking at me with a kind of a bored interest. He turned a bit around in his seat and he asked the two in the back did they know in the fuck what the woman was talking about.

Not a fuckin clue, bud, one of them said, and I knew the voice, I knew it well. Penrose spoke then. If you don't mind, missus, we have to go. The one who must have been Dowel started spouting out of him then, and Penrose roared suddenly, SHUT YOUR MOUTH! And he looked at me for a second before his window rolled up and he nodded, a bare tip of his head.

A few days after that Marek came into the kitchen while I was getting ready for my evening shift. He was just coming off the early shift. This was on the mat, he said. Someone must have thrown it through the letterbox.

And in his hand was Peter's watch, and the time was showing on its face, the hours and the minutes and the seconds, and one of the hearts that my Peter left behind him, thank God, was still intact.

Jason

THAT WHOLE THING about how you shouldn't marry your cousin is bullshit. How come the poshest of posh cunts do it the whole time if it's so bad? Everyone looks down their noses at the Travellers for doing it, but no fucker says a word to the royal shitbags and the crowd with the alien heads that own all the banks. I know. I read all about them. Trying to keep their bloodlines clean, making sure they're always separate, never polluted by scum. So they spread it around that poor people shouldn't ride their cousins while they're flahing the holes off each other in their ivory fucking towers.

Fuck that. I know their game. It's all about control. Do as I say not as I do. I'm gonna marry my cousin Sonya. I fuckin love her. I don't give a shit. Our grandparents are all dead anyway so there'll be no awkward shite at the wedding with Granda and Nan not knowing which side to sit on. We'll go out foreign anyway, I'd say. Cheaper. Bring no cunt only my boy Jayden and Sonya's little one, whose fatherage is contentious but I don't give a fuck. No rows that way. I seen Sonya in a bikini last summer in Kilkee and she was fuckin gorgeous. I nearly passed out. I had to stay in the water for ages, even after they were all calling me, Come on, Jason, to fuck will you, and I had to tell them to fuck off and leave me alone.

See all them cartel cunts? All the Johnny Big Balls and Dangerous fuckin Dans? They're thick bastards. They're like fireworks, all dazzle and flash, everyone looking, admiring them, and then they're gone in a bang. Or a pop or a fizzle. They all want to be famous. They love being in the papers. Why would anyone want that? I have it sewn up. I keep a low profile. I live in the same little house my grandparents lived in. Middle of the terrace, grey on grey. Granda kept it beautiful but it doesn't stand out. The corporation tried to get it back off me to give it to a family of refugees or something but I'm a registered disabled so I told them fuck off and there was shag-all they could do. They even put in a downstairs shower for me cos I have the back thing.

I drive a twenty-year-old Scooby. The shades don't even notice it. The Big Ballses, the Dublin lads, go round in fuckin blacked-out brand-new Mercs and Beemers, all blinged, standing out, showing off. Then the CAB come and say, Hey, lads, how'd ye pay for them? And if they can't show proper accounts from a legitimate business and receipts and all, then that's the motor gone and the shades are driving around in it, using it for shits and giggles. But I can drop five grand decking out my Scooby and no fucker knows a thing. It has the bones of six hundred horsepower now. Garrett blower. Suede buckets. Bilstein coilovers.

OEMs. P Zeros. They were a grand each. No fuckin problem. Lowest of low profiles, just like me. Beautiful.

I told Sonya she can be my carer. They'd pay her and all, hahaha! Prolly more even than she gets now. Ever since the bust they're watching her like hawks. How comes you never seen nothing going in or out, Sonya? Cos they fuckin did it when I wasn't there, she says back. See how it pays me to keep my profile low? I'm gone off their radar years ago. They'd never link her to me, the dopey bastards. When I need to see her I slip in the back entrance. Of her block of flats. Fuck it I'm getting a horn.

That was a lovely operation for a while, clean as a whistle, nowhere near anyone's radars. Your man Trevor the fuckin blanket-muncher was unreal at the cutting. Down to the fuckin milligram. Fuckin Rain Man. And the speed of the cunt. But everyone has to make sacrifices to stay in the game, and that was mine. The shades are happy now for a while. They got a big one, they think. It was mostly shite in them boxes that day they went in but they don't know that. Or if they do they're keeping it to themselves. Street value of three hundred grand. Hahaha! They pluck the numbers out of their holes.

And old Trevor won't be a problem. There's no way he can finger me. He never even knew my name. There's a dozen cunts like me between here and the city centre and anyway he's a fuckin looper so his word isn't worth a fuck. He never knew Sonya was supervising him, keeping him happy, mesmerizing him. He's probably happy out, back in the loony bin, doped to his eyeballs, smearing the walls with his own shit.

I'm back in it now for a while, hands on. Pokey's auld

fella kicked the bucket so we're in his sheds. We used to use them for a bit of overflow storage of the cut and bagged gear before Augie's boys made their pickups but now the whole place is a proper operation and it's the dog's bollocks. I was never happy about leaving gear there with the old man knocking about but Pokey always said he never went through the door, only ever stood looking out the window, or watched the bore box all day. Pokey drives us up from town, or sometimes I run the Scooby out. I don't have a big mad exhaust like some doughnuts do. Shade magnets, the big pipes. She burrs under me and only whooshes from the dump valve.

The house is on the side of a hill. It's peaceful there. I don't mind the work. It's kind of soothing after a while. You have to wear a mask or you'd be off your box. I spent my life avoiding labour but when you're engaged in a profitable enterprise it's different. I'm more or less self-employed. I'm disciplined and organized. I'm actually a new man, to be honest.

I sometimes catch myself feeling proud and I know to pull myself back. It's dangerous to ever congratulate yourself. You're only ever one step from disaster, one fuck-up from shitting in a bucket in a cage with an arse bandit smiling at you, holding your jacks roll, telling you make sure you wipe it nice and clean.

THIS'LL SOUND GAY now but my young lad is beautiful. He's why I'm the way I am now. Clear, busy, in control. I seen his mother one day at the pitch shouting over the fence at him, Go on, Jayden, go on, Jay. I knew her straight away, mostly by her voice. Used to drill into my head, the screech of her. Although when I knew her first I loved her voice. She was always gas. My first instinct was to avoid her, though. I never seen her out this side of the city before. But something made me have a look. Some impulse that must be just in us when it comes to our children, put there by nature. I fucked away the rollie I was smoking and straightened myself up and sidled over. Howya, Suze, I said to her. Well, fuck me, she says back. Look what the cat shat out of itself. She always had a wicked dirty tongue on her. Here, I said, is that my young fella? Ya, she says. Left wing. Number seven. As if you didn't know.

I really didn't know. I hadn't seen him since he was a small yoke, and I remember thinking he was mad-looking but still I hadn't the heart for it and I walked. But I knew then, straight away, and I know now. Jesus, I'll never forget the feeling I got when I seen him. I nearly fuckin started crying or something. I was shocked at myself. I had to lean up against the railing. Is that really my young fella? I said to Suze. She only shook her head at me and told me fuck off. But I said nothing back, only stood like an ape with my mouth open watching him out on the left wing, crossing in the ball beautiful, putting it right on his mate's forehead so the cunt had to score, and then celebrating his assist real cool, one hand out, bit of a smile, classy.

I remember thinking, Thank fuck I wore the North Face gear and my newish tackies. Suze had a Superking on the go. She was sucking it down to the burned lip. She had the same lips she always had. Talented. She was wearing a wedding ring. She's the size of a house but still I was a bit disappointed. This was before I fell in love with Sonya.

Jayden looked over at her and she waved at him and

roared, Well done, love, and he winked. Jesus. I knew straight away he was a chip off the old block only better. Way better. My life changed that day. He could have fucked me off there and then and he'd of had the right. But he come over after the game and Suze says, all casual, like she was telling him to pick up his jocks off the floor, This is your father. And he looked me up and down a bit and he says, Ya? Fuck me. And he laughed and so did I, and old Suze rolled her eyes and lit another fag.

He's taller than me and he has wide shoulders and fair hair and blue eyes. He's a fuckin heart-throb. He has to fight off the flange non-stop. He's as sound a skin as ever you'll meet as well. That's why I'm better now than I was. Everything I do now since that day three years ago when I accidentally met him again is for him. Even the Scooby, my only weakness, is going to be his someday, if he wants it.

He's in college now. He comes in to me some days, between his classes, on the bus from the university. He thinks the place I work is a right laugh. Fuck, Dad, he says. This is some con job. You're a security guard in a college with no students. What the fuck do you do all day? And I tell him I pull my fuckin wire and think about his mother and he roars laughing. He can take a joke, my boy.

I HAVE THIS fantasy life all worked out, and it's starting to look like it might actually happen. Me and Sonya in a nice house, nothing too flash like, just a semi maybe out in Castletroy. Jayden working in some posh knob job in Plassey, living in a more fuck-off place, detached maybe, with one of those flakers you see on Instagram for a wife. The only problem is how to make it all look legit, buying the house and all that. The bank cunts'd tell me to fuck off if I asked for a mortgage. Even if Sonya threw in with me. And if I pay cash for a house the filth will sniff it out. No cunt trusts a cunt like me, with the tattoos on my face and all. Why the fuck I ever let Suze talk me into that I don't know. The thing is, though, it forces me to stay out of sight, to keep my head down, hoodie up, no sudden movements, no loudness. I used to be always shouting and roaring, looking for trouble, wanting to be seen. I don't know why. One of those counsellors tried to tell me why one time I was on remand in Arbour Hill but the cunt was so boring I forgot to listen.

Anyway, I stay in the shadows now. It's why I have the beard. It hides nearly one full spiderweb. Jayden slags me over the tattoos but I tell him they're his mother's fault. She told me they'd be rapid. I'd of done anything she told me. We were teenagers. As thick as shit. I was anyway. Suze always knew what she was doing.

I go running now. Five, ten miles at a time. I check places, spots, watch the runs in and out from a distance. No one ever suspects a cunt in running gear. I watch the towpath and the riverbank and the lads on the scooters. They're all working for me and they don't even know it. They're working for me, I'm working for Pokey, Pokey is working for some cunt from Malta or some fuckin place.

But that could all change soon. Pokey isn't as smart as he thinks he is and I'm way smarter than he thinks I am. And I have hidden talents. They were hidden so well and so deep I didn't even know about them myself for a long, long time.

Hillary

THERE'S A LANDMARK case in criminal law in the areas of *mens rea* and *actus reus*, the principles of the formation of mental intent and the commission of a voluntary act, both of which are required to be shown beyond reasonable doubt in order to find criminal liability. In the case, a man got up out of his bed in the middle of the night, drove twenty miles across Toronto to his wife's parents' house, and shot the two of them to death in their bed. But he was acquitted on the grounds that he had neither formed any intent nor committed a voluntary act. He'd been asleep the whole time.

I often think about that case now. How the man must have felt the next day. Apparently he drove back to his own house afterwards and got back into bed. He probably woke up thinking he'd had a really weird dream. He might even have woken his wife up to tell her about it. Then the door-bell will have rung and the real nightmare will have started.

I think a lot about how responsible we really are for the things we do, whether we're all just sleepwalking through our existence, following along a groove that was indented for us by some force far beyond our understanding in some other place and time. I spend my days advocating for people who say they had no choice. It was the drugs. It was their syndrome. It was their childhood. It was society.

I don't know why I tried so hard to become a solicitor. Well, I do in a way. It was the way the solicitors always looked at us, even the ones who were genuinely sound. That mixture of pity and amusement, that barely concealed contempt for us secretaries, even when we were the ones working non-stop up to our necks in maps, land registries, wills, codicils, appendices, shite, so that they could send out bills that'd make your eyes water to poor misfortunates just trying to make their tiny stakes, get themselves behind a door they could call their own, even with thirty years ahead of them of giving banks back twice the amount they were loaned. Actually, they didn't even send the bills out: we did. But still I was always in awe of them, like they were in this secret circle, this elevated, separate society that I could never occupy. Then I realized it would only take a few bursts of really intense effort for me to get through the FE-1s. Georgie was delighted, of course, because he got to take me on as an apprentice, after all my years working there in his *highly respected firm* as a secretary, and pay me peanuts for doing the same work.

Anyway, here I am. All these years of stress and study and vomiting from nerves later, qualified. Réaltín did her ACCA exams to become a certified accountant before I did my FE-1s to become a solicitor. She only did them because she couldn't let me get one up on her. The second she heard I'd applied to Blackhall she was on the internet looking for a course she could do so she could get out of Georgie's practice before me. And she's long gone and here I still am.

I can't believe sometimes that I'm still friends with her. Every single day she rang me crying that she had nothing done, she was going to fail, what the fuck was she going to do, and every time she did I stayed on the phone, soothing her, placating her, encouraging her. When we met for coffee or drinks she went on and on and on about herself, about Dylan, about Seanie, about Dylan's trauma and how it might affect him. I said once, Sure he'll hardly remember what happened to him. He was only gone a couple of days. And weren't they nice to him?

She started screaming at me. Right there in the wine bar on O'Connell Street, in front of loads of people. *NICE* TO HIM? ONLY GONE A COUPLE OF DAYS? YOU FUCKING BITCH! THEY COULD HAVE KILLED HIM! THEY *DREW* ALL OVER HIM! YOU WOULDN'T KNOW! YOU HAVE NO KIDS! FUCK YOU, HILLARY! Then she stormed off, hegging and snotting all over her makeup. So of course I had to ring her and apologize, like I always do. And she made a real favour of forgiving me, reminding me over and over again how I was Dylan's godmother, how I was meant to be one of the people who loved him most in the world, whose job it was to protect him and care for him, and on and on and on.

I didn't actually sign up for any of that, by the way. But being Dylan's godmother is tough going. Not because of Dylan, he's a pure sweetheart so he is, but because of the way she watches and judges every birthday and Christmas present. I don't think anything I've ever bought him has met her approval. I got him a Canada Goose jacket for his twelfth birthday last year. It cost an absolute fortune. I saw her rolling her eyes. I heard her whispering to Seanie, That's what all the scumbags wear. And Dylan, the dote that he is, smiling at me, and admiring himself in the mirror, saying, Thanks, Aunty Hill, and the sound of those words from his mouth bringing tears to my stupid eyes. God, I love him. I wish he was mine. Réaltín doesn't deserve him.

WHEN I WAS studying for the FE-1s I lost nearly two stone. I puked every day, sometimes twice. I smoked around thirty fags a day and drank a bottle of wine every night. Then I'd be so hungover I'd convince myself that I'd forgotten everything I'd learned the day before and I'd cry and puke again. Some of my hair fell out; my nails went to shit; I got pains in all my joints. I went home to my parents one day and Mam was in a tear of a mood and she started giving out that I hadn't gone to some random ancient person's funeral and I snapped. I started screaming at her to fuck off, to leave me alone, that I didn't care if everyone she ever knew popped their fucking clogs on the same day, it was nothing to do with me, she wasn't to ever ring me to tell me anyone was dead ever again or to mention funerals ever again unless it was either her own or Dad's.

That doesn't even make any sense, she said. And we both started laughing, and she came over and put her arms around me and said, Oh, my poor love, you're up in an awful heap, stop worrying, my darling girl, and Daddy came in then from the garden and stood beside her and cleared his throat and said, You know, Hillary, you can do those exams as many times as you want, and if George McSweeney won't pay for you to repeat them I'll pay for you myself. And that's the happiest moment of my life so far, imagine.

I was happier in that moment than I was the day I got my results and I'd scored so high they actually gave me an award. When I told Réaltín she said, Jesus, they give out awards just for passing exams? Well for you. *I* wasn't given any award. Then she started on about how accountancy was a real-world occupation, how accountants were, like, *facilitators of commerce*, while lawyers were bureaucrats, exploiters, advantage-takers. Fuck her and her *real world*. A lot she'd know about it.

The day I finally got to stand up in court and introduce myself to the bench, Mam and Dad came in with me and Dad started clapping but no one joined in. The judge looked around the courtroom at the speeders, the fine non-payers, the breachers of the peace, the handful of remanded prisoners shackled to prison guards off to one side, the rat-faced court reporter with his twitching nose and beady eyes, and she said, Are you sure this is what you want? And I smiled and said it was, I was committed to my role as an officer of the court and a servant of the law and of my clients, and she rolled her eyes and said, Right.

GEORGIE ACTS NOW like I was this charity case or something. Like I was an orphan he found on the street and brought home and turned into a solicitor. He makes me go for these dinners with his corporate clients. Corporate my arse. Car salesmen and builders, mostly, all teeth and flashing eyes.

Hillary, now, he goes. Rolling the *r* in my name just a tiny bit. Hillary came to us straight from school. Isn't that right, Hillary? And the so-called corporate clients look at me with a mixture of curiosity and boredom and that weird know-it-all superiority that business people often have, and I always nearly say, No, actually, I came from the School of Professional Studies, but there's no point, because Georgie is usually droning on: And we put her through college while she secretaried for us – and I want to scream then that *secretary* isn't a goddamn verb – and we sent her to Blackhall Place to do her FE-1s, and we apprenticed her and qualified her, and she's one of our bright young stars now, well, youn*ger* stars, fwaw haw.

And I feel myself redden and sweat and I have to settle myself, steady my voice before I speak, and I tell them all about how grateful I am to have been given such wonderful opportunities and to be working in a firm that places its clients' needs above everything, and I think about the day that Georgie made a guy wait for over half an hour in the little lobby on the ground floor even though he had nothing else in the world to do except meet his client at the appointed time, but he made the guy wait anyway, because that's the kind of prick he is, only happy when his foot is on your throat or his hand is on your arse, and when finally he came down and stood there with his big cheesy smile and his sweaty paw held out, the guy said, Did you not have a client with you?

Georgie put on his fake quizzical expression, eyebrows up, lips curled down at the corners, head a little sideways, and the guy said again, Did you not just have someone in your office with you? I know this is the only door out of here, and no one has come through here since I arrived. So it looks like you made me wait down here for no reason. Half two our appointment was for. It's after three now. You were above sitting in your office on your own and I was down here like a spare prick, like a boy, waiting for you to get up off of your hole. I have milking and foddering to do.

Georgie stood his ground awhile, in fairness to him. We all kept our heads down at our cubicles but we were straining to hear every word. Georgie was using his court voice now. Strident, loud, not quite aggressive but heading in that direction. I came down for you as soon as I was ready for you. Came down myself, mind you. I didn't phone down to have Rosemary send you up as I most often do. I was preparing for a deposition, if you must know. Just because I'm alone in my office doesn't mean I'm not working. Your man was having none of it. Georgie, he said, I was told you were a bollix, but I was prepared to give you the benefit of the doubt. Georgie still had his hand out. He withdrew it slowly.

Well, you waited this long, Georgie started to say, and he smiled his grisliest smile. And the guy said, To be honest, George, I only waited the last ten minutes to tell you to fuck off. And Georgie stood back to let the man leave, and shrugged and waddled back upstairs, but he was rattled. He wasn't used to having people cut through to the craven core of him. Because the guy was right. Georgie does that all the time. Keeps people waiting so they know their place. The length of the forced wait is inversely proportional to the level of wealth or influence of the person waiting. I promised myself I'd never, ever do that. I hope I never do.

STILL, THOUGH. JESUS. Sometimes I get so sick of every-thing and everyone. It's just. I don't know. The selfishness. Everyone always suiting themselves. Allowing themselves every pleasure, every luxury, every mistake. People feeling entitled to experience everything, no matter the cost to other people. I'm on legal aid for my sins, the main sin being the sin of having only just qualified. I have to deal with the petty fuck-ups, the recidivists. They sit there acting all wounded, victimized, reeling off the excuses. Or worse, for the ones with no imagination, they'll sit there waiting for me to make up the excuses for them. You're the solicitor, they'll say, or they'll think, at least, You're the one getting the big bucks. Now just tell me what to say so's I can get away with it, so the judge will think I'm a worthwhile person, that there's more to me than just stupidity and selfishness and meanness.

I hear my own voice getting shriller and shriller while I try to convince young lads to borrow a pair of trousers, or to go down to Penneys and buy a pair, and a white shirt and a dark tie, they have packs in Tesco for a tenner, just not to turn up to court in runners and tracksuits no matter how expensive they were. No tracksuit, no matter what label is on it, will look as respectful as a tucked-in shirt and trousers and shoes. They look at me like I'm mad. They smirk and gurn and rearrange their genitals. Their eyes are always shiny and glazed. Their noses are always red and runny. Everyone is taking cocaine. My vision blurs. My voice wavers. I hold on to the edge of the desk to steady myself. Then I tell them not to worry. And to make sure not to miss their appointment with their counsellor.

And the odd day the legal-aid crowd send me down a

frightened first-timer, who's been caught on the street with a wrap or an ounce, and they're shivering with fear, they can barely speak, their whole world has narrowed itself down suddenly to this grim cul-de-sac of crime and punishment, and I feel something clicking into place, something suddenly making sense about the crazy cartography of my life, and I know I'm in the exact right place in that moment to make a difference, to help this person through this time, to lift them up from the rushing waters and onto the safety of the shore, to make them feel like someone in the world is on their side, is backing them, is ready to help them to hold their hands up to their mistake, and to make amends.

A fella came in the week before last. I knew his face, knew he was a friend of Seanie's, but I didn't let on, and neither did he, though I could see something in his eyes when he came in first, a little flash of shock and embarrassment. Hello, Brian, I said. His eyes widened a bit. How do you know my name? We have an appointment, Brian, I said, and he reddened, and laughed. Oh, ya, ya, course.

He was caught with a few bags in the toilet of a country pub. Just enough to get done for supplying. But it turned out he had something worse hanging over him. He half told me and I inferred the rest. He was being threatened. By the real dealers, the guys who'd sucked him down into their hell. His story was so familiar. Now they were making demands of him, and holding a threat over his family as collateral, a dangling sword. He wanted to know if coercion was a defence. Was it too much of a stretch?

A defence for what? But he couldn't say. The pitch of his voice rose, he was almost shrieking; then he broke down to a wobbly whisper. What if I did something terrible because not to do it would lead to something worse being done? I told him he'd have to give me more detail and he closed his eyes and screwed up his face so that his teeth showed. Straight and white. He was quite a good-looking chap. You're in enough trouble as it is, Brian, I said, and he looked down at his hands, which he had placed palms down on my desk as though to steady himself. His fingernails were clean for a builder, and clipped. He had perfect half-moons. I told him that it was worrying to me that he was talking about stretched defences for unspecified crimes. Go to work and go home, I told him. Do not fraternize with the people who got you into this mess. But he went on. His voice was high and reedy again, pleading, wheedling.

What about that nurse who took an axe to the US Army plane out in Shannon? She pleaded lawful excuse because our collusion in extraordinary rendition could have caused us to be attacked. How much of a stretch was that? How much of an excuse do *I* need? He raised his two hands then and banged them back down and then he lifted them to his face and he cried like a child. I stood up. I think I nearly hugged him but I caught myself. I stood beside him and rested my hand on his shoulder. I shook it a little, as though to rouse him, to wake him from his nightmare, or to remind him he was a man. But he wasn't. He isn't. You'll have to speak up, Brian, I said. I can only help you if you tell the truth.

I felt awake and alive and *important* in that moment, as helpless as I was. It was one of those moments when I remembered that I can do good, I can be good. But those moments are few and far between. The rest of the time I'm sleepwalking.

Seanie

IT WAS I set Bobby and Triona up. In Nenagh, in Frankie's. Weeks before the first night they shifted, I lit the flame. I handed him my cue to play her even though it was winner stays on and I'd just beaten Pat Shee. It was my twenty pences he used for that game, too. Bobby never had twenty pences of his own. I fuckin knew. I'd seen him eyeballing her. I think he forgets that, you know. Or pretends to forget. The chances are now if you asked him how they got together he'd have a different story altogether, or he'd have the same story only with me left out of it. I wouldn't blame him. I wouldn't include me in a story about young love, either. Love's young dream.

Love. I always thought I knew what it was, but it turns out I had a fierce distorted view of it all along. I used to go in to a woman in the city and she'd sit across from me looking at me and I'd sit looking up at the ceiling or down at the floor. How are you feeling? she'd go, and I'd say, Grand, grand, finest now, A-wan. Then she'd go, Really? And she'd just be quiet then, her eyes drilling into me. It was like being fuckin tortured at the start. After around five goes I answered her honestly. I don't feel great sometimes, I told her. Some days I don't feel good at all.

Jesus. The relief of it. I couldn't believe I was after saying it at last. It was the best thing I ever did. Of course I couldn't shut up then. I went from there to telling her every single thing that ever happened to me. And the weird thing was there was nothing bad in all the things I told her. My parents were brilliant. They still are. My auld fella rings me every day. We go to matches together the whole time. Dylan came with us for a good few years but now he goes with his pals from the club on a minibus so it's back to the two of us. We usually try and meet him around the stadium some-where, though, to make sure he isn't up to anything. They're well supervised, in fairness, but he's my son at the end of the day. By the time I was twelve I was fit for anything.

We have whole routines worked out for Thurles, Limer-ick, Cork, Dublin matches, me and Dad; we park in the same spots, get a bit to eat in the same places, the Dergvale in Mountjoy Square when we're going to Croker, Clon-gibbon House in Mitchelstown on the way to Cork. Lar Corbett's for a pint in Thurles. I always drive so the auld fella can have his one pint, two at most, and he's happy out. He left his teeth on the table in Clongibbon House one time. Beside his plate after having the fry. We were nearly at the Jack Lynch Tunnel before he told me. Fuck's sake, Dad, I said. I rang the hotel. The lovely English bird who served us our fries answered the phone. She knew straight away when she heard my voice. Don't worry, she said. I have your dad's teef. You boys enjoy the match and call in to me on your way home. Poor auld Dad hardly opened his mouth the whole match out of embarrassment. He was too shy then to go in for them on the way home, but he gave me a tenner to give the one as a tip for minding his teeth. Then he says to me, getting out of the car, Don't try and ride her. It was a bit shocking to hear those words out of his mouth but we roared laughing anyway.

The therapist fuckin landed on this. She was obsessed suddenly. She leaned right forward towards me. The top button of her blouse came open. She wasn't in bad nick at all, in fairness. Around the block and back a few times. Knew all sorts of tricks, I'd say. She goes, Why would your father say that to you? For a joke, I said. A joke? She sat back and crossed her legs. She was wearing nylons, sheer. I'm nearly sure I got a glimpse of a frill high up on her thigh for a second. Stockings. Jesus. I could feel myself starting to sweat a bit. I could feel that buzzing in my head, that bristling I get on my skin. This need comes over me, sometimes, it's like something takes me over, like I'll go mad if I don't get something out of myself.

I stopped going, not long after that session. Once I got it in my head about her stockings and the suspenders and the expensive silky knickers she was probably wearing it was all ruined. There was no cure for me in sitting across from a foxy auld one, nursing a half a horn and trying to look like I wasn't thinking about what it'd be like to ride her. And anyway I started feeling like something that was being examined, probed, opened up and looked into. So all I got from it was that I saw love wrong, or felt it wrong, and that I used sex as a balm for my feelings of inadequacy, to mitigate my self-loathing. But that can't be right. I loathe myself way more after I do the dirt. But still I can't stop doing it.

I KNOW I shouldn't have been acting the prick with Bobby. It was dirty, taking that picture. I was delighted with myself, is the worst thing. I couldn't wait to show Réaltín. She was always oohing and aahing about Bobby, how great he was, how he started his business from practically nothing. That was nearly worse than the time years ago when I was sure he was tapping her, when the whole town had it that he was, even though deep down I knew the truth of that. But the way she admired him fuckin tormented me sometimes. Like I couldn't have done any of the things he done. Like I was only a boy alongside him. I'm his oldest friend. It was me he always came to when his father was acting the cunt. He'd arrive at the door and I always knew before I even opened it, by the shape of him through the frosted glass, the hump of him, that auld Frank was on the warpath.

I pushed him in through that door in Amsterdam and I think I actually prayed to God that he'd get off with the hooker. That's how fucked up in the head I am. I actually prayed that my best friend would do the worst thing in his own eyes that he could do. I wanted him to be like me, so I wouldn't have to feel so bad about myself. I threw the money in behind him and all. I could see the one kneeling down picking up the notes as I closed the door. Bobby was out of his head, in fairness. I put a bit of something in his shot glass. I was pissed, though, when I did that. I waited then to make sure he was okay. And to take his photo coming out. I couldn't believe how well it came together, with the one blowing kisses after him. Réaltín acted like all her Christmases were after coming together when I showed it to her. I got a bit nervous then. I only sent it to the stag WhatsApp group but she fuckin sent it everywhere, that photo. Jesus, I wish I could go back in time.

BOBBY IS ON about sorting out Augie Penrose and the three musketeers he carries around in his car, Pitts, Braden and Dowel. They're running the whole show, he says. Every day now nearly he says it. We have a responsibility, he says. As fathers, as men. They're running drugs around the countryside and they're ruining lives. Any of our kids could get sucked in and hooked. He never says too much about exactly how he's going to sort them out.

I don't know if he realizes how bad those boys actually are. I heard stories about some of the things they did to people that owed them money. And how the debt once you're in it gets deeper and deeper so there's no way of climbing back out. That's how they get people to deal for them, to handle the goods, to take all the risks. I've heard of people selling land to pay them off. Parents of kids who got hooked inside in town. I've heard worse stories, too, way worse. I wouldn't tell Bobby. He's close enough to the edge as it is. He does this fucking mental thing where he pulls in his van right in front of Augie's black Audi where he parks in Summerhill, and he eyeballs them through the windscreen, Augie, Pitts and the two cunts in the back. He sits there with his teeth gritted and he says fuck-all, and when they start mouthing he just pulls off again, real slow.

Penrose got out one day last week and so did Bobby. Right there on the street inside in town. There was no space in front of Augie so Bobby stopped out in the lane and cars started building up behind the van – there was pricks blowing and everything. I was only with Bobby that day because my own van was in the garage for a cambelt. I'd swear that's why Bobby done it. He knew I'd have to back him up. Penrose just kept saying, What the fuck is your problem, Bobby? And Bobby just stood there with his forehead right into Penrose's forehead and his face was blood red and his lips were back from his teeth like a dog's and he goes, You're my problem, you filthy little drug-dealing cunt, and Augie just kept saying, Come on then, big man, fuckin try something, try something.

I got out then because Pitts did, and I pulled Bobby away, and Augie Penrose spat on the ground, and eventually I managed to finagle Bobby back into the van, and Pitts shouted after us, Tell your mate Pat Shee he owes me a grand, and Bobby fucked Patsy off the job the minute we got back. Literally kicked him in the hole the whole way out the yard of the house we were doing. The missus of the house was there watching and all. Bobby just looked at her and said, Drugs. And she blessed herself.

IT'S LIKE SOMETHING is wired wrong inside in me. The way I think, the way I act. It's like I'm split in two, light and dark. Most of the time the two sides can mingle so I'm just kind of stable, half normal, a bit okay, a bit worried, but level; I can act the bollix, slag away, take a slagging, have the craic with the lads on the site, in Ciss Brien's, on the phone.

I can give a hand out at the hurling with the coaching here and there, and Dylan doesn't even get embarrassed.

He's a great lad, so he is. The day me and Bobby went at it there last month he got all worried. Fair play to Bobby that day, though, the little speech he made about friendship. When I heard him telling Dylan that me and him were kind of like brothers I felt unreal, this weird sensation, this sudden brightening, and the whole thing nearly seemed worth it, the whole way I tried to make Bobby look like he was as big a fuck-up as me, that he wasn't the goody-goody hero everyone thought, it kind of clicked or something, like it made sense suddenly for me to have pulled such a low stunt.

When I think of how Réaltín caught me by the balls. I didn't even want to go into the one's room in Torremolinos. I was just passing her door and she was standing there in her bikini bottoms. Fuck it anyway. Why didn't I just stay going, down the corridor to our room, and have a wank like I'd intended, while Réaltín and Dylan were out by the pool and I had a bit of peace? It wasn't worth it. I should have known Réaltín would cop it. Any other time I done the dirty on her there was a good gap of distance and time between us so I could have myself convinced nearly it hadn't even happened. It's ages ago now but I don't think she'll ever forgive me, to be honest, and I don't deserve to be forgiven. I can't forgive myself. I never could. Only for Dylan I'd be gone long ago.

I PUSHED BOBBY and I pushed. I kept on acting the cunt, even after we had the dust-up and even after the thing with Augie Penrose. It was like there was someone else inside in me saying shit and I couldn't stop them taking over my brain and my mouth. It was like the Devil was lining things up for me to be sure that I had no choice but to shoot my stupid mouth off. There we all were at the back of the vans, mine and Bobby's, sitting out for three o'clock break. Rory was there, and Timmy Hanrahan, and Brian Walsh, and a couple of the new lads. One of them was reading his phone. I wonder if it'll be Niall Scannell or Rob Herring that starts for Ireland at number two this year, he said. His mate said, I don't know in the hell. It's hard to know who's the best hooker.

I couldn't fuckin help myself, I swear to God. Before I knew my mouth was going to open it was out. Ask Bobby, lads, I said. He knows all the best hookers! And Rory Slattery nearly choked on his tea. Even Timmy Hanrahan laughed, and you wouldn't be sure half the time does he even know he's alive. Bobby was sitting on a small blue bandstand about ten feet from me. Right, he said. Just that. It was like we were ten again. He was up and he was coming towards me and I fucked my tea at him, mug and all. He just swatted it and he kept coming. I took off running, out the yard, out the gate, down the road towards the weir, I kept running. Bobby was shouting behind me. I crossed the stile onto the path by the Newtown River. I was fuckin laughing. I knew he was going to kill me and I couldn't stop laughing. Seanie, Seanie, Bobby was going. Just stop, just fuckin stop. At the end of the path there's another stile. But it was blocked off. There was a whole bale of razor wire spread out from tree to tree either side of it so the only way through was by dropping down off the bank to the right and into the river or down to the left and through a high electric fence. It was all the one.

He was behind me. And I could hardly breathe. I turned around to face him and I waited for his fist to smash into my face. His hands were up, his face was red. I shook my head. And then he was up to me, my old friend, my friend Bobby, and his arms were around me, and he was holding me up, and I was holding him up.

Kate

THERE I WAS with nothing. Only for the urgent-needs payment I would have starved at the start of it all. And I nearly had to beg for that. I was about to tell the little prick to shove it up in his hole when he stamped the form and fucked it at me. Well, I knew I could have gone home to Dad any time I wanted, but I couldn't really, you know? I couldn't face going back, back to my old bedroom, my old bed and shelves and books and locker, the same grey wall at the end of the garden, the same flowerbeds and vegetable drills and the two ancient apple trees. I loved the thought that those things were all there still, and that Dad was still there among them, whistling softly, moving quietly through his little world, his green kingdom. But I couldn't go back: I couldn't abandon my own life, the shreds and remnants I had left of it.

My father talked to my mother all the time after she died. If anyone saw him they'd have thought he was mad but he actually used to do it so as to stay sane. He said he knew exactly what she would have said about everything that happened, exactly what her opinion would have been, and so he let her words form themselves in his mind and then he answered her out loud. He roared laughing sometimes out of the blue and when I asked him what was so funny he'd start saying, Oh, your mother just said . . . Then he'd get a bit embarrassed, the end of his nose and the tops of his cheeks would pink up, and he'd correct himself . . . Oh, I was just thinking what your mother might say if she were here. Oh, Dad. You shouldn't have minded me. You should have talked to her away.

SO THERE I was, rightly landed. My husband in prison for killing a man. The worst recession ever to happen in the history of the world raging all around me. My business closed down because one of the kids from my crèche was kidnapped. From *my* crèche. By a person I had working in the crèche. Who wasn't on the books. Who I hadn't fully done the Garda clearance for. It was in train, like. It takes way too long. And, it turns out, he would have been cleared anyway, because his part in the kidnapping was his first offence. How was I supposed to know he was a fucking psycho? How did no one spot it when he was doing his Montessori course? Why had I to take all the blame? They found the child, anyway, totally unharmed. Still, the mother was in here threatening all sorts. I should have pressed charges against *her*. It blew over, though, that part of the madness, like all storms do. You have to weather them, I know that now. Batten the hatches and cling on for dear life.

Ten years is a long time. But it all still feels like yesterday. And in another way it feels like it happened to a different person, in a different world. I remember every single moment, every single word, of the exchange between me and Denis when he told me he was after killing a man. It was only a few days since the kidnapping. I was still holding out hope that I'd be able to reopen. The regulator hadn't struck me off yet. I'd hardly noticed Denis for days – his presence around me was like a fly, a nuisance on the edge of my consciousness; I swatted at him when he came too near me.

For a finish I came on him lying down in the spare room on the unmade bed, curled up like a child, rocking himself. I exploded. I was demented with anger and worry. He let me shout myself out. Then he said, in a whisper, Do you know that man that was killed out near Nenagh? That man that was killed in his own house? And I could feel the next moment flooding over me before it happened; his words echoed and vibrated through me before they were even spoken. I did it. I did it, Kate. I killed him.

AND MY FIRST thought was, How do I make sure he doesn't get found out? How do I get us through this new nightmare? For a second or two I thought about killing Denis. Going to the kitchen for a carving knife and stabbing him right in the throat. Claiming self-defence. I'd never have done it but I can't deny the vision that appeared to me. Then I moved towards him and he put a hand out to me from where he was lying on the bed and I took it and I lay down on the bed beside him and we lay there together holding hands in silence for ages, listening to the wind and the rain on the window, watching the shadows on the wall. We turned to face each other. He kissed me and I kissed him back. I'd forgotten what his kiss was like, the way it used to feel.

We got up as the light fell and we dressed ourselves and we drove into Henry Street and Denis walked up to the hatch and the pretty young Garda behind it looked at him and then at me beside him and I'd say she knew immediately from the looks on our faces that we were going to ruin her nice quiet shift. She knew we were big news, big trouble. Before Denis even opened his mouth she was over to the door to let us into the inside of the station. And into the belly of the beast we slouched, my love and me.

They charged him with manslaughter and he pleaded guilty. His solicitor pleaded provocation as a mitigating factor for sentencing. Denis had told the cops the truth when he made his statement, and the truth was that the man he killed had taunted him. That Denis had lashed out in rage. That he'd been under severe financial pressure. But he'd been armed entering the house. That was what fucked him. The old man's son and daughter-in-law came to the sentencing. The judge asked if there was a victim-impact statement and the prosecutor looked down the courtroom at those people and the man shook his head, no. Denis got eleven years. You'll do seven, max, the solicitor said, as she snapped her briefcase shut. Bobby, the son of the man he killed, started to visit him in prison after the first year. They're kind of friends now. Denis doesn't say much about it and I don't press him.

I HADN'T MUCH personal debt. That was the saving of me. Thank God, Denis had built the extension himself for the crèche. Credit cards are unsecured so I told the bank they could forget me paying those off for a start. The one I was dealing with, a right little madam, huffed down her witchy little nose and said she'd clear them and cancel them and add the balance to the end of the mortgage. Ha, I said. Mortgage my arse! I have sixteen euros in my purse, love. You can put me on interest only or you can try to sell the house. Best of luck to you in this market. I'd say she wasn't used to being on the back foot. She narrowed her eyes and laced her fingers together. If we did that, she said, and then she called me *madam* in a really sarcastic voice, we would pursue you for the deficit between the sale price and the outstanding loan. I laughed again and I meant it this time. You wouldn't have to pursue me, I said. I'd be easily found. In my *fucking house.*

I swore to myself in that moment that I'd never miss a mortgage payment. There was no way I was losing the house. So I started working in a chipper. Chippers and hairdressers are the two recession-proof businesses. I took every shift going. Once I had my twelve hundred euros a month for the mortgage nothing else mattered. It was my only focus. I walked to work and the owner or his wife drove me home. I ate at work. Every day I had a shift, some days I had two, some nights I babysat for the owners. Once a fortnight Dad drove me down to Cork Prison to see Denis. Then they moved him to Limerick, and I was able to work on visit days. He was always quiet. He always said, It's fine. The grub is good. The lads I'm with are all right. We play pool most nights. The wardens have me doing bits and pieces of fitting and carpentry.

We held hands across the table and before I left we always hugged. I found myself missing him, longing for the visits. I put on weight. All the chips at work, I thought. The new job is suiting you, Dad said. You're looking fine and strong. I was nearly six months pregnant before I realized.

I'D THOUGHT THE stress of everything had stopped my periods. Or that maybe I was in early menopause. I'd never meant to be a mother. Denis and me used to fight about it. He made out once or twice after we got married that I said we'd have kids once our businesses were up and running and we had people we trusted working for us and we could relax a bit. I could never remember saying that but maybe I did. I could have been pissed or anything. We used to go out a lot before we got married. I saw the words *geriatric mother* written in the nurse's notes in the obstetrician's office. A geriatric mother with a husband in prison and a job in a chip shop. How the mighty had fallen.

That's what I expected Nuala to say when I met her in town one day after a scan. I was never big with my Laoise, but it was obvious I was pregnant. Her eyes were like saucers. Oh. My. God, she goes. In Brown Thomas, this was, over by the shoes. I was looking at a pair of boots I couldn't afford that wouldn't even go over my ignorant swollen toes, and when I saw her there, staring at me with her wide eyes and her big smile, I said, Ah, fuck. Out loud. And she laughed, the way she always used to when I was giving out to her in the crèche for slacking off, smoking fags, letting nappies overflow, being a right little strap.

And I laughed, too. Kate, she said. You're blooming.

Oh, my God, you look so beautiful. She sounded like she meant it. And the weird thing is I felt beautiful. I stood there, in a 1970s maternity dress from Mammy's wardrobe that she must have kept out of some prescient maternal instinct that told her I'd need it someday because I'd be a pregnant prison widow a half-step from bankruptcy, and I knew that everything had happened exactly as it was supposed to. All the horror and the heartbreak and the crushing shocks and disappointments and struggles. I felt a burst of happiness, like a wave breaking inside me, rushing to fill every part of me, to the top of my head, to my fingers and toes. I felt as well a swell of pride that I was here, that I was carrying a new life inside me, that I was in love again with a man I'd nearly hated once.

It's never really faded, either, that new-found joy. I look at Laoise now, my little eight-year-old goddess, heading off to her camogie match, holding her daddy's hand, and I hear my own father's voice from heaven, saying, Thank God for her. The beautiful child. Lord, can't life be good?

And I answer him out loud, like I always do. Yes, Daddy, it can.

Lloyd

I SUPPOSE I expected my father to turn up looking exactly the way he looked the moment he left. In the same jacket and T-shirt. With the same voice, the same smile, as though he'd only made it to the end of the street and changed his mind. Laughing, catching me in a headlock, mussing up my hair, kissing me, saying, Gotcha! I was only messing! I'd never leave you! Come on, we'll go the flicks.

I used to go to the cinema a lot when I first got out. Matinees only. I was often the only one there. There aren't even projectionists any more, it's all programmed. I used to try to feel what I felt as a kid. The thrill of expectation. The smell of Dad's cologne, the sound he used to make through his nose as he chewed his wine gums, kind of a half-laugh of anticipatory pleasure as the movie started. He loved movies. He'd talk the whole way home, going through every scene, laughing again at all the funny parts.

It was a mistake meeting him. Everyone said it'd be good for me. That it would mean a lot to him. That I could get some answers, some closure. But he was so different. He was old, bald on top, grey at the sides. He had a big belly and skinny arms. And his smile was gone. He didn't smile once. He was wearing a *cardigan*, for Christ's sake. My dad would never have worn a cardigan. I suspected for a minute that it was a prank. That my dad was setting me up for a laugh, that the dour old man at the table in front of me was in on the joke and that my real dad was hiding somewhere, watching, and he'd jump out and shout, Surprise! And he'd be wearing his leather jacket with the collar turned up and his hair would be dark and combed back and his eyes would be sparkling with fun.

IT'S STILL HARD sometimes to hold on to what's real. I wish I could ask people around me if things are real, like Russell Crowe's character at the end of A *Beautiful Mind*. And have everyone smile and laugh like it was really cute, just a charming affectation. But I can't, so I cling on, still myself, centre myself, concentrate on my breathing the way I was taught. It's a lot easier now, though, and it's getting better all the time.

Maybe you should try to meet someone, Mom used to say. How would that have worked? How does it work? And she'd start saying things like, You just walk up to someone you like, and . . . Imagine if I did. A convicted child kidnapper. Out on licence. Tagged and curfew-bound. Walking up to random women and . . . I don't know what. I didn't used to let Mom finish when she started that kind of silly talk.

Even if I hadn't been so horrendously hamstrung by my list of proscriptions and the lingering manifestations of my crimes, it would have seemed impossible.

It still seems a preposterous act, to attempt to initiate any kind of anything. To ask someone out, precipitously, spontaneously. It sounds like nothing. Would you like to go out with me? Would you like to go for a drink? Has anyone actually ever said those words to another human? I can't imagine it. People meet online now, of course. But I was monitored for the first two years. It was almost a comfort to know there was a bored police person sitting in a room somewhere watching a screen of activity, waiting for red flags.

I was tempted sometimes to push the boundaries just to see if it would elicit any warning, any communication. To google 'primary schools' perhaps, half expecting a masked SWAT team to abseil down from the apartment roof and smash through the picture window. I never would have, though. I was only allowed to use one PC, the monitored and restricted one in Mom's apartment, and they gave me a set of login credentials, and they even, mortifyingly, gave me a list of admissible porn channels. I never looked at them. I was embarrassed nearly all the time. And scared. Of myself, mostly. Of how much I despised myself. They thought I was a danger to children but really I was only a danger to myself.

Poor Mom. I gave her such hell for so long, then landed her in a living nightmare. And still there she was every week, across from me, putting on a brave face. I felt so bad for her sometimes. A faithless bastard for a husband and, hands up, a wack job for a son. But she seemed able to exist happily, or peaceably at least, within her own little world, her routines, locked inside her own set of shibboleths and comfortable prejudices.

I actually love her company now. The apartment is quite spacious and filled with light. We have a view of the river and of Limerick's three bridges, the blunt greyscape of the ancient city. I work every day on my play at the desk she bought for me and she brings me coffee. She buys the beans on Saturday mornings from a roaster in the Milk Market. She grinds them herself on the kitchen counter, timing her little contraption to the millisecond. It reminds me of how I always used to grind my teeth and how I don't any more. I love her coffee. Her cooking, too, is much improved. Or maybe my palate has atrophied. Either way, I appreciate her efforts.

WHEN TREVOR SAT beside me on the bus a few weeks ago I genuinely thought I was hallucinating. I said nothing for a few seconds. Then his long grisly face swept around and I was looking into his flat eyes, his open pores, and smelling his foul breath. It smelt the exact same as it always did. Stale milk, rotten meat. He was about to speak when I jumped up. I had to almost climb over his gangly legs. We weren't at a stop but the driver let me off, thank God. I shouted at Trevor, What the fuck are you doing? I watched from the street as the bus drove off. He was just sitting there, staring forward.

It was so obvious in the end. When my trauma was pointed out to me I felt so stupid. The reason I had created an alternative reality. I tried to depopulate the universe. If no one existed outside of me then no one could hurt me. The moment my father left. That's what it was, that's when the fracture happened, invisible, the barest of hairlines. But it opened out. I held the broken pieces of myself together inside my clothes, inside my skin. The day I heard Mom talking about Dad's new girlfriend being pregnant all the pieces fitted themselves back together and I had this clarity, suddenly, this absolute knowledge that nothing was real. Not even my body was real. Everything was a figment of my consciousness.

I loved prison in a way, after a while, after the shock of it had worn off. It just all felt so right. Everything was ordered, timed, supervised. I had to make no effort. There was a school there, unbelievably, with blackboards and desks and actual teachers. Ben, the guy I spoke to twice a week in a white windowless office on the ground floor of the school wing, hardly even reacted when I told him about the solipsism. He just looked at me kind of bored, resigned, and he smiled, a kind smile, I think. This place is full of solipsists, Lloyd, he said, and he laughed, and I did too. The idiotic paradox of it.

We talked a lot then about perspective, our positions in the universe, how every single point is necessarily the centre in a space with no defined or visible parameters. How reality is composed somewhere between the optic nerve and the occipital lobe. So I'd been completely right all along, and also completely wrong, and those two states of being existed comfortably together in one place and time, like Schrödinger's dead and alive cat. It was a great relief. The burden of Godhood was lifted from my shoulders.

I WROTE A lot in prison. Daubs and scribbles initially. I was still playing some kind of part. I had visions and notions of myself as Ed Norton in *Primal Fear* or James McAvoy in *Split*. Eventually I calmed down and settled into myself. Ben asked me to write a letter to the parents of the boy. I did so but I don't think they ever read it. Ben said they would have to agree to receiving a letter from me, we couldn't just, like, pop it in a letterbox. But he said my letter was really good. Coherent, contrite, and an expression of full acceptance of my responsibility. He put it in my file for my parole hearing. Keep writing, he said. You're good at it. So I did.

I composed a series of monologues. I gave each speaker a unique voice and I allowed them to reveal their deepest secrets. Some of them had only banal, anodyne, humdrum confessions to make. Some of them were darker, more shocking, more fun. I lost myself completely in them. In a way it was as though I was a solipsist again, a single force of creation, generator of everything, controller of everything. Language was unwieldy at the beginning: I had to learn to marshal it, to make it do my bidding. And when I had the language leashed, the characters were suddenly beyond my control. They were crazy! The things they said and did. The wild joy I felt. The rightness of it all.

I READ A book by a local journalist. It was reportage, non-fiction, but lightly dramatized and padded out with plausible fiction. It wasn't very well written. The journo was a hack, I suppose, slashing their way through the briary overgrowth of their story to find the truth of things. And I found in her inelegant efforts the seed of my play. The book was about a guy called John Cunliffe, or Johnsey, as he was known to those who loved him. The name was familiar. I'd often heard it spoken when I was young, Mom and her friends in the kitchen discussing it. He'd lived not that far from our old house. The far side of the valley, to put it colloquially. He'd been shot by the Garda Armed Response Unit because he'd pointed a loaded gun at them. They'd tried to get him to put it down, they'd waited and waited, but he kept walking towards them with the shotgun raised to his shoulder and pointed outwards at the world. He'd been holed up in his parents' house for a few hours beforehand.

The journo who wrote the book didn't do a bad job, I suppose. She pieced together what she could about the last year of the guy's life. He died near Christmas so she wrote it as twelve chapters, January to December. I couldn't stop thinking about him. She interviewed his neighbours and friends and family but they didn't seem to give her very much. You can't blame them. Who in their right mind would volunteer information to a journalist? The rest she extrapolated from hearsay, circumstance and conjecture.

But it was his last moments that fascinated me. I spent whole days trying to imagine how he must have been feeling as he walked through the door, as he took his last steps. The book was pretty detailed about the mechanics of that part of the story, the positions of the armed responders, the exact words that were spoken through a loudhailer before he opened the door, and without the loudhailer as he walked across the yard towards the wall and gateway where the marksmen were crouched, their weapons trained on him. Did he know he was going to die?

He's alive again now, anyway. In my monologues he has lots to say, about love and loss, life and death. Mom sits across from me some evenings in the kitchen and we read through scenes, and we correct things that don't ring true. It's amazing how things can change when they're spoken aloud, when they're shared. I never realized how lovely Mom's voice was, how perfect her diction, how adept she is at loading a phrase with just the right weight of emotion, just the right swing of drama.

Mom was a great help with my grant application, too. We filled it in together over one Friday evening. I kept waiting for the question about criminal records, but there wasn't one, and the day I got the email saying we had a development grant from the Arts Council we danced for joy around the apartment. I'm so proud of you, she said. I hope she'll play the part of Johnsey's mother, but she probably won't. She's just too shy. I've told the director not to cast the part yet but he's anxious to do so. Mom has less than a week to forget about her self-consciousness and allow her truest self to shine through. Ha! I hope that kind of saccharine bullshit never infects my writing!

MY FATHER WAS giving me a lecture. I tried to find a memory of a time in my childhood when he'd spoken to me angrily, or even with authority or sternness. We all have to take responsibility for our actions, he was saying, for our lives. We were all very let down by you. I laughed then, a kind of shrill, disbelieving laugh. I hadn't known I was going to do it.

I looked out the window of the café. The car my father had arrived in was parked at the opposite kerb. The word *dad* had dissolved for me completely now, before our coffees were even drunk. Dad was somewhere else in time, wearing his leather jacket and his Converse. He still had all his hair and his devilish smile.

The car was an older Mercedes, one of the austere, blocky, slab-sided ones. I could see that there was someone sitting at the wheel. Male, dark-haired, curly. I realized who the person must be. My brother. Half-brother. My brother from another mother as one might say if one were so euphonically inclined. Or a simpleton.

I excused myself but instead of going to the Gents I sneaked out the door and crossed the road. I walked back up away from the car a little bit, then joined with a small squabble of office workers and approached at an oblique angle across the wide footpath, until I had a clear view of my long-lost semi-sibling. I watched as he hunched forward in his seat, then swung upright and shook his head violently from side to side. I startled him by standing still by his window and looking at him. His eyes were wide, his pupils wildly dilated. He lowered the window.

I don't think he knew who I was. He sniffed expansively. A thin skim of powder ridged his nostrils. His nose and cheeks were very red. Can I help you? he said. I could hear in his voice a dim distant echo of Dad. Real Dad, not the cardiganed, censorious father from the café. And that new old man was beside me suddenly, and his voice was truly angry now, and he was asking, What do you think you're doing? And he called my name as I walked away, but I didn't slow down or look back.

At the corner of Henry Street I stopped and turned around and he was still standing there, looking. I shouted back at him, Love you, kiddo.

And I walked on, towards where the Savoy cinema used to be.

Rory

WE USED TO have a howl in work most days. It's all gone to shit at the moment, though. Bobby is like a bull going around. There's no pleasing or placating him. Every man has his head down. Him and Seanie made up after the whole thing with the hooker and the photo. Lampy Shanley ran down towards the weir after them the day Seanie took off running and Bobby after him like he was going to actually murder him. He sent a photo back up from the towpath of the two of them hugging. He zoomed right in. Pair of apes. That's what happens when you spend your whole life repressing your feelings. I can't really talk, in fairness.

But still there's a feeling off Bobby like he's about to explode. He's up in arms over Augie Penrose and those lads and the way they seem to have a kind of free rein. They're smart, though. Jim Gildea said it one day in the Dapp Inn inside in Nenagh. Jim is all talk since he retired and he doesn't seem to give a fuck who hears him. It was nearly like he was hoping someone connected to Augie's gang would report back. He said you could search them and search their cars morning, noon and night and never will you find a dust on them. The only chance you might have is catching them with cash but they'll always have a story ready. Gambling or they just sold a car or something like that.

Bobby says we all have a duty to stand up to them. That if the cops can't do anything to protect our children then we have to. That was grand all along but now Eugenija is expecting I'm included in the sermons. Do you want your child born into a world ruled by those scumbags? No, Bobby. Do you want them pushing drugs on your children? No, Bobby.

So far, though, Bobby has only questions and no answers. The only stand I've seen him make was against Patsy Shee. He fucking kicked him down the road to his house. He went in roaring to Pat's poor mother and father. Did ye know this fuckin eejit is taking drugs? Poor Paddy and Agnes got a terrible hop. Patsy said his mother keeps trying to get the priests out from town to talk to him or exorcize him or something. It's nearly worse than the time his wife did the dirt and got knocked up and fucked him off, he says. Patsy is actually *grounded*, and he well into his forties. Paddy and Agnes have him locked in his room. It's like something out of fucking *Trainspotting* in there by now, I'd say.

I NEARLY FEEL guilty being so happy. I'm half afraid to think about it. When Eugenija told me she was pregnant she was afraid I'd be cross. Imagine that! When did you ever see me cross? I said to her. Last year, when Limerick won the match? Haha, I wasn't cross, I was only worried about having to listen to the fuckers going on about it inside on the Castletroy site. They were waiting a long time, in fairness to them. Anyway, they're only a flash in the pan, that team. Tipp will win it this year and order will be restored. Eugenija actually loves the hurling. She's some bird, in fairness. Jesus Christ, I won the Lotto the day I tripped over her dog's lead inside in the castle field in Nenagh.

Oh, my gosh, she said. Are you okay? Her accent was foreign, sexy. She was standing over me. I was after making a bollix of myself, in fairness. It wasn't just a little stumble. Her dog saw a cat and darted out from the bench where she was sitting with her friend just as I got to them, and it was too late for me to stop, so I fell over the lead and landed flat on the path. Then I rolled a bit into the grass, then fell again when I was trying to get up because the grass was wet. I ended up kind of lying on my side to get my breath back until she stood up and tried to help me and her dog was sniffing my crotch and her friend was looking disgustedly at me behind her and I actually think it was love at first sight. I'd never seen eyes like hers before. Pure green, and full of light. She wasn't laughing at me but her eyes were.

The palm of my left hand was skinned to bits and dripping blood. Oh, my God, you are bleeding, she said, and her eyes opened wider and I fell in deeper. Then I said something fucking ridiculous like, Ah, don't worry one bit, I fall the whole time. And she laughed again and said, Oh. Okay. You are good at falling, then. Yes, I can see this. But please come to my café and I will make it up to you. You have a café? I said, like a fool. Yes, I have a café. And she looked a little bit pissed off suddenly at the suggestion of surprise in my stupid voice.

I wasn't surprised, though. If she'd told me she was a brain surgeon or an astronaut I wouldn't have been surprised. The shock of her beauty was coming through in my words, is what it was. I told her that months later. She was delighted. She kept repeating it. The shock of my beauty. Haha, Rory, you are a gas man. When she says that kind of thing, an Irish phrase in her Lithuanian accent, I get a bit dizzy.

SHE TOLD ME that her café was on Friary Lane. Where Ryan's bookshop used to be before they moved out to Pearse Street. Oh, ya, I know it, I said, but I was lying. You know it but you have never come in? I did, I said, you mustn't have been there. I have never not been there since the day we opened, three weeks ago. Her friend rolled her eyes. I found out later the friend was her cousin, Lucija. She's actually sound, in fairness. She came over from Lithuania especially to give Eugenija a hand setting up. But she was no help to me in that first moment of meeting her, when I was after getting caught in a lie.

Eugenija was standing facing me now with one hand on her hip. She'd picked Milky up and had the dog tucked under her oxter. You're not there now, are you? I heard myself say. Eugenija's lips pursed a little bit and something flashed in her green eyes. Lucija made some kind of surprised sound, ooh, like the fake noises we used to make in school when a fight was about to start, to encourage the fighters to get stuck in. Today is Sunday. We don't open on

Sundays. We are café, not restaurant. Do you work on Sundays, mister, when you are not running around parks and falling over my dog? No, I said. That was all I had. I could feel the old hotness, the redness, the familiar itch of mortification starting up along my spine and neck and onto my cheeks and forehead.

Milky wasn't too impressed with me on that first encounter, but she loves me now. It actually makes Eugenija a bit jealous, the way she favours me. I say it's only because I'm physically bigger and dogs are attracted to those they perceive as the alpha but Eugenija still looks hurt when Milky hops off her and over to me the second I sit down on the couch in the evening. I actually googled dog repellent, just to see if there was something I could do about it. There are sprays you can get.

I ran off anyway, that first day. I was on one of my weekly ten-milers at the time, from the village, into Nenagh, six laps of the track up at the Christian Brothers, and back to the door of Mam and Dad's, exactly ten miles. The whole rest of that run all I could think about was whether I'd have the balls to call into that café. She'd actually shouted after me, Make sure to call to me! For all I knew she could have been married, or going out with someone, or not into fellas; she could have thought I was some kind of a special-needs case. But since I started the running and lost the bit of weight I've been more inclined to do things I wouldn't have done before. So I said fuck it and I went in the very next day. I was doing the first fix on a conversion out the Old Birr Road so I was able to slip away into town at lunchtime.

That was the worst time, of course. Half of Eastern Europe seemed to be packed into the fucking place, all sorts of chatter bouncing off the ceiling and the walls and none of it English that I could make out. I nearly turned back out the door again but she had me spotted. Ah, Mister Fall Over! And everyone turned to look at me. I knew a good share of them, lads I'd met on sites here and there, or in the factories. How ye, boys, I was saying. I felt myself flexing, sucking my stomach right in. I'd spent ages that morning picking just the right T-shirt.

THAT WAS IT, then. She came out from behind the counter and she put me sitting at a tiny little table tucked away near the jacks, and she brought me over a cup of coffee that tasted like it had cinnamon in it, and something else, that had me remembering years ago, from my childhood, something to do with summer and sun but I couldn't quite place it. It was like a magical coffee. And she gave me this pastry yoke with meat and potatoes inside in it, and she said the name of it but I still don't know what they're called. I just call them the meaty spud yokes. Just as I finished eating that, and was starting to wonder what the fuck I was going to do, how I was going to go about leaving, whether I should offer to pay, she came back to my table again with a chocolate muffin on a plate with a dollop of cream on it and I remember thinking, Shit, that's a lot of calories, and she asked me would I go with her to a church in Limerick to listen to her friend Anna singing in a choir.

I borrowed the auld lad's MG roadster. He keeps it beautiful, in fairness. He must have waxed it four times for me, and checked the oil, brake fluid, fan belt, coolant, over and over again. He was more excited about my date than I was.

Himself and Mam were acting like I was going to my debs as I was leaving. The fucking pressure. Jesus. Thank God it all worked out. I couldn't have broken their hearts again. I'm enough of a let down to them, all their hopes for me actually doing something, being someone, dashed over and over again, and all their days wasted worrying about me.

Eugenija was thrilled when she saw the MG. Dad had the roof down. I offered to put it back up for the drive but she said, No! and she ran back upstairs to her little apartment over the café and she came back out with a headscarf on and big sunglasses. Like Eugenija Pleškytė, she said, the actress for whom I was named. Someone whistled at us as we rolled up Pearse Street. I took the old road to Limerick.

The choir were singing in the old Protestant church by the courthouse. Hymns, a mixture of Lithuanian and English and one in Irish, even. The sound of them floated around me, then washed gently down over me. There were nearly tears in my eyes, it was so beautiful, so peaceful. I forgot myself. I moved my hand so it touched off hers, and she linked her fingers in mine and left them there. I could have sat there for ever listening to the choir, smelling her perfume, feeling her hand in my hand, the soft perfect weight of it, the thrilling rightness of it. We drove home by Ballina. I kissed her on the wall above the river. I was in love. I still am.

I DO MY best to keep it to myself. You can't be going around acting too happy. When lads start moaning about shite, giving out about wives and children and wages and tax and cars breaking down and horses not coming in and the weather and the price of everything, I nod and agree away, and sometimes I pretend to be just as pissed off over things as they are, but inside myself I have this secret cargo of happiness. When Bobby comes around the site with that heavy silence all around him and that dangerous look in his eyes, like he's about to kick off, I feel like saying, Fuck's sake, Bobby, will you just take life easy, enjoy it while you have it.

It's only the very odd day now that the cold wind blows around me. When I feel myself getting too smug, when I start counting all my blessings, I start to think about all the things that could go wrong. I remember that I have to die someday. That Eugenija will die someday. That the child inside her, that I love already more than life itself, has only one sure destiny and that's death. Everything falls apart. All things tend towards chaos. I close my eyes against the mad torrent of panic. This is okay, I think. This is life, this is life, this is how it's meant to be.

Millicent

IT WAS ACTUALLY a relief when Augie told me I had to turn off my phone when I was with him. I started to kind of remember things about myself that I'd forgotten, the way I was when I was younger, the things I used to wonder about, the things I used to notice.

The first day I met him I was standing out at the yellow bridge with my friend Rachael and we weren't even thinking about going anywhere, we were just hanging around watching the cars go past. But sometimes people thumb lifts at the yellow bridge, into Nenagh in one direction or Limerick in the other, so the odd car would stop for us, and we'd say, No thanks, we're grand, but it was always kind of exciting seeing who'd stop, and hearing what they'd say.

A fella stopped one day in a big huge black car and he was kind of good-looking but a bit suss too, his shirt was open too many buttons down and he had a manky hairy chest, and he spent ages trying to get us to go for a spin with him and in the end Rachael shouted at him, Fuck off, you pervert, and he spat out the window at us and called us mickey teasers. We roared laughing but it was a bit scary too.

The one thing Daddy says to me every single day is to never get into a car with a stranger. So when Augie pulled up that first day I was about to say, I can't, I have to go home, but Rachael said, Oh, hi, Gus, to Augie, and hi, Jordan, to Pitts, and then she looked into the back seat and said, Hi, Tyrone, hi, Lee, to Dowel and Braden. That actually might be the only time I ever heard them called by their first names by anyone but me, except Augie. Everyone always calls him Augie.

Augustus, his full name is. After a Roman emperor his father read a book about one time. So straight away they weren't strangers. Augie is Rachael's cousin. I knew he had a bad reputation but I still wasn't going against Daddy by getting into the car. I'll do anything to go against Mammy but I can't bear upsetting Daddy. I love them both equally, though, so I don't know why that is. Something about the way Daddy's face looks when he's worried, all kind of pink and scrunched up, like he could be about to cry any minute, and his voice actually gets softer and quieter, but Mammy goes mental, shouting and screaming, and then I start shouting and screaming too and we end up nearly actually physically fighting until one of us storms off and slams all the doors in the house and the whole place literally shakes.

THAT FIRST DAY anyway I couldn't stop looking at Augie. I couldn't even think of anything to say. He was staring at me and his eyes were really dark and his lips were a deep red and his chin and cheeks were a bit stubbly and I could see the top of the dragon tattoo on the side of his neck. He was wearing his Bulls cap. Then he said, Come on and we'll go for a spin. And Rachael said, There's not enough space in the car. And Augie said, There's loads of space. Braden is getting out here. And Lee said, Am I fuck, and Augie turned around and said, You fucking are, and Lee just opened the door and got out and went over and sat on the wall of the bridge and started turning and spitting into the stream, trying to let on he didn't care about getting left out on the road miles from town.

I felt sorry for him but I got into the car anyway, into his seat, and Augie turned around then and looked at me and said, Hold on, you go in front, and Jordan made a pissed-off sound but Augie just looked at him and said, What? And Jordan got out and him and Rachael got into the back with Tyrone, who put down his window as we drove off and shouted something at Lee, See ya later, sucker, or something stupid like that, and Lee just gave him the finger, and Rachael straight away started saying, I'm your cousin, Gus, I should be in front, not her.

Augie said nothing for ages, just drove, with his left hand kind of draped on the gearstick and his right hand on the top of the steering wheel, and I could feel the vibration up through me of the exhaust pipe, and then a feeling like a hand on my stomach as I was pressed into the seat while Augie drove faster and faster and I heard Rachael screaming as he turned suddenly off the main road and the car kind of skidded and we were on the tiny little back road that goes up into the mountains.

I LOVED THAT day. I close my eyes sometimes and try to remember it exactly, down to the last detail. Augie parked up by the pylon and told Tyrone he was to stay with the car. He threw him a fag box and a packet of Rizlas. I wondered for a second why he'd need papers with proper fags, then I copped that it was to skin up, and I felt proud that I knew that. I wanted to say the words *skin up* but I couldn't find a way to get it into the conversation. Jordan and Rachael walked back down the road we'd just driven up, because Jordan wanted to see if it was true that the black pond down at the bend was bottomless. How are you going to find out? Rachael asked him. By fucking you into it, he said, and seeing if you hit the bottom. That's stupid, she said, but I knew by her voice and by the way she was looking at him and acting around him that she was definitely going to shift him.

Augie and me watched them walking off and Augie turned to me then and said, Come on, we'll go over to the Millennium Cross. I want to say a prayer for my uncle. His uncle Eugene only has one leg since this mad old bastard shot him years ago down in the village and he was in hospital at the time because there was something wrong with his other leg and it was looking like he might end up with no legs at all. Most of the lads I ever knew would think they were too cool to pray, but Augie doesn't care what anyone thinks and he talks straight to Jesus all the time.

I remember how Augie opened the boot of his car and took out his jacket and looked up at the sky and said it probably wouldn't rain, and he offered me the jacket then. I think he only wanted me to see that it was Canada Goose, and I shook my head, no, and I smiled at him then because he didn't seem as sure of himself all of a sudden. I looked at the black and white dragon that wound all down his left arm, its wings folded along its back and just a tiny flame coming from its mouth down near his left wrist, and then I noticed that there was a tattoo of a knife on the back of his left hand and a tattoo of a gun on the back of his right hand.

I tried to think of something to say about his tattoos that wouldn't sound stupid, that wouldn't make him think of me as a kid, all full of wonder at the world. But I was wondering about him – I wanted to know everything about him. I only knew tiny little bits from Rachael and some of the girls in school. We'd be going back in a few weeks and I was looking forward to telling them that I was with him, the fella they were all afraid of, who everyone, even Rachael, was warned to stay away from.

I KNOW I sound stupid. I'm not stupid at all. I know I should have run away the minute he took my phone out of my hand. I should have just left him the phone and taken off down the narrow path that only deer normally use. It leads straight down to the lake road and I've known every step and turn of it since I was a baby. But Rachael kept sending me Snapchats the whole walk over from the station to the cross, and he didn't say anything, just walked along beside me, and then when we got to the cross he just flicked his hand out and suddenly my phone was in his hand and then it was in his pocket and then his hand was around my wrist when I made to grab it from his pocket and it hurt a bit and he just looked into my eyes and said, Stop.

Then he put his hand on my other wrist and he stepped up onto the platform at the base of the big metal cross and I stepped up after him, and his grip was gentler now and he put his right hand then inside the neck of his black Nike T-shirt and he lifted out his silver chain and closed his eyes as he kissed the little cross that was on it. Then he looked up at the big cross, and if this was described to me, if someone, Rachael or someone else, told me they were with someone who did this I'd have laughed and thought it was stupid, but when Augie did it there seemed to be something so beautiful and pure about it. He put his chain back inside his shirt and he held my two hands in his and he said, Please, God, look after my uncle Eugene. Keep my family safe. Keep Millicent safe and all her family, too.

Then instead of blessing himself he raised up my hands one by one to his lips and he kissed them the exact same way he'd kissed his silver crucifix and then he pulled me in tight to himself and I could feel this heat off him going into me. It was nearly unbearable and it was the most beautiful feeling at the same time, and his lips were burning on my lips, his kiss hurt me, and I wanted it to never end.

HE TOLD ME on the walk back down into the valley that I couldn't ever have my phone on when I was with him. I didn't ask him why, I just said okay. I knew it was because he didn't want anyone to be able to track him. Then when we were walking back up the opposite hill path to the car he held my hand tight the whole way in case I tripped. He told me he had no phone of his own and that he'd get one of the lads to send a text to my phone when he wanted to meet up. A number for the day, he said, one to seven Monday to Sunday, and YB for the yellow bridge, or MW for the mill wall, and one number for the time. If he wasn't there on the hour I could wait or go home, it was up to me.

Do you understand that? he said. I said I did. I couldn't really understand why it was so important to me suddenly that this boy who I hadn't ever really even seen properly before in my life, except through the dark glass of his windscreen in town when Rachael pointed him out, saying things like, There's my cousin Gus, he thinks he's so cool, he thinks he's such a bad boy, *ugh*, why it was so important to me now that he knew I'd do exactly what he said, that I'd be waiting for his text, that I'd wear my best clothes and my good perfume that Daddy got me and my makeup from Brown Thomas that I bought with my birthday money.

I WAS HIS girl then. Rachael told me her parents were hopping over her meeting Jordan so she stopped, and she said he was too old for her anyway, and I told her fuck off because Augie is older than Jordan so she was saying he was too old for me, in a sneaky way, and I knew she was trying to break me and Augie up because without me she had no one because no one would put up with her moody shit except me.

She snapped me the day of my birthday, a photo of herself in bed, looking like she was only half awake, and there was a little rhyme, *sixteen is sweet, seventeen is sweeter, Red Riding Hood was happy till her granny tried to eat her.* Fucking bitch. I got so mad I threw my phone against the wall. Only for my new case it would have been in bits.

She was slagging my granny Lily. When we were small we used to all run over to her cottage when we were swimming down at the quay and the big dare was always to run right up to one of the windows and look in, and only a few of us ever actually did it, and we used to say that a witch lived there, and that she ate children. I didn't know then that there really was a witch living there, and that she was my grandmother.

One day after we got back home I told Mammy about the game, how I'd gone right up to the window when no one else would, and I'd actually seen the witch sitting inside at a table in front of a fire, and that the witch had looked right at me, and Mammy went crazy, and shouted and roared at me that I was to never go next, nigh or near that house ever again, and I knew better than to ask why.

I never saw the witch again until the day we buried my uncle John-John. Mammy acted then like I should have known all along, like it wasn't some big family secret. She's your father's mother, she said, in that kind of weird posh accent she puts on for certain situations. They've been *estranged*.

I WAS SO happy when I started calling first. My other grandparents are nice but I hardly ever see them, except the very odd Sunday that Mammy makes me go with her to their little house inside near Limerick. It's always roasting and there's always too much food and there are pictures of Jesus everywhere, with his eyes rolled back and a bloody hand raised up, like he's saying, Stop, please, will you all just leave me alone.

Granny Lily has no holy pictures. She says she was never at mass but she must have been. I know the way things used to be and no one could have avoided mass for a whole life. She says she doesn't believe in a separate God or the Devil or in heaven or hell, just in the power of nature, and we're all part of nature, part of the universe, so we're all little bits of God in a way, and we're all eternal, but we change our forms over and over again. I asked her once if she was a witch and she said she supposed she was. It was one way of putting it. I told her about the game we used to play and she roared laughing. She said she remembered me looking in. Why wouldn't I? she said. It was only eight or nine years ago. That feels like more for me because it's half my life, but it's only a tiny bit of her life, Granny says.

Daddy and her made up, and even Mammy talks to her sometimes now when she drops me down. I thought that she and Augie would be great friends. I told her all about him and I made her swear she wouldn't tell on me. I told her how much he needs me, how I'm the only one that can calm him down when things get on top of him, how he holds on to me so tight and makes me swear I'll never leave him. I tell her about all the places he takes me, all the secret places we have that are just for the two of us, that no one else knows about, up in the mountains and down by the lake and the little flat in the middle of Limerick that we can use whenever we want. She doesn't like him, even though I've only ever told her how good he is to me and how much he needs me, how I'm the only person in the world he really trusts. That's why he went so mad when he thought I'd broken that trust, the day he saw me walking down Church Road with Patrick Cantwell. It's a sacred thing between us, and I nearly ruined it by walking with Patrick in my new skirt. I know it sounds like nothing but I should have known that it was disrespectful to Augie, and especially the way I was laughing at Patrick's jokes, but I couldn't help laughing because he's so funny, and we only kissed once ages ago at the laser disco but that was my second mistake, telling Augie that.

When he pulled up he said nothing, just sat there looking at me and looking at Patrick, and then after ages of no one saying anything, he just said, Get in. Patrick said, Bye, Milly, and he walked off. And I waited a second for Jordan to let me into the front seat like always but he didn't move. So I got into the back with Lee and Tyrone. There was a horrible smell of Lynx off them. Or that worse one. Axe.

AUGIE DROVE US out from town and Jordan was smoking in the front and there was a thick cloud of sweet smoke in the car. I could hardly breathe. We drove down a tiny little narrow lane and Augie parked in a gateway. It was getting dark. He got out and then he opened the door and told me to get out. I didn't move. I didn't like the way he was acting. So he reached in and he grabbed my arm and he started pulling me. I told him to fuck off and I wouldn't move so Tyrone pushed me and I fell out onto the ground. Augie pulled me up to my feet and through the open gateway and across a field of knee-high grass. He was dragging me really fast and I tripped over a little hill of grass and my skirt flew up and I landed on my back. I saw then that Tyrone and Lee were following us. Jordan was still over at the car, leaning on the bonnet, smoking. I was saying, Augie, please, I'm sorry, but his face was dark and closed off and his hand was so tight on my arm that I couldn't feel my fingers.

I couldn't breathe properly. We got to a little pond and

there were thousands of hoofprints in the muck around the edge of it. Augie threw me down in the muck and I landed face first and he was behind me with his knee in my back and he pushed my face down into the muck and cow shit. He had my hair wound around his fist. He kept pushing my face down until I started to breathe in the shit and swallow it and I was choking and crying. It was in my eyes and up my nose. I could hear Tyrone and Lee laughing. Over and over Augie was saying, You fucking stupid little slut. I'll fucking kill you. I'll kill you.

Then I heard Jordan shouting from a distance, For fuck's sake, man, come on, will you leave it, and then it was really dark suddenly and it felt like I was floating above myself looking down, but all I could see was dim shapes and the circle of the pond. After a while I felt like I was back inside myself and I was able to get up and see properly. They were gone. I sat there screaming, Augie, Augie, please come back, I'm sorry. But they didn't come back. I cleaned myself in the pond but my clothes were destroyed. I thought for a minute about going to Granny's, but I couldn't bear to let her see me like that, so I went home. Thank God Mammy and Daddy were in bed. I just knocked on their door passing like I always do and I heard Mammy saying, She's home, and Daddy sleepily saying, Goodnight, baby.

IT WAS MORE than a week before I got a text again. After a few days I was starting to go mad. I couldn't sleep or eat. I asked Granny Lily for a love spell but she only laughed at me and told me there was no such thing but I know it's because she hates Augie so much. Then it came: 2. YB. 3.

So last Tuesday I waited at the yellow bridge at three, but it was after four before Augie came for me. On his own. We drove in silence for ages. Then I said I was sorry. I kept saying it until he told me to shut up. He asked me then what time did Granny Lily usually go out into the forest and the fields. He knew she went gathering every day, because I'd told him all about her. I always told him everything. I wasn't able to keep anything from him. He'd have known if I did.

I knew why he was asking. I begged him not to. I told him I'd do anything he wanted if he just didn't do that. But there was no way to stop him, and so I went with him. I even opened Granny Lily's door for him with my key, but he said we had to break it anyway or she'd know it was us. And he smiled at me, his beautiful smile. I know now that Granny Lily is wrong. There is a God and there is a Devil, and I could feel them struggling inside me when I smiled back.

We've been together eleven months, two weeks and four days. I have a ring got for him for our anniversary. Gold signet, with my name and his stamped on the inside of the face of it inside a love heart.

I haven't gone back there yet. But last night I dreamed that Granny Lily was outside my window looking in. And she didn't speak but I could hear her all the same. Saying, Don't worry, child. There's nothing to forgive. I love you. And when I woke this morning I knew I'd never see her again anywhere outside of my dreams.

Denis

I SUPPOSE ANYONE on the outside looking in would think it was the queerest thing that was ever known, me and Bobby Mahon with our heads together, making the smallest of small talk about the weather and the hurling and the price of timber, making bigger talk about work to be done, and being so at ease with one other. Considering our history, it might even seem perverse. But since the first day he sat opposite me in prison I kind of had an idea that in a different world we could have been good friends. We'll never be that, I know. I'm not sure even if he's the kind of man that has close friendships, or that knocks around in groups with other men. There's something kind of boyish about that, like fellas having a desire to allow themselves any sort of profanity and loud talk, clinging on to the freedom that youth affords, freedom to say what's on your mind, to plumb the depths and come up laughing.

The first time he came into the prison they gave us a private space in a little room off the main visiting area. He'd looked for the meeting, and the privacy, and they'd been amenable. There wasn't much I could say except okay, right. There was a white line across the table and we were told to stay either side of it. There was a screw in the room and one outside the door, and there was a camera. He stood up when I came in but he didn't put out his hand to me, he just nodded and reddened a bit and sat back down. I was going to write to you, he said. But then I thought, I'll see about going in. I hate writing letters, he said. I told him I was glad he hadn't written. Because I'd have had to write back. I told him I was much happier to meet him man to man and I meant it, as hard as it was.

He asked me then how was I doing. Grand, I said. How are you? Arra, I'm kept going anyway, thank God, he said. And we started into talking about the trade then and all the jobs that were after being cancelled, the amount of fellas laid off, the talk of them setting up some kind of an outfit that was going to take over all the big jobs and bail out the lads who borrowed the serious money while all us small lads could paddle our own canoes right up the creek and drown. That was always the way in Ireland, he said. You'd be hung for robbing an apple and made king if you robbed a castle. And we talked like that about nothing at all for nearly the whole forty minutes we were allowed, and when the screw said, Five minutes, gentlemen, he seemed to get a bit quiet and nervous and he started looking up at the ceiling and down at the floor and so did I. For a finish we said nothing at all about the things that people might have expected us to talk about, if they'd known we were meeting.

He came back again later that year. We started off about the hurling and gave out about Clare being let back into it and how hard it was to listen to them, it was nearly worse this time than it was in the nineties, and then I could see that he was going to force himself to ask me what he had to ask me and I steadied myself for it: I had it all worked out, what I was going to say, the form my apology was going to take.

I tried even to get there before him. It had been on my mind a lot all those months since the first visit, the fact that I hadn't said how sorry I was, that I'd offered nothing by way of explanation beyond what the barrister had read out in court. Lookit, I said. I'll just say this. I didn't mean to hurt anyone. My mind was gone from me that day. I had you tied in with Pokey Burke in my head and I knew Pokey was long gone so I was going to have it out with you over what I was owed.

But he only shook his head and put his hand up towards me palm out as if my story was of no use to him, or as if it was too painful for him to hear it, I'm not sure which. He told me he knew how I felt. He said to me, Denis, I know the kind of a man my father was. And I think I know the kind of man your father was. Our fathers were cut from the same cloth. And I had nothing to say back to him except Thanks.

I KNOW THE look of a man about to blow. Even if he's silent and unmoving it comes through, maybe even more so then. I've been on building sites every working day since I was fifteen years old, except for the few months before I landed in jail, when I was driving the roads trying to get paid what I was owed. You get used to reading the tides of men, tuning yourself to the carry-on and the shouts and the way lads move around each other so that you know well in advance when things are going to boil up and spill over.

That skill served me well in jail. I was always able to stay out of trouble. No one ever had an issue with me and I stayed out of the petty rows over pocket money and fags and tuck-shop treats, and I never went near the lads who were running the drugs around the cells. I've seen one or two of those lads out around the place since I got out. If they recognize me they don't let on, and neither do I. The warden had me working with the maintenance crew, anyway, so I never had to mix too much with the hard chaws. The maintenance boys were sound out. I was useful to them, and I gave no trouble. They were sorry the day I was leaving. I would nearly have been sorry myself, if I hadn't been going home to Kate and my daughter.

My daughter. How is it I got so lucky? I'm nearly afraid to think too much about it. I have to stop myself sometimes thanking God out loud for her but I do it in my head a thousand times a day. When I got out first she was nearly six but she knew me well. We made no story of it for her: she was told the truth, or a version of it anyway, before she even knew what the words meant. Daddy had been bold and was in jail but now he was home. Kate had a new bed bought and we all slept in it together the first night and when I woke up Laoise was cuddled into my back and the heat of her was pulsing through me like life itself, like the whole power of the universe was squeezed down into the particles that were moving from her body into mine. Sometimes I think that something must have gone wrong in the universe. Some blueprint got mislaid or was read upside down and something came into existence that was never meant to be. Like the church in Nenagh that was only meant to be half the size but the builders were given the plans for a cathedral by mistake, and by the time anyone noticed it was too late.

That must be what happened with me. I was surely never meant to have what I have, and all of it I came into without effort. For all the years I broke my back from dawn to dark I ended up with nothing, only debts I couldn't pay, and money owed to me that I'd never see. But lying on my back in a prison cell looking up at the ceiling I became a father, and I got back the fire I thought was long gone out for the only girl I ever loved. I had no child going into prison. I thought I was going to die in there, that I'd either be killed or I'd kill myself. But I left prison as happy as a man can be.

Looking back I don't know was I ever really happy before. The day I married Kate, maybe. I was mad about her, in fairness. But we kind of lost each other after a while. We never stopped working. We never slowed down to listen properly to each other, to take care of what we had between us. I was wiser about the world, after my six and a half years away from it, and about the workings of the heart, and I had a sense that this new wisdom was going to serve me well. My daughter took me by the hand and guided me back into the world and back to the truth of myself, and she's holding my hand ever since, even when we're apart.

ANY KIND OF connection between me and the son of the man I killed will always have a weight of strangeness attached to it. The fact that he subs jobs to me is the talk of the town. You can't keep up with the retrofitting and the attic conversions and the extensions, and no one ever wants to turn work down. Well, I don't, anyway, and nor does he. It makes good sense to channel overflows to someone you trust, someone you know will do the work in your name without causing any damage to that name. All people really care about is whether the job will be done right, and on time, and for the price they've agreed. No one wants to deal with a cowboy or an add-on merchant. People prefer an honest killer to a crooked builder any day of the week, thank God.

We only meet the very odd time. And when we do it's mostly the same old yarn over and over again, the weather, the hurling, the Premiership maybe, the rugby now and then, and always the work, what needed to be done, where, when, what price it could be done at. I met him earlier this week. I could see straight away that there was something up. This sounds very wishy-washy now but there was a kind of an aura around him, like a kind of a glow, a feverish glow coming off of him.

He was telling me his mother-in-law was in Milford hospice and that it looked like she was near her end. I told him I was sorry and he shrugged it away like all men do, saying, Arra, it'll be an ease to her, God help us. But there was something more, I knew. I could feel something radiating off him. I got this crazy notion that he was possessed, that there was something inside in him that wasn't him, that could at any moment leap out of him. Something about the way his eyes were shining, the way he was forming his words, the way his focus was never on me as we were talking but on a point in the distance.

We were standing at the side of his van and the sliding door was fully open. He reached in and he handed me a folder of plans and specs for two jobs, one in Newcastle West and one in Killaloe. And as he leaned his head down to examine the sheets in the folder, tidily clipped and snug in their clear A4 pockets, to go through the few bits with me, I looked past him for a second and I saw, standing behind the driver's seat of the van, held in place by a length of new rope that was threaded through the bars of the cage between the cab and the cargo space, a black leather gun case.

I didn't know you were a hunter, Bobby, I said to him. And he looked up at me and he smiled a funny smile that was barely a smile at all, and he said, I'm not.

Mags

WE NEVER STOP being children. Or at least we never fully leave our childhood behind; we drag it with us and we stretch it out along our years and every now and then when we let our grip fail it snaps and reels us back. Despite all the things we thought we'd learned in life, all the toughening and hardening and strategies for coping, those memories can assail us without warning, leaving us bereft of all our armour. They can descend from the ether or rise up from the earth, or they can be carried on a breeze from the lake, concealed inside the soft mineral scent that contains the essence of a moment lived long ago, and that essence breaks over us and suddenly we're being dragged back, back, back. What power does time have, really, except to weaken our bodies and cloud our minds? It doesn't heal any wounds. If we're lucky it attenuates our trauma to the point of invisibility, but it's always there. Even the happiest child-hood has its trauma, and it never ends.

That's nearly word for word what Ger said to me. I added the bit about the smell of the air from the lake because it was that smell that buckled me the other day when I took the dogs for their walk. I was suddenly six again, holding Daddy's hand, looking out across the bay from the little quay, and Daddy was pointing at the lake island and telling me it was where the fairies lived, that the king and queen of the fairies had their castle there among the trees. I asked him if we could row out there and he said yes, we could borrow Mickey Briars's boat, but we'd have to wait until the right day. You couldn't just arrive out to see the fairies any old time. There were particular days when they were more amenable to humans. How will we know what day is good? Mickey Briars will tell us, Daddy said. Mickey knew the fair-ies well.

It was two or maybe three years before I stopped expect-ing to be told that today was the day, and to be rowed across the lake to the fairy island. I had a little backpack all ready in case we got word from Mickey at short notice that it was safe to strike out. I had presents for the fairies in it, a Cinderella flask and a mirror and hairbrush. I never asked Daddy about it because I knew not to be asking for things, I knew to be patient and to wait, not to be always whining like Pokey, clamouring and reaching and sulking. No one wanted to be like Pokey. Some things definitely never change.

That hardly qualifies as a trauma. To have been falsely promised a citadel of fairies on an island in a lake. Yet there I was on Monday, not having thought about the lake island or the fairies for I don't know how long, standing on the quayside, with a memory opening and expanding inside me, delivered in a parcel of morning air, so vivid and stark that every intervening moment sloughed away and I was dragged suddenly and violently by the elastic tether that joined me to my six-year-old self, so that I could feel his hand in mine, I could feel the thick, living mass of him, I could hear him saying, Oh, yes, love, they sure do, they live and reign out there on that island, and I could hear myself saying, Really, Daddy? Is that really true?

IT WAS POKEY that found Dad. What Dad was looking for in the small shed is anyone's guess. His tools were all locked away in the metal press in the big shed, and there was no way he was going to start into any kind of DIY job with the shake and the pains in his hands. There was nothing in there except boxes of old tat, vinyl records and broken lamps and little bits of furniture that Mam had been sentimental about and refused to throw away. But he obviously had taken some kind of a notion to do something when death crept up on him. Pokey said he was lying on his side when he found him, like he'd just lain down to take a nap. I wish he'd died outside on the grass so that his deathbed would have been softer, soil and grass and daisies.

Dr Roche said he's sure that he'd have felt a weakness and lowered himself to the ground before his heart stopped. That's comforting. I can't stand the thought of him falling. Sudden cardiac death with ischemic heart disease as substrate and underlying cause, I think it says on the note we got back from the coroner. Pokey did compressions for ages after he found him, but he knew he was gone. He had his phone on loudspeaker and the dispatcher talked him through putting Daddy in the recovery position and pressing down with his palms on his sternum, and the crew used their paddles on him when they arrived but just for form, I'd say.

His time had come, Dr Roche said, as he shook my two hands up and down with both of his, and I could see tears in his rheumy eyes. He looked funny in his sadness, indignant almost, in spite of his sanguine words, as though death was dismantling the world he'd known all his life, gradually evacuating all of his certainties, deposing him from the seat of authority he'd occupied with such quiet firmness for so long.

DAD TOLD ME after Mammy died that she'd left instructions about me and him. How we were to get back to being as pally as we always were. Before . . . For fuck's sake, Dad, I said. You were doing well there for a minute. Before what? Before I was gay? I was always gay, Dad! But instead of reddening and muttering and throwing his hand in the manner he'd developed over the years to passively abnegate any possibility of an embrace of my reality, he laughed. I might have known I'd make a balls of this, he said. And your mother knew, too. Then he told me exactly what she'd said.

Eileen told me I was to remind myself every day how much I loved my little Margaret. And he stopped there. His tears were flowing in a shocking deluge. I'd never seen him cry. It was only a month since we'd buried Mam and he was straight-backed and dry-eyed through the whole ordeal of ritual and remembrance, even through the lowering of her coffin, when I heard a long keening sound echo off the handball alley wall and realized it had come from me. He'd given me a cross look then. He couldn't help it. He couldn't bear anyone making a show of themselves, to have a show made of him. Now here he was, tear-soaked and open, more vulnerable than the day he was born, and his arms were around me, and I was on my island at long last.

WE WERE A sorry sight I'd say, assembled in the front room around him before the closing of the coffin. Looking down at the man who'd made us, who'd made a thousand other things, who'd been making things since he was in his boyhood.

The best thing about sudden death, someone from the long stream of sympathizers said, is you look like yourself in the coffin. When it's slow, they went on, death has its way with you and it makes you deathly. You can thank God for that mercy, anyway. That he wasn't made to linger and suffer. That this is how you'll remember him. As the man he always was.

Eamonn thanked her and looked at me smiling, thinking I'd be rolling my eyes and suppressing my offence and annoyance, but she was right. I was so glad that Daddy's hands weren't skeletal and death-hued, that they'd kept their bigness and their appearance of strength in death, the round knots of his knuckles with their patches of dry skin and the dark rims of grime around his fingernails that neither soap nor Swarfega could ever shift. I was glad his cheeks were full and red, that his eyebrows bushed like wild hedgerows, that his mouth was set in a line, straight and serious, as though it might open at any second to enquire about this foolishness we were all at.

But there we were, the three of us. Not the closest three siblings in the world, but well-disposed enough towards one another to offer each other comfort, to be able to joke about what our dead father might have made of his own end, and of the words spoken about him, about the long, droned homily of the new curate of whom he'd been suspicious, saying his face was hard to read, his jokes always too rehearsed, and his fondness for himself too apparent by far.

That same curate was in the room suddenly, to ask if we wanted to say a decade of the rosary before saying goodbye, and Pokey suppressed a skit, and Eamonn chuckled softly, and I told the slender boyish priest that we were fine now, thanks. We'd take a few more minutes on our own with Dad before Chris and Roger came in to screw the coffin shut and take him to the church, and the curate left, with a slight air of offence about him, and Pokey started then, finally, to allow himself to be pulled back fully into his childish self, whispering over and over again, Dad, Dad, Dad, Dad, Dad, and Eamonn put his hand on Pokey's shoulder and I felt a wave of love for those two men that nearly knocked me.

I KNOW THAT Pokey's up to no good. I could never close my heart against him, but neither can I close off my instincts or my sense. I know he had Dad's name down as a director of this Mickey Mouse college inside in Limerick without Dad having any clue, God knows how he managed it. I know he bought the car he's driving for cash because Ger's cousin, who was her bridesmaid at our wedding, has a gossipy friend who works as a secretary in the dealership and she told her that Pokey specced it to the last, every single extra you could think of, and the all-in price came to well over a hundred grand, and he put it all through the college's books, paying from a college account and registering it as a company vehicle.

What's he into? I asked Eamonn, and Eamonn only shook his head and said, Mags, all I know is we're as well off not knowing. He can't upset Mam and Dad any more and that's all I care about. Eamonn always let Pokey off the hook, though. He was always moon-eyed about him, his little baby brother, even when Pokey was doing his best to sabotage him, smashing his train sets to bits, stealing the sweets that Eamonn used to secrete under his bed after me and Pokey had devoured ours in seconds. Eamonn is annoyingly nice. Ger calls him Principal Perfect Pants. She's wicked at times.

I MET JIM Gildea this morning in the village. He was standing by the pump holding a bag of groceries from the Spar shop and looking intently at the pump's seized and rusty handle with a kind of sorrowful expression on his face. He looks very old, these days. Retirement does that to some people, men especially, I think, robs them of purpose so that they quickly deflate and atrophy. I was walking Izzy and Poppy, and Jim broke from his reverie to admire the dogs. Then he turned back to his inspection. Isn't it a shame the way we allowed this pump to fall away? Jim said. I felt a tiny dart of indignation at the collective pronoun, as though I were vaguely implicated in the dereliction. Wouldn't you think it would be minded and appreciated, something that served this place and its people so long and so well?

I nearly said, Like yourself, Jim, but thought better of it.

Instead I reached across him and tried the handle and it actually moved, and a spurt of rusty water landed on the worn flagstone beneath it. After a few more pumps it ran clear. That's it, begod, said Jim, and his face brightened. Good girl you are. Arra, aren't you an expert on water pumps, anyway? Didn't you give a good share of years showing them how to draw water from the ground beyond in Africa? Lord, your father was proud of that, God rest him.

And I laughed at this, the talk out of him, and told him they already knew how to draw water, that we just resourced people and trained them in best practice and sustainable irrigation, and Jim laughed again, and said, in a strangely pointed way, How's the lad these days? Is he as busy as ever? Do you mean Pokey or Eamonn, Jim? I asked, though I knew who he meant. Oh, Pokey, of course. The bould Pokey.

And while I was telling him how Pokey was indeed very busy with his various enterprises, Jim's gaze broke from me to the hills to our east and he said, Look at that. There's rain coming. You can see it in the distance, coming down across the mountainside.

Go on and take shelter, he said, and he squeezed my arm once before we parted with his strong and gentle hand, a father's hand.

Jim

THERE'S NO SUCH thing as a sixth sense. It's just a handy way of describing the skill that a good detective must possess. I was never a detective myself. I never had the assuredness or the impetus to go for the job. I was grand as I was. I was able to leave most things in the station or at the scene. That way, I hadn't always to be mulling things over, putting things together in my head. I was better able to be a good husband to Mary, I was better able to keep myself from losing my mind the time of the accident when we lost my little nephew Peter to the sea. I was better able to keep a lid on things the time that auld Frankie Mahon was murdered and the young Shanahan lad was snatched.

They gave me a medal the time of that kidnapping. Because I entered the premises alone and confronted the kidnappers and safely extricated the child, with no injury, loss of life or damage to property. Not ten years ago that was but this is a new world now. These days you'd be up on charges for not sticking to the letter of the law. Endangerment or some kind of a mad yarn like that. It's hard to be a policeman, these days. I don't envy the young men and women joining now. Every bigmouth ball-scratching do-nothing bastard watching their every move and filming it or writing all about it on their mobile telephones and every other gom with their mouth open reading all about it.

Anyway, there's no such thing as magical powers, no matter what way you look at a thing. Everything can be explained somehow. I knew something was going to happen before it happened, but I was as good as told in advance. After it happened, though, I knew exactly how it had come about, the ins and outs of it, every road taken and river rowed. The boys were in from Limerick, Philly at their head, my ambitious old comrade and he a chief inspector now, and there was a crew down from Dublin and there were experts and professionals and consultants and every kind of a fuckin know-it-all looking at the ground and examining bits of the stone of the wall of Mickey Briars's cottage and taking away sods of the earth to laboratories and what have you and no fucker was stopping for a second to examine the truth of the matter: that Mickey Briars was prepared to tell them the whole story if only they'd listen to the man.

He was determined, he said, to tell the story, but only if they were prepared to listen to it from beginning to end, and when Mickey said beginning he sure meant it. And not even his own beginning. According to Mickey, the story of what had happened at his house last Sunday had started before Ireland was free. I'll hear it eventually, because I heard from Carol Morris, the little girl I trained in a few years ago, who has a right good head on her shoulders, that he has them told now that the only bollix he'll talk to is me, because I'm the only bollix who won't keep interrupting him.

I know the parts that have immediate relevance to the facts at hand, and the rest of it, the way things are going, will remain inside in Mickey until they realize he's as stubborn as a butt of oak, and harder again to get the better of, and they give in and send a squad car out to collect me.

BOBBY MAHON AS good as told me there was something on his mind, something welling up that was going to break through even in spite of himself. Bobby is one of these rare men who measures himself against the well-being of the people around him. If there's a problem he takes it personally and does his damnedest to solve it. After Pokey Burke banjaxed his father's good business and ran for the hills, it was Bobby who gave himself the task of building back up the whole village, giving every one of them lads a job again.

Himself and the wife went from door to door, to bank and credit union and every kind of a backstreet moneylender and shyster to get started again, and by God did they get started. Even in the shadow of auld Frank's murder they toiled. Once your man from Limerick owned up to it and Bobby came back to his senses there was no stopping them. It was like two fingers to the doubters, in a way, a declaration of war on the sad fate that so many were prepared to accept. There's men alive today, I know for sure, because Bobby Mahon wouldn't lie down for anyone. The very same as when he hurled. He was unstoppable.

Goodness is a hard thing to define. It's inexpressible in its nature. I'd say that's the right word anyway. You can only know it from what you sense about a person, and not just their deeds. Sometimes, often, a person's deeds and their nature have no alignment or connection at all. It's always best to try to divine their motive before you allow yourself a reckoning of their character. If a person is showy about their good acts, you can discount those acts from your reckoning of them. If they're looking for recognition or thanks or some kind of satisfaction or gain outside of the simple pleasure of having given of themselves for the good of others, then the merit, for me, is gone.

You'd never in a million years have heard young Mahon going around boasting about himself. How he was giving employment. How he was sailing his ship into the stormiest seas and keeping it afloat by sheer force of his will, his giving heart and his indefatigable spirit. You'd never hear him admit to taking on jobs at cost or at a loss, just to keep lads working. But I know these things: I have sources like every good Garda who ever wore a hat, and I was able always to add my instinct and intuition to any received intelligence, putting it together like a collage of tiny bits to form the clearest picture of the truth of things.

I SAID IT before. Madness comes circling around. Ten-year cycles, as true as the sun will rise. I got a funny feeling when I heard about that Cain chap being shot inside in Limerick city the other week. Jason Cain. His parents were given a house out here years ago but they moved on again. He was involved in beating up young Cunliffe that time, the bones of twenty years ago, but we couldn't get him for it. Not enough evidence. The DPP fucked the file back at us. The tattoos all over the fucker's face should have been evidence enough but there's no knowing what way those lads make their calculations. Coldly, objectively, I suppose. They have their secret equations and they wouldn't be sharing them with us rank-and-file nobodies.

The lad Jason anyway was nowhere near anyone's radar, but he must have quietly climbed a few rungs of the ladder and gotten bigger notions than he was entitled to, or crossed someone a few rungs higher up again, because he was taken out in fine style, a proper hit. A single bullet while he was stopped at traffic lights in a souped-up Subaru inside near the train station. And his son in the car beside him, God help us. A grand boy, by all accounts. A student inside at the University of Limerick and a good soccer player. He wasn't hurt, but he'll have a long road ahead to recover from something like that. May the Lord heal him.

And Bobby Mahon sat into my car beside me this day last week, the bones of a decade after I sat beside him inside in Henry Street in an interview room with four windowless walls and told him to tell the truth, to speak out in the name of God and say what really happened. He said my name this time. Jim, more statement than query. And with no further preamble he told me someone was going to have to do something about the drug dealers around the town and the villages, and did I know what kind of a plan was in place, was someone going to do something, someone at the top, or near it, or what in the name of God was the story?

Bobby in that moment reminded me of the story of Our Lord in Gethsemane. Like Jesus in the garden before His

Passion, it's as though he was asking could the cup be taken from him. He was willing to sacrifice himself, but if there was another way he'd be as happy. *O my Father, if this cup may not pass away from me, except I drink it, thy will be done.*

Or maybe now with the gift of hindsight I only think that's what I thought. Maybe I have a false memory of my prescience and perspicacity. Though I know that I knew, I could feel it in the pit of my stomach and crackling along the skin of my arms, the danger that Bobby was in, the terrible conviction that had a hold of him about his obligations as a man.

I said, Bobby, do you know why Rentokil will never go out of business? And he only looked at me, but on I went, and I feel nothing but a burning shame now at the memory of the feeling I had in that moment of smartness, that I was possessed of a rough and stout and hard-won wisdom after all my years' policing a backwater. I should have known that pride comes before a fuck-up, every single time. But on I went with my stupid analogy.

Rentokil will never go out of business, I said, because every rat you trap or kill will have a dozen more on its tail, and each of them dozens will have a dozen more to take their place. You might clear out a spot of infestation for a while, but they'll always come back. And I used that Jason Cain and the absence of consequence for the drugs trade brought about by his pitiful end as an example to prove my point. His place was taken before the trigger was even pulled. God forgive me my callousness, but I was desperate to impress upon Bobby the futility of vigilantism.

So no one will do anything about this whole place going

to shit because if Augie and the boys weren't poisoning the place then someone else would be, is that it? Bobby's face was red now and his eyes were flashing bright. I was keeping an eye on the door of Tesco for Mary to come out. She takes her sweet time, though, in fairness, and I don't begrudge her one bit. She likes to stop and chat to people. But Bobby was in a temper and I was worried he'd worry her if she came out and he was still reading me. Still and all I couldn't very well tell him to be quiet. The last thing that'll calm a man down is being told to calm down.

And in the name of all that's good and holy, Jim, will you explain to me, if I know Augie Penrose is running drugs around here, and that Pitts and Braden and Dowel are his brother rats, and you know it, and every other fucker knows it, how is he left sitting pretty in his black Audi up around Summerhill, and young lads passing up and down to school past his car every day? And I had to explain to Bobby then about Augie Penrose's constitutional right to wander abroad, and his right not to be searched without due cause, and anyway that no search that was ever sanctioned bore fruit, that Augie and the boys were junior management, that senior command, whoever they were, had countless removes of distance between themselves and the trenches, and that the poor gobshites who were hooked were doing all the dirty work.

Bobby was glowing now with frustration and rage. There was a sheen of it on the surface of his skin. His nostrils were flaring like a bull's. His two hands were in his lap and I felt a sudden mad impulse to reach over and pick one of them up and hold it tight in my own and tell him he was a great lad, that he was loved beyond reason by all who knew him, that we were all proud to have him among us, but that this was a fight he couldn't win, this was a sport he couldn't even play, but he started speaking again before I had the chance to embarrass myself with such nonsense. I find lately that my mind takes its own paths sometimes, even in the most inappropriate moments.

The drugs have to get here somehow, he said. They're surely not coming by helicopter. How in the fuck are they getting them in? And again, all I could say was that as far as I knew nobody knew. NOBODY FUCKING KNOWS ANY FUCKING THING, he roared, and he pummelled his two fists on my dashboard. Then he quietened and came back to himself and he looked at me and said he was sorry, and I said, Son, I'm sorry too. And he was gone.

It was early in the evening of the next day that I got a phone call at home from a private number. The voice was familiar but I just could not place it. Quiet and deep, a small bit of a drawl on the vowels. Bobby Mahon has a gun in his van, the voice said. And he's not planning on using it for sport. Will you please pass that on to whoever needs to be told? And I said I would, and they were gone.

And I did, but what happened next no one could have predicted. Not Philly inside in town with all his big detective notions, or any of the natives or blow-ins hereabouts for all their looking and their talk, or I, for all the things about the world I thought I knew.

Frank

JOSIE BURKE AND Lily Coyne passed down the road the other week. I was standing at the threshold of the door, which is still the furthest I can go. They both looked in at me and Josie raised his hand in salute and he said, Frank. Just like that. No hello, no comment on the weather, no how do you do. Just my name, the way he always saluted me the very odd times he passed my gate walking. Josie, I said back. Lily. Just their names. Josie. Lily. He nodded then in acknowledgement of my returned salute, and she smiled her wicked smile and her eyes shone black. And I gave the rest of that day to wondering how in the hell they could have seen me standing in my doorway. Then it hit me like a punch in the stomach. Not a breath have I in this body, this body made of memory, but still the wind was knocked out of me. They were dead. Josie Burke and Lily Coyne were dead, and walking freely together through the earth, bound for where, I don't know.

Why wouldn't they be? Old men and old women die and, as a rule, their expirations aren't shocking or overly mourned. You'll see now and then a scene being made by a graveside, by women usually, or homosexuals. Thinking back now, was I at more than a handful of funerals my whole life? There was a small procession of deaths in my boyhood, of grandparents and grand-uncles and grand-aunts and a sickly cousin, and I was dragged to a number of them but they're a morass now, a vague jumble of images and echoes. The only one I have a clear memory of is my father's, and I just out of my boyhood, and most of the memory is of feeling nothing. I often stopped at the cross at Youghalarra, though, and watched the goings-on, the rote business of exequy and interment.

I often wondered what kind of a crowd I'd draw myself. I wonder still, because I was stuck here for the whole thing, and not one jackass that walked in here in the ten years since thought to mention it. *Gor, wasn't there a fine crowd all the same? He couldn't have been that much of a bollix: the church was packed to the rafters and there wasn't a blade of grass to be seen below in Youghal!* Something like that would have been reassuring.

More likely if my funereal emoluments were discussed it would be in leaner terms. *It was quiet below. Only for Chris O'Halloran and Roger Spain parking the hearse out by the cross you'd never have known there was a man being buried.* That kind of a thing. They're a tiny and fleeting comfort, these imagined conversations, but they're all I have.

But there were Josie and Lily, sauntering down along that road out there, not a bother on them, his face red with health and satisfaction, her face glowing with all the secrets of life and death, the auld witch. Why in the fuck did I not shout out after them, Hey, Josie, hey, Lily, how did ye know I was here? I've been waiting since to see would they maybe walk back up the way they came, leaning myself against the bounds of the territory I have by some mysterious hand been assigned, the line of the threshold of this old door, the rafters of the ceiling, the boards of the floor.

Down or up I can't go, nor can I move beyond these walls. I can't sleep or take any kind of ease except in my contemplation of the world, or as much of it as I can see from this redoubt, as it brightens and darkens, the odd small bird that perches on the sills and stares blackly in at me, the blow-ins and rubberneckers tramping up and down my road the very same as people who have bones below bones in Youghalarra graveyard.

Was Josie Burke a better man than I am? Than I was? All told, I suppose I'll have to allow that he was. It wouldn't have been hard for him. I was never too fond of him. I never knew him, really. The Burkes were big shots but my father always said they came from nothing. The same way he came from something and ended up with nearly nothing, besides a scrap of a farm that I drank on him. I always liked that Lily Coyne though, even in spite of the way she only ever had a cold eye for me. She paddled her own canoe, that lady.

I'm looking forward to meeting my father and asking him what he thought of my stewardship of his beloved acres, but time is stretching itself and compressing itself again in maddening sequence, like the vacuum pump on his auld Dairymaster, and I don't know if I'll ever break free of it, or out of this place.

THIS IS MY punishment, my penance, my taste of hell. No eternal immolation, no flaying demons, no bottomless pit of sighs, just this unending existence in the shell of my father's house, with only my thoughts for company. It occurred to me early on that this house might not be standing at all, that I might occupy some kind of a facsimile of my earthly home, that it might just be a receptacle of my sorrow, a trap to keep me from passing to the next world. But then my boy arrived, and sat down there at my table, his table now for all the use he makes of it, and he's been a frequent visitor ever since, just the way he always was.

I got the impression from his demeanour that first time he visited after my mortal flesh and my eternal spirit were separated one from the other and things were settled a bit, that he'd come to his senses, that he'd told Jim Gildea or whatever yahoo was in charge of investigating my murder what had really happened. He arrived on and he sat down and he stretched out his long legs like a man relaxing his weary muscles after a day's labour, and I suppose he was.

I looked out the window and saw his van. *Mahon and Son* he had on the side of it in big yellow letters. Imagine that, and the boy that time not even weaned from his mother's teat. Shaping, that is. Mahon and Son. I ask you. The sound of it from my soundless lips is sweet.

SO MY SON sits across from me the way he always did in my living days, staring at the space where I used to sit looking back at him. Some days he does little jobs, running repairs so that this place is kept liveable, and only me living here, and I not even alive. He has a good hand and eye, in fairness to him. He has a surer hand than I ever had, anyway. The amount of times I wrecked this place I cannot count. Splintered tables and chairs, and pictures torn off the wall, and screamed curses into the rafters and the roof. It was fitting, I suppose, that I was killed here, and that it was a man's rage that did for me.

I always knew, from a few digs he'd thrown over the years, that Bobby had big plans to burn this place or to knock it back to stones when I was gone but I knew as well that he never would. He's not the sort for grand gestures, or at least he wasn't up to now. I often wish he would throw a match on this place or swing a ball at it to see if I could be released.

He arrived one time with the wife and the young lad. Little Robert. He was only a child, barely walking. The wife was giving off a bit, laying down the law the way women do. You have to do something with it, Bobby. You can't just leave it here. You can't let the garden run wild, either. It'll be worse than Mickey Briars's place up the road. It's bad enough as it is, the way Frank had it.

I think she felt me beside her then because she pulled her coat tight around herself and made a kind of a shivery, disgusted sound. The small boy looked straight at me and he pointed a little finger at me and he smiled. I smiled back at him and I smile now every single time I think about that moment. If only I'd been alive for it. There's a gang of lads that passes up and down the road on bicycles to the handball alley and the lake on summer days. I'm nearly sure one of them is my grandson, a fair-haired lad, tall. He never stops, though, or slows even as he passes. Maybe someday his father will pass this pile of stones and patch of earth to him. Maybe I'll still be here. That'll be heaven enough. More than I deserve.

IT'S ONLY THE very odd time that Bobby comes now. Mostly on a Sunday, I think, but only once or twice in a season or some seasons not at all. I have no hold on time any more. Go home, son, I say to him, and leave me be. And when he goes I set myself again the task of waiting for him, of watching out the window at the turning world, greening and browning and baring itself, watching for a sign of him. He was here more often recently. Does he feel me? I don't know. Does he think I have some kind of an answer for him, something that might soften the darkness that has itself draped around him? His grim face, I can't bear it, and yet I long for it. All I do is long for it, for all of these eternities I must endure.

Don't do it, I said to Bobby, the last day he was here. There was a heavy black weight around him, a shifting dense shadow, something dancing darkly in his eyes. He was looking, like he always does, at the empty space across the table where I used to sit. He does that for I don't know how long every time he comes and never a word does he speak but I hear him. I hear him telling me about the pain he's in. I say, Will you for the love of God knock this place down, or sell it, or burn it to the ground, and free yourself of the past? What's bringing you down here with a face like a slapped arse, dragging all our wearisome histories behind you?

OH, HERE HE'S on now again, look out. With a sense about him of a man walking along a cliff edge. I feel all around me a terrible miasma of danger, of something imminent, like something is about to crash through the filament that separates me from grace, from my wife's kind eyes, blue and forgiving, from her beautiful hand, held out to me in greeting. Whatever kind of foolishness you have in your heart, forget about it, son. Sit down there now and take your ease awhile and then go home to your family, go home and be the man I should have been.

I SEE THROUGH my window a lad walk in the gate, a lad I knew from somewhere, from some other time, and he carrying the same dense weight as my son, a shroud of blackness about him, a burden of things as yet undone. I know his name. Brian. I'm shouting his name, God help me, I am. I'm shouting to him the same thing I said to Bobby, over and over again, in the hope it might get through to him from death to life. The boy Brian's left hand is empty and his right hand is the Devil's hand. Don't do it, son, don't do it, for the love of all that's good, don't do what you're about to do, but he's coming still, he's stopping at the window and he blocks the sun, and his shadow is the shadow of death, a shadow I well know, and my son has his eyes closed, his hands across them rubbing them, he's weary, is he weary of life, oh son, my son, please don't be weary of life. Please open your eyes, there's a gun pointed at you, the boy outside has a gun and his eyes are full of tears but his shot is clear . . .

A moment, and then the shadow is gone. Thank you, God, the shadow is gone, the boy has disappeared from the window and I can see his narrow back as he vaults the wall. He's standing now on the far side of the road and he's looking across the low hedge and the scrap of a field towards the callaghs, and the sky above the callaghs is filled with a brilliant light, and a noise like a demon's bellow is filling this house. The back windows are shattering inwards and the front windows are shattering outwards and my son is flying from his chair and landing on the floor like half a bag of wet cement but he's whole, he's alive, thank his blessed mother my boy is alive, he has work yet to do in this world. And at last at last the vault of heaven is opening to receive me: I see through the glassless window from the lake shore a plume of smoke rising and billowing outwards against the blue sky and my son is on his feet and out the door and I'm following him and I'm calling out to him as I go, Bobby, son, come back, son, and at my gate I'm stopped and the metal heart at the centre of it that my wife loved so much the heart I had made for her one time in the foolishness of love that I thought would say for me the things I couldn't say myself is stopped

IT ISN'T SPINNING any longer even with the clean breeze blowing from the mountains to the lake I look across the land to see can I see my boy but he's gone from my view my beautiful boy and I feel myself resting into the whispering wind received by it and I'm part of it now and I'm lifting fading now I'm away

Triona

MY MOTHER DIED the day after the explosion. Poor Mam, people barely noticed. When I told Bobby that they'd rung to say she was going, that we had to get into the hospice quick, he acted all confused, like he'd forgotten she was dying. Marjorie? Yes, Marjorie, my mother, Jesus Christ, Bobby, where the fuck are the keys of the car? He told me later that he'd meant to call to her the evening before, but that he'd gone down to his father's house instead, on a kind of a notion. What kind of a notion makes a man forgo his dying mother-in-law's bedside for his dead father's kitchen table? But I didn't ask him that. He felt badly enough as it was.

I knew from Nuala, my friend who nurses on the downstairs ward in Milford, that Bobby called in on his own two, sometimes three evenings a week to see Mam. For some reason it was his little secret and I let him off with it. Like a weird affair they were having, him and my dying mother. I'd just thought it was a part of her doting the few times she was lucid and coherent, and she said, Bobby, you're here again! Did you go home at all? Then Nuala said to me, All the girls upstairs love the evenings that Bobby comes twice! And she laughed her dirty laugh. She's a bold bitch.

LEE BRADEN, TYRONE Dowel, Augustus Penrose, Jordan Pitts. Their names were read so mournfully on the news. Like they were killed on the front line of a war or something. They looked innocent in their photos, suited and slicked, like ordinary young lads off to a do, a debs or the races. In a way, I suppose, they *were* killed on a front line. Of Mickey Briars's one-man war, his secret crusade against local organized crime, which culminated in the detonation of a hundred-year-old home-made barrel bomb, and the immediate deaths of the four lads inside the small thatched cottage near the shore of Lough Derg, five miles from the town of Nenagh, County Tipperary. That's something like what they want to say in the papers and on television but they can't. Not yet, anyway. The reporters are buzzing around like flies on dead meat, but no one is letting them settle. Ethel Hartnett, who's a cousin of Mickey's, put a sign on the door of her guest house in Dromineer saying NO PRESS.

Jim Gildea told his wife, Mary, who told the rest of the parish that Mickey's nephew was being harassed and threatened by Augie and his crew. That the nephew's adopted parents had their life savings and more already handed over but that the lads were visiting weekly. Until Mickey lured them somehow into his house and trapped them there, and whatever way he had the barrel bomb rigged it blew them into dust. What nephew? was the first question everyone asked. No one had known that Mickey had any living family, or who these adopted parents might be. There's more to that story, a lot more I'd say, but it'll be told elsewhere, I'm sure.

Mickey was out on his boat at the time of the blast, fishing. He was on the lake island, actually, when the guards caught up with him, reclining on a little hill of grass, dozing. I heard this from Shauna Nugent who works as the civilian attachment to the Garda station in Nenagh. Hello, boys, he said to the two cops on the little launch who'd been dispatched to bring him in, and he offered them some trout from his pan, and a cup of tea from his billy-can. He's a smooth operator, our Mick.

There's not a thing they can do to him. His story is that they must have been robbing his house and for whatever reason they went at the barrel that held up his kitchen table. They must have thought it was full of money but it turns out it was actually filled with gelignite cased in a thin layer of concrete, one of a pair of barrel bombs that had been deployed against Crown forces at Templekelly, Ballina, in 1920, by Captain Jeremiah Cranty of the North Tipperary Brigade IRA, Mickey's father. Its comrade was detonated in the battle, and Captain Cranty carried the unexploded ordnance home on his mighty shoulders, in the lee of the Arra Mountains, along the mass rock paths worn by his ancestors.

Mickey says he never really believed that story, that his father had a thousand other stories like it, and that it was kind of a running joke for years and years that the barrel was never to be moved or molested or they could all be blown to Kingdom Come. He liked the idea of death being always so close, Mickey said to Bridie Connors and a crowd that had assembled around him in the bar of the Abbey Court where he's been staying since the big bang. He felt like he had power over it when he was eating his breakfast off of it every morning. And he laughed his soft, wheezy laugh. He's getting to be a bit of a celebrity.

There was a public meeting in the Scouts' hall in Nenagh. The chairman of the new local drugs task force stood up at the podium and made a powerful speech. It's a tragedy, he said, that those young men lost their lives. But from the ashes of that terrible conflagration rises for us an opportunity. To keep drugs off our streets. To keep our families safe from the evil of organized crime. It's up to each and every one of us to play our part in ensuring that the void they have left is never filled.

He got a standing ovation. People were slapping him on the back, saying, Good man, Pokey Burke, more power to you, Pokey. It's not too long since the same people would have tarred him and feathered him and thrown him into the lake. But everyone deserves a second chance, I suppose. And he really seems to mean it when he talks about the evil of drugs. The passion of the saved, I heard someone say as we left the hall. The prodigal's new-found wisdom. *He was dead and is alive again; he was lost and is found.*

I CRIED WHEN I heard their names read out. We knew, of course, long before the official announcement, because Augie Penrose's car was parked on the road outside Mickey's cottage, half melted from the heat of the sudden inferno. The site of the cottage itself was a crater with a ring around it filled with bits of its own stone, clumps of thatch, ash-edged pages of books. Mickey was a secret reader, it seems.

Every house for a half-mile around had broken windows from the shockwave of the blast. But most of Mickey's little forest of undergrowth survived, and the hawthorn tree at the corner of the plot was unmarked, not a leaf did it lose. Legend has it that Bride Cranty, Mickey's mother, was often seen beneath a full moon, incanting and dancing around that tree. People see what they want to see, of course, and there were plenty of noses poked over that wall for the sixty-odd years that she reigned over that little patch of earth, hoping to get a glance of a witch, some of them even hoping I'd say to be tempted, to be beckoned into the darkness, if only to test the mettle of their faith.

I cried when I heard the names of the dead because they were young men. But also I cried for joy, and pure relief, God forgive me. I wouldn't have to see that cursed car ever again with its blacked-out windows idling by the kerb outside the school, I wouldn't have to lie in bed thinking about the danger my children were in, the danger all the children of this parish were in. I wouldn't have to think about Milly Coyne and her little heart and her bruised face, and she driving with the Devil round the roads. I saw her shortly after it happened, white and thin and washed out, with a single blood-red rose in her hand, standing on her own at the police cordon. She's free now, but it'll take her a while to realize it. May she keep her gift of freedom all her days.

BEFORE MAM WAS diagnosed we went on a city break. Zürich. I'm not exactly sure why. Not because Réaltín

Shanahan recommended it, that's for sure. She was here going through the books and I was sitting across from her, regretting, as I do every year, ever getting involved with her. But Seanie was so sweetly supportive of her when she qualified as an accountant, and he practically begged Bobby and me to give her the work, and I have to admit she's good at it. She was all talk about herself and Seanie and their few days in Zürich, and how Seanie loved the city, the clean air and the galleries, and I laughed in spite of myself at the thought of Seanie in a gallery surrounded by priceless works of art, his pervy eyes bulging out of his head at the bare arses and cleavages of the Rubenses and Caravaggios. With the straightest face you ever saw in your life she told me they went to see a Roni Horn exhibition and I spat coffee all over the table. She had a puss on her then but I don't care.

We ended up there, anyway, Bobby and me. And it was lovely. Bobby is never usually himself when we're away just the two of us; he's never relaxed the way you want someone to be. There's always an edge of discomfort and worry about him. He's always sure we're about to get mugged or ripped off or run over or that we'll miss our flight or that something will happen to the kids while we're gone. On a flight to London once to see AC/DC in Wembley when they were small, as safe as houses at home with Mam, he announces, If this plane crashed now they'd be orphans. And they mightn't be left with your mother. They could end up wards of court. They could be separated, even. I nearly fucking killed him. I barely looked at him until we were checked into the hotel and I had a half a bottle of wine drunk.

But on this trip to Zürich he managed to relax and even I think enjoy himself. He loved the order and the quietness of the place. No roaming bands of pickpockets, no hawkers or buskers or rubbish or any sense of edginess or danger, just cleanliness, unforced sophistication, and impeccable manners; even the air was undramatic, still and cool. We walked through narrow cobbled streets and along a winding rampart to a geometrically treed park above the east of the city and we saw, set into an ancient wall, a little monument to a child who had died before Christ was born. Bobby translated the Latin without even using his phone. He remembered what he'd learned from Brother Boniface in the Christian Brothers School, like he remembers everything he's ever read, and understands more about things than he ever lets on. The boy was five years old, his parents' only child. They must have been big shots to say they could afford to put this here in his memory, Bobby said. *Diligitur in infinitum*. He is loved to infinity.

He squeezed my hand then as he spoke. And I felt the pain in those ancient people's long-dead hearts. They stood where we were standing once, holding hands the way we were, and they reread their own inscription and held their palms against it, I'm sure. The inscription, and the dead stone into which it was carved, was eternal and unmoving and they could transfer some of the heat of their living bodies into it as they would share the heat of their child's living flesh.

Bobby was whispering now. Jesus. Can you imagine it? Can you imagine how they must have felt? And I said that I could imagine, of course I could. He looked at me then and I saw on his face, just for a moment, an expression of fear and helplessness that was so pitiful it nearly made me cry out, Jesus, Bobby, come on, it's not going to happen. But I can't make promises like that.

We walked back down towards the cold still city and it felt like we were the only two living people in the world for a while, and he pulled me in close to him like he used to when we were young, when we were teenagers, and I had everything he wanted, was all he wanted.

YOU HAVE TO reimagine the world when someone dies. Those four families who lost their boys in the blast have to recast everything to accommodate this new reality. You can't just go about your business as before when someone you love departs: the dead take something of the world with them, something of your being, because they were part of your being. I haven't reimagined this motherless world yet. I still pick up my phone to ring her twice, three times a day, like I always did. I still catch myself with the keys of my car in my hand to drive over home. And the shock of her absence isn't abating. If anything it's becoming more acute, stinging a little bit more each day.

I'm a grown woman with children of my own to mind. I can't be wallowing in this grief. But I remember Sister Laelia in the Convent when we were doing *Hamlet* for the Leaving. Why, girls, was the prince not allowed to grieve as he wished to? He is scolded and mocked for his sadness. *'Tis unmanly grief. It shows a will most incorrect to heaven, a heart unfortified, a mind impatient, an understanding simple and unschooled.* Poor Hamlet, Sister Laelia would say, and shake her pretty wimpled head in sorrow. Maybe if he'd been allowed to cry things wouldn't have gone so terribly wrong! I always gave Hamlet Bobby's face, but now I hear myself say, *But break, my heart, for I must hold my tongue.*

I FOUND THE gun the day after Mam's funeral. When I asked Bobby about it he said, There's a photo going around of me coming out of a whorehouse. And I said, I know. And *whorehouse* is a filthy word. It's as if he thought I'd care about some stupid laddish antics over in that godforsaken place. I know the foolish strut of men among men, the way they have of insisting on reducing the world to a set of basic rules, reverting to all their adolescent types.

I know what he's capable of and what's beyond him. I know his goodness better than he knows it himself. When he realized that I knew about the stupid photo that Seanie Shaper's bitter little strap of a wife was sending around the country I could nearly see something lift from him, some physical presence emanate and dissolve in the air around him. I know that he still doesn't know, after all these years, after I loving him boy and man, that I know the deep core of him, that I know him better than he knows himself. Sometimes I wonder does he know himself at all.

I SAW THE gun in the garage, tucked behind the lawn-mower and the wheelie cabinet of tools. Not quite hidden, but definitely meant to be out of sight. I smelt it before I saw it, that deep rich oily scent. I remember it from my father's guns. I remember him striding in with a string of pheasants over his shoulder and down his long back, singing, *'Tis my sorrow sorest, sad the falling forest, the north wind brings me no rest, and death is in the sky*, and the feeling I always got in my stomach, the sick knot of grief for the beautiful dead creatures, and the depth of the blackness in their tiny round eyes, staring into infinity.

My kind gentle father always seemed in those moments something beyond a man, something cruel and monstrous, and mighty and brave, and I forced myself to watch him as he hung the pheasants in the back kitchen and cleaned his gun, and then a few days later I watched again as he drew them and cut through their necks.

I've told Bobby to take that gun out of my house and to get good and rid of it. I've told him he's never to bring a gun near my house again or near my children. But first I want to walk with him through the forestry in the valley of Slieve Felim and Keeper Hill, with the rifle strapped to his back, and I want him to show me how he'd have done what he was going to do.

I want to hear the bolt sliding and the round clicking into the chamber, I want to see the flash of fire from the muzzle, and feel the shockwaves in the air around me and through my body. I want him to feel that power in his hands of death over life, and then I want to feel his hands on me, and I'll lie beneath him on the forest floor, and I'll tell him that he's my man, my good, good man.

Acknowledgements

MY LAST NOVEL, *The Queen of Dirt Island*, was written in tribute to the indomitable living spirit of my mother, Anne Ryan. This novel was written in her memory. I love you, Mam, and I miss you every day.

THANKS TO YOU, Reader, as always, for making this writing life possible; to the booksellers and librarians of the world for keeping all of our writerly and readerly fires burning; to my editor, Brian Langan, and my publisher, Kirsty Dunseath, for helping me so much in every way; to Larry Finlay, for a working life spent championing and shepherding countless great stories and literary careers with such passion, skill and kindness; to Bill Scott-Kerr, Alison Barrow, Patsy Irwin, Milly Reid, Hannah Winter, Sorcha Judge, Louise Farrell, Michael McLoughlin, Keltie Mechalskie, Tom Chicken, Hannah Weatherill, Kate Samano, Hazel

Orme, Catherine Wood, Holly McElroy, Georgie Bewes, Catriona Hillerton, and everyone at Doubleday, Transworld, Penguin Ireland and Penguin US for all of the wonderful work that you do; to everyone at the PRH rights team and to all of my international publishers and translators, for giving my characters voices and lives I never thought they'd have; to Antony Farrell and The Lilliput Press, who welcomed me thirteen years ago and set me on this path; to Kennys of Galway for lifting me up time and again; to Sarah Bannan and the Arts Council of Ireland for a helping hand at just the right time; to Sarah Moore Fitzgerald, Joseph O'Connor, Fíona Scarlett, Eoin Devereux, Emily Cullen, Kit de Waal, and all of my incredibly supportive and inspiring colleagues, friends and students at the University of Limerick; to my dear Mary, John, Christopher, Daniel, Aoibhinn, Finn, Katie, Lucy, Thomas, and all of my family, in-laws and friends; and to Anne Marie, who looks after my heart and my spirit, gives me courage, and makes me better in every way.

DONAL RYAN is an award-winning author from Nenagh, County Tipperary, whose work has been published in over twenty languages to major critical acclaim. *The Spinning Heart* won the Guardian First Book Award, the EU Prize for Literature (Ireland), and Book of the Year at the Irish Book Awards; it was shortlisted for the International IMPAC Dublin Literary Award, longlisted for the Man Booker Prize and the Desmond Elliott Prize, and was voted 'Irish Book of the Decade'. His fourth novel, *From a Low and Quiet Sea*, was longlisted for the Man Booker Prize, shortlisted for the Costa Novel Award 2018, and won the Jean Monnet Prize for European Literature. His novel *Strange Flowers* was voted Novel of the Year at the Irish Book Awards, and was a number-one bestseller, as was his most recent novel, *The Queen of Dirt Island*, which was also shortlisted for Book of the Year at the Irish Book Awards. Donal lectures in Creative Writing at the University of Limerick. He lives with his wife, Anne Marie, and their two children just outside Limerick city.

My Silent Scream:
Finding Hope & Grace to Endure
Inside a mother's struggle to raise a child with
OCD, ADHD, & Asperger's Syndrome
ISBN: 978-1-936314-54-6

Copyright © 2011 by Dee Phillips-Goodnight
www.mysilentscream.org

Published by Word and Spirit Books
P.O. Box 701403
Tulsa, Oklahoma 74170

"Mom?"

"Yes, Ross."

"I'm just not, you know, as easy as other kids.
Am I, Mom?"

FOREWORD

Nobody knows a child better than his mother. A mother just has that God-given innate sixth-sense which tells her when something is wrong with her child. Many times I've witnessed mothers consoling crying babies with the words, "Mommy knows, Mommy knows." Mothers know when something is "not quite right" physically and mentally with their child.

Dads may notice as well when something is "psychologically off" with their child, but they rarely have that sixth-sense type of intuition. It's actually not unusual for a father to be oblivious to his children's thoughts and feelings. An old saying in psychiatry is that if Mom and Dad disagree on what's happening with their child, the mom will be right at least 100% of the time. While this is not meant to be taken literally, it does emphasize the superior insight of mothers.

Moms are also committed to do whatever it takes in finding out what's wrong with the mental state of their son or daughter and then getting them the help they need. Dads don't always want to know. I'm certainly not trying to beat up on fathers—nor question their love and devotion to their offspring. But many times I've heard men attempt to explain away their son's

unacceptable behaviors by statements such as "well he's all boy" or "he's just a little rambunctious."

It's not uncommon for fathers to resist searching for psychological help for their child for the following reasons:

1. I don't want people knowing (or asking questions) about what goes on privately in our family.

2. If my child thinks there is something mentally wrong with him it could damage his self-esteem.

3. My child will be labeled by others now (especially the school).

4. If there's something wrong with my child, that's a failure on my part as a father.

Much of this resistance deals with concern of how others will perceive the family rather than confronting the specific psychological challenges facing a child. Mothers can get caught up in this as well. And in parents' defense, there is some truth to these four statements—a huge stigma still surrounds mental health in this country. And parents are often the first who are blamed when their child has problems.

The overwhelming majority of mothers that I've dealt with in my practice as a psychiatrist are willing to do whatever it takes to find help for their child—no matter the price. And I'm not talking money here, but personal sacrifice. A mother will abandon her dreams, well being, and security in life for her child if needed.

We've seen shows and read books about women trapped in Middle Eastern countries who risked their own lives in order to enable their children to escape and lead a better life. I know a mother who drove her daughter six hours every Friday to Houston to get the cancer treatment she needed on Saturday—then drove back on Sunday. On top of this, that mother worked a full time job Monday through Thursday.

Dee's story about her son Ross is a perfect example of a mother's instinct and insight. Dee's unfathomable love for Ross and her unshakable faith in God propelled her onward to find answers.

My Silent Scream is a rollercoaster ride of a family's trying, tragedy, and triumph. You'll fall in love with Ross as you discover the wonderful heart and charisma of this young man; though there will be times that you'll feel like sending him to his room and telling him not to come out until he's twenty-one. *My Silent Scream* is also a story of high expectations, hard work, and hope. Most of all, it's the journey of a mother struggling to raise a son who's "not quite right" in today's world. On this journey she discovers the real meaning of God's strength and blessing.

I consider myself among one of the privileged few because God has allowed me to play a small role in Ross and Dee's lives. Their story continues to remind me that life is not always what we expect nor originally hope for, but no matter what circumstance we find ourselves in—magnificently splendid or utterly horri-

ble—<u>God is with us</u>—whether we realize it or not—He's providing for us; all of the time.

Todd Clements M.D.
February 2011

INTRODUCTION

"Adversity causes some men to break; others to break records."

—WILLIAM A. WARD

Therefore, since we have been justified through faith, we have peace with God through our Lord Jesus Christ, through whom we have gained access by faith into this grace in which we now stand. And we rejoice in the hope of the glory of God. Not only so, but we also rejoice in our suffering, because we know suffering produces perseverance; perseverance, character; and character hope. And hope does not disappoint us, because God has poured out his love into our hearts by the Holy Spirit, whom he has given us.

ROMANS 5: 1-5

This book is a raw look inside our daily lives. As I look back over the years since Ross was born, my life has been one big puzzle. Some pieces fit together; while in other areas, I'm still trying to bring the pieces

together to make sense. Everyday, I strive to find one more piece that fits to make the puzzle recognizable, to be able to understand the total picture. My goal is to share with you the way Ross expresses himself and how the characteristics of his disorders manifest themselves in our everyday life. Perhaps I will describe an account along the journey of our lives that may be similar to what you are facing with your own child. I hope to bring validation to you as you read this book. I hope to make you smile, and above all, give you hope.

I want to encourage you to keep pressing forward and never give up! As I begin, I pray that my words and the recounting of my experience will be a blessing to those who read them and will, in some way through God's grace, present each individual with something that can be useful in their situation.

Fall 2008

The room was dark, it was still daytime, but I had closed all the blinds. I knelt beside the bed and sobbed. It was hard for me to get a deep breath. My body ached and my heart felt broken. Visions and voices played over and over in my head. I had just finished meeting with Ross's teachers...all of them. I could tell by their facial expressions when I entered the room, that it wasn't going to be a pleasant meeting. The air in the room was heavy. There were times I tilted my head back, just to get a deep breath of air.

As I sat there listening to each teacher describe Ross's behaviors, I felt weak. It was like someone stuck a needle in me and deflated my strength. Some of the teachers seemed compassionate and others, highly frustrated. I kept wishing the words they were using to describe my child weren't true, but I knew the sad reality all too well myself. One teacher commented that she had over 25 students in her class, and she simply didn't have the time or energy to give that Ross demanded.

- "He's argumentative."
- "He can't keep up in class."
- "I can't get him to do his schoolwork."
- "He just wants to go to the library and read non-fiction books."
- "He's obsessed with building a spaceship."
- "He's paranoid to go outside."
- "He's not in touch with reality."
- "Dee, I think he's close to a breakdown."

We all agreed that something needed to be done, but exactly what that "something" was, was always the question. If I knew what to do, I would already be doing it! Ross seemed to be growing increasingly agitated and was "melting down" in class frequently.

Ross was not only struggling at school, but things at home were on the decline as well. He now had added a

list of phobias to the mix of issues we were already confronting. In addition to the traditional Asperger's characteristics, Ross was now experiencing unrealistic fears. He did not want to walk from the car in the garage to the house for fear that a wasp might attack him. He didn't want to take a shower without me standing right next to the shower door. He thought a dinosaur might come through the wall or hot lava might spew from the faucet. He refused to walk upstairs without someone with him. He became hypersensitive of crossing bridges while riding in the car. He wanted his window in his bedroom concreted shut so that no "predators" could enter. He especially was concerned about cougars. If the heater in the house came on, he jumped as if he were on edge. He refused to walk from the bus stop to our house. He would literally go door to door to find someone in the neighborhood who would walk him to our door.

My son was crumbling right in front of me. *How had I failed him so miserably? Why was this happening to my baby?*

As I knelt there beside the bed that day in the Fall of 2008, I did the only thing I knew to do—pray: *Oh Father, help me! The pain is so deep and real. How do I live above this? I suffer for another's pain. He's my child. How do I free him from the pain? Not only now, but the pain that awaits him as he tries to make it in the world?*

About Me

Trust in the LORD with all your heart, and lean not on your own understanding; In all your ways acknowledge Him, and He shall direct your paths.

PROVERBS 3:5-6 NKJV

In order for you to best understand the story contained in this book, you have to know a little about me. Before Ross was born, my life was centered, of course, around me. My goals in life concerned, of course, me. My ambitions were to go to college and graduate with skills that would lead to a high paying career. I was performance driven.

I can remember back to the first grade, not wanting to take home any papers that were not A's. I would get rid of them, one way or the other, before I made it home. I wanted to please my parents and their acceptance, or rather their praise, was a big deal to me.

Maybe this was a function of being the oldest child in my family. By birth order definition, oldest children have a tendency to be higher achievers than younger siblings. (Don't get offended, those of you who are younger siblings. I'm just repeating what research suggests.) I don't remember my parents prodding me to study or do homework. The mere thought of going to school unprepared was something I did not want to experience. There was just something inside of me that hated failing.

Academically, I excelled. I graduated with the highest grade point average in my class. I was the high school yearbook editor my senior year. My efforts resulted in a full ride scholarship to any school of my choice within the state of New Mexico.

After high school, I left my small rural town and went to college, though not in New Mexico (I should have rethought that one). In college, I excelled again academically. I received the Woman of the Year award. I was a residential assistant. I served as vice president in student government. I was co-chairman of the Race Across America qualifying event. The list of my activities and achievements could go on and on.

I graduated college with a bachelors degree in business administration with an emphasis in marketing. My first job was selling radio ads in Garden City, Kansas. I was successful and set sales records, though I'm not sure how I did that. I was an absolute failure at role

play in our sales meetings. I'm sure my co-workers and supervisors thought, *How does she ever sell anything?*

There is one thing I need to point out in all of this: My achievements were a result of application. I was a committed student. I worked hard and spent the time to learn the material. I applied myself. I was not naturally intelligent. I was just disciplined to do the work.

I'm a Type A personality with a day planner and a To Do list. I'm not an impromptu person; I like to have a plan. I like to have a schedule and follow the schedule. I want my ducks to be in a row and if possible, I like to know the kind and color of the ducks.

So now that I have established a little background about myself, you can see that I was nowhere near prepared for what lay in store for me!

CHAPTER TWO

Pregnancy

"For I know the plans I have for you," declares the LORD, "plans to prosper you and not to harm you, plans to give you hope and a future."

JEREMIAH 29:11

I got married in July of 1993 and found out in September of 1995 that I was pregnant. I was elated! It was a planned pregnancy. I wanted a baby so badly. I couldn't wait to know if it was a boy or a girl. What would it look like? Would it be intelligent, an athlete, or maybe both? My mind took me through a thousand "what ifs," but the one thing I knew was, I loved this baby!

I didn't have a normal pregnancy. The pregnancy "glow" was nowhere to be found. The only glow I had came from the sweat beads on my forehead when my stomach once again decided to reject partially digested food. They may call it morning sickness, but the nausea

lasted all day. I felt awful, like I had the flu that never went away. Not only did I feel bad, I looked bad. Some say they never looked or felt better than when they were pregnant. What's up with that? My face broke out with multiple large blemishes. My normally blond hair turned dark. My cheeks lost all of their natural color. I snored profusely, and even started drooling. Yuck! I was tired and very emotional.

At nine weeks into my pregnancy, I started bleeding. I was afraid I was going to miscarry. My mom had had several miscarriages and I was hoping this was not something that was hereditary. I lay in bed, still as I possibly could be, as if moving might cause a harmful effect. I just lay there and prayed.

I had a doctor's appointment scheduled for the next day. At the appointment, my doctor checked me and said, "Time will tell." Like that's encouraging. I wanted someone to say, "You're going to be fine," but I kept faith and the bleeding eventually stopped. I think this situation made me realize more than ever how precious life is, and just how quickly it can be taken away.

My morning sickness, or shall I call it "day sickness," continued. Every day was a struggle to get up and go to work. I worked at two museums doing public relations and marketing work. I had a 45-minute commute and often times, I had to pull over alongside the road in the freezing cold and vomit. I couldn't even eat my favorite foods. I guess if I look on the bright side,

I didn't gain very much weight during my pregnancy—only 22 pounds by my delivery date.

Spring rolled around and I welcomed the rain. It is almost always wet in Missouri in the springtime. I've always loved the rain. It is calming to me. Work kept me real busy and this was a good thing. It kept me focused on what needed to be done and made the time go by quickly.

A week before my delivery date, my mom came to stay with me. She lives in Dalhart, Texas. This was her first grandchild and she didn't want to miss a thing. She had me out walking laps around the neighborhood because she wanted to see that baby. It didn't work. The doctors decided to induce labor a few days before my due date. My stomach wasn't growing as it should and I was not gaining as much weight as expected in my last trimester.

William Ross Phillips was born April 29, 1996, at Heartland Hospital in St. Joseph, Missouri. I was at the hospital at six that morning and they started the inducement about seven. Ross was welcomed at 2:01 p.m. He was nineteen and a half inches long and weighed five pounds and fourteen ounces—not very big for a full term baby. I had elected to do a natural delivery. (Big mistake!) My doctor said that medication would delay labor and he felt that natural was the best approach. I did my breathing as I had learned in class, but the pain was intense.

I finally made it through labor only to find out there were other complications. I had what they called a calcified placenta. The placenta was stuck internally and did not pass after the baby was born. I experienced the worst pain I had ever felt as the doctor tried to pull out the placenta. They took me to surgery and performed an emergency procedure to remove the placenta. They were pushing me through doors and everyone was talking to each other like they do in the movies. It was very unsettling. I didn't know what was wrong with me or what they were going to do about it. The last thing I remember was counting backwards as they put me to sleep.

When I came to in the recovery room, my initial impression was that I could feel heat. I guess they had put a heat lamp on me, though I'm not sure why. I think it had something to do with the healing process and stopping the bleeding. I felt like I was in one of those dreams where you are in a compromising position without any underwear on. (Has anyone else ever had those dreams?) They soon took me back to my room. I remember feeling so weak. That morning, I had also begun suffering from a sinus infection. I couldn't breathe very well and had drainage running down my throat. If you've given birth to a child, you know this is not the time you want to be coughing!

Upon being wheeled into my room, I saw that my mom was holding Ross and she said, "I think he's hungry!" I was so excited to see my baby and hold him.

I couldn't believe he was finally here. He looked so perfect. I think all parents are relieved once the counting of the ten toes and ten fingers is successfully completed for their child. Ross had started to fuss, and though all I really wanted to do was sleep, I tried to give breast feeding my best shot. I felt exhausted, but was so thankful that Ross had made it into the world and that he was healthy. As I held him close and he began to eat, I will never forget the feeling I had: The intense love, deep in my soul that was there for that child.

I finished feeding Ross and they took him back to the nursery about 9:00 p.m. I was ready to lay my head on a pillow and rest. I had had enough excitement that day. My mom left for the evening and said she would be back in the morning. I was so glad she had been there with me. Her presence gave me a lot of comfort. I drifted off to sleep at about 10:00 p.m.

At approximately 11:00 p.m., in came the nurse. She was pushing Ross in his roller bed and said she was bringing him back to me because he was screaming and keeping all the other babies awake. I thought to myself, *What? You can't bring him back to me. I'm tired. Have you forgotten the whole surgery thing? I need some sleep.* But without hesitation, I held my baby. He ate and then slept for a little while. Then he ate and slept a little while longer. And so the story began, eat and sleep... a little while.

Motherhood
Blissful...or not!

So many new mothers feel overwhelmed and emotional, especially when it's your first child and you have nothing with which to compare the experience. You have spent your full existence in life up to this point worrying about and taking care of yourself. Now taking a bath or going to the restroom alone is a rare occurrence. You're now taking showers as fast as you can – if you even get to take a shower—and forget about having time to shave your legs. The skin that stretched to accommodate your bundle of joy is now hanging over the top of your pants. The only thing that really excites you these days is the thought of a nap – alone!

I now welcomed cone-shaped breast aerators that made me look like something straight out of a Madonna music video, even though they made me look ridiculous, because the touch of my bra on my raw breasts was more painful than I could handle. I found myself doing things I would have sworn I would never do. I would shamelessly whip a breast out in public and offer it to my son, just for a moment's peace. Anything to stop the crying.

CHAPTER THREE

Infancy and the First Year

Come to me, all you who are weary and burdened, and I will give you rest. Take my yoke upon you and learn from me, for I am gentle and humble in heart, and you will find rest for your souls. For my yoke is easy and my burden light.

MATTHEW 11: 28-30

Ross's Infancy Characteristics

1. Cried a lot and for no apparent reason
2. High maintenance
3. All consuming of my time
4. Difficult to console
5. Did not require much sleep
6. Strong willed and would not cry it out
7. Loved rocking and swinging
8. Loved watching movies, even at a few months old

We left the hospital on Thursday morning. They had kept me an extra day since I had the surgery. I had read that infants usually slept a lot. I was looking forward to the rest myself. However, this was not the case with my baby. Ross's screaming was piercing. He seldom seemed content. I tried everything I knew to do. I checked his diaper, I fed him, made sure he was the right temperature, made sure all the tags had been removed from his clothes so that nothing was poking him. I followed a strict diet of "do not eat foods" when you are nursing. I read everything I could find on colic and things that might help, nothing worked. There were times when Ross was not crying, but those times only came through constant effort and never lasted very long.

Night after night, infomercial after infomercial, I sat in the rocking chair trying to console my baby. He seemed calmer and less irritable when I was rocking him. He clearly liked rhythmic movement.

Leaving the house became more difficult. I watched as other parents of infants took their child to dinner and the child slept in their car seat for the duration of the meal. I remember seeing a parent taking an infant into a movie theatre as multiple thoughts ran through my head. *How is this possible? What are they doing that I am not? How do they seem so together? Why am I failing so miserably?*

When Ross was a few weeks old, a co-chairman of mine from the museum wanted to come over and talk to me about an upcoming event. I tried to discourage her

from coming by, telling her that my baby was pretty fussy. She assured me that would be fine and we would just work as long as we could. She came over, but ended up leaving about thirty minutes after she arrived. I think we talked for a total of five minutes and the rest of the time was spent trying to keep Ross from screaming. My colleague sat there just looking at me, or at least that's what it felt like. I kept wondering what I was doing wrong. I felt embarrassed. When I was around other people, Ross's constant crying made me more nervous than normal. I guess I thought his crying was a reflection of my lack of parenting skills. By those standards, I must be the world's worst mother!

Going to bed was no longer part of my routine. If I made it to my bed at all, it was only for periods of time just long enough to catch a minimal amount of sleep. Nights and days rolled into each other with no sense of routine. I felt like I was losing my mind. I was so alone and defeated. I was so tired I didn't have the strength to cry, silent tears that came when I blinked, ran down my face. A pain took up residence in my soul, so deep it made me sick. I experienced complete exhaustion and frustration. Was this what they meant by "the joys of motherhood"?

What happens when the hype of the peaceful baby sleeping in the crib turns into the reality of a screaming baby who never sleeps and is difficult or almost impossible to console? Then what? My reality was not the same as that idealized in commercials. When you

are pregnant and you are dreaming of holding your baby, the baby isn't screaming in the dream. You don't think about sitting on the toilet, nursing while you go to the bathroom. No, you read every parenting book and you come to believe that if I follow these guidelines, this will be a piece of cake. If you follow these certain steps, then in just a matter of time the child will go to sleep on their own; fuss for a few minutes, maybe, then drift off into peaceful slumber. But what happens when this doesn't work? There was no chapter in the books that I read that said, "If your child screams relentlessly…this is what you do." Remember, I'm a Type A personality, I had done my homework, I had looked. Any suggestions I did find claiming to aid with a screaming child, failed to work.

I was now living in survival mode. All I could think about was getting from one moment of sleep to the next. I was so tired, I fell asleep in the shower. My eyes burned and often watered. I ran into door facings. I felt like I was in a fog. I couldn't focus. My body ached like I had the flu.

The crying seemed to never end. Although it's difficult to admit, there were days I thought about jumping out a window. Not that I wanted to end my life, I just felt like I was going insane. The constant thought, *What am I doing wrong?* went through my head hour after hour.

Once Ross did go to sleep, he was restless. I remember the echoing words said to me by well-meaning people, "He will sleep when he gets tired." What, exactly, is that

supposed to mean?! Everyone, no matter how young or old, has to have sleep, right? That didn't seem to be true of Ross. How can an infant survive with no sleep? For that matter, how can anyone survive with no sleep?

Two Months

My sister was getting married and we went home to go to the wedding. This was an eight-hour drive. I'm not sure how many of those eight hours in the car Ross cried, but my nerves were frayed and my hands trembled by the time we arrived.

The trip was a disaster. Ross cried through the whole rehearsal. He cried through the entire wedding. At the reception at my dad's house, I got a piece of wedding cake (my absolute favorite). Hours later, a dried out, half-eaten piece of wedding cake still laid on the plate. There was no reprieve. Ross just cried and cried!

While I was visiting for the wedding, some of my extended family came to visit the baby. As usual, Ross was fussy, irritable and all consuming. My aunt turned to me with a look of disgust and said, "I don't see how you deal with that." I didn't know what to say. I felt my shoulders sink and all I could think of to say in response was, "What do you want me to do, put him back?" To be honest, I didn't know how I did it either. I was on edge, completely exhausted and didn't know what to do.

Going Back to Work

A whole book could be written about all the emotions a mother feels about leaving her child. I was no exception. Part of me was excited about going back to work. I loved working. I had never envisioned my life without working. That's why I had worked so hard in school, right? But now, I was experiencing all sorts of feelings and emotions I didn't even understand. (It could have been from the lack of sleep!) I was uneasy about leaving Ross. Could his care providers handle him? Would they be loving and kind when he cried and cried?

I was blessed to have found someone to care for Ross who loved babies. She wasn't able to have children of her own and adored spending time with Ross. She loved him. Looking back I know that she was God sent, this is the only explanation. She kept only Ross and all her attention was devoted to his every need. She rocked him, took him on strolls outside, read to him, and spent her hours entertaining him. She watched Ross for about a year. She commented on several occasions that he was the smartest and most alert baby she ever saw.

Moving to Kansas

When Ross was about one year old, we decided to move to Wichita, Kansas. I was not excited about the move to Kansas. When we had moved to Missouri just two years before, there was no family close by and I

knew no one. Through my involvement with the museums, I eventually made a lot of friends and was not anxious to leave now and start the process over again. This meant new doctors, a new pediatrician, learning my way around another city, and frankly, I was worn out.

We moved to an apartment while we waited for our house to sell. Living in an apartment with any one year old is challenging, especially when the one year old is fussy, high maintenance and rarely sleeps. Ross was active, often seeming to have an endless supply of energy. He had one volume and it was loud! When he did sleep, he was restless and never seemed to be really well rested. As most mothers know, a tired baby equals a fussy baby and a fussy baby equals exhausted parents.

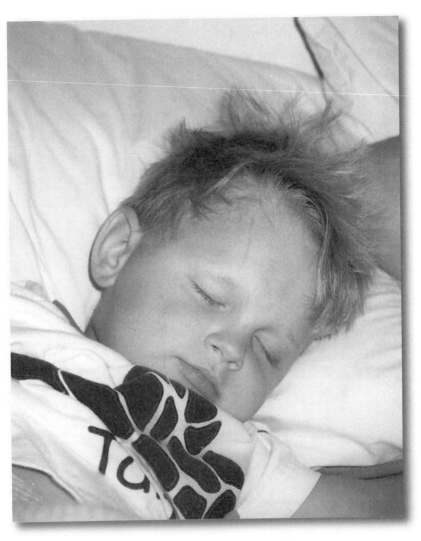

Since birth, Ross has been a restless sleeper.
He's as active when he's asleep as when he's awake.

The Toddler Years

Train a child in the way he should go, and when he is old he will not turn from it.

PROVERBS 22:6

Ross's Characteristics During the Toddler Years

1. Difficult

2. Cried a lot and very hard to console

3. Strong-willed and defiant, would not cry it out

4. Loved books, being rocked, and watching movies

5. Did not require a lot of sleep

6. Difficulty going to sleep and then was restless

7. Lined up plastic animals in particular sequence

8. Re-enacted scenes from movies

9. Difficult to take in public places

10. Demanded a lot of attention, wanted to be close to me

11. Always on the go, very active

12. Loud

By the time Ross reached the age of two, he could communicate his strong preferences to me. It was clear he liked repetition. I would read the same books over and over. His favorite was *The Foot Book,* by Dr. Seuss. I read this book hundreds of times. Probably more. Let me give you a sense of what the book is like...

> *Left foot*
> *Left foot*
> *Right foot*
> *Right*
> *Feet in the morning*
> *Feet at night*
> *Wet foot*
> *Dry foot*
> *Low foot*
> *High foot*
> *Front feet*

Back feet
Red feet
Black feet

Left foot
Right foot
Feet Feet Feet
How many, many feet you meet.

In addition to liking to hear the same books over and over, Ross also liked to watch the same movies time and again. He watched them over and over and over. Ultimately, I found that television had the most calming effect on Ross. He would actually not cry, sit still, and watch it. It was like he craved it.

Along the way, everyone had a discipline theory to offer that would "straighten Ross out." You know what I mean, the "if you would just" approach. It was even suggested that a good old-fashioned spanking surely would do the trick. People are so critical. The criticism I received was rough for me to take. I already felt like a failure. The truth is, I couldn't control Ross.

I want to point out that all these characteristics I've mentioned that Ross was displaying can be seen in any child at one time or another. But when these problems are consistent and seem to be excessive, a problem may exist. Such was the case with Ross.

Sixteen Elephants

It was summertime and Ross and I packed up to make an 8-hour road trip. I knew before I left that the trip would be a challenge, but I told myself that I could do it.

Ross didn't like being in the car seat, as most children don't, but with the help of "Silly Songs" and another tape we had listened to a hundred times at least, I thought I could occupy him for part of the time. Ross and I usually traveled alone and this made it especially challenging, since Ross was in the back seat and I couldn't readily hand him what he decided he needed at that moment. Ross wasn't patient and was relentless in his requests. For road trips, I would pack treats, all his favorites and several sippie cups of drinks. The sippie cups would be filled with apple juice or Tang. Ross was very specific about what he liked and disliked and a road trip wasn't the time to start new introductions. By the time we would reach our destination, there would be about five sippie cups in the floor, all half drunk, that Ross had decided to send airborne over the side of his chair when he was tired of holding them, only to want them again once they hit the floor. Ross had favorite sippie cups, of course. I guess the color and the feel of the cup were pleasing for one reason or another, because a drink from his "favorite cup" was always more pleasing to him.

I'm sure many of you are thinking, *If that was my child I would....* Oh, do be careful what you say! Once

upon a time, those words were uttered from my lips. I had been very dogmatic about what I would and wouldn't accept in a child's behavior. I had firm boundaries set in my mind that I would not tolerate being violated. But then I had Ross and I decided that if I wanted to survive, I was going to have to use my energy to address the big things and let the smaller things go.

For this trip, I had packed Ross's favorite toys, or shall I say "things." I packed his blue blankie, a grey elephant that made a noise when you squeezed it, and a green squishy alligator. He liked to carry things in his hands.

While we were visiting, my sister gave Ross a tube of animals, safari animals that included elephants, tigers, lions, zebras and hippos. He played with the toy animals the entire time we were on our trip. I noticed he was more content than normal and that playing with the animals held his attention longer than any other toy he had ever played with. I had never before found anything that had kept him occupied or entertained for any period of time. When Ross played with something, he played a matter of minutes, then he was done and on to the next thing. But this was different. On the way home I looked back at him and he had lined up the tigers and the lions on the bar across the front of his car seat, lions together, then a space, and then tigers together. He gazed at the animals intently. What was most observable was that he wasn't as agitated as normal. He was quieter and less fussy. Of course, I

couldn't make sudden stops or turns or I would have to pull over and retrieve the animal that had fallen off and put it right back in the exact spot it had fallen from.

By the time Ross was almost three, he had acquired sixteen elephants. They were plastic elephants of various sizes. I noticed he lined them up on the coffee table the same way every time. One day I knocked over a few of the elephants with the vacuum cleaner cord and placed them back on the coffee table in a different order. When I came back in the room, Ross had moved them back in the proper order. At the time I didn't give it much thought. I just knew Ross really liked playing with those animals and he preferred them to be lined up a certain way. Everywhere we went, he was looking to add animals to his collection. But not just any animals, only the animals he showed an interest in. Ross never actually played with the animals. He either held them in his hands, or lined them up.

In addition to lining up animals in a sequential pattern, Ross had another love—movies. He had his favorites and watched them over and over. This had a calming effect on him. The most amazing thing was that when Ross was watching a movie, he was quiet. From a very early age, movies held a certain fascination for him. He memorized the words to the movie and said them back to me by rote memory. This made Ross sound much older than he actually was. He had an ever-increasing vocabulary and seemed to be ahead of

the guidelines in the "What to Expect" books by a decent margin.

However, behaviorially, Ross was still behind. He still didn't sleep well and seemed fitful when he slept. He was fussy and never seemed to be appropriately rested. He had dark circles under his eyes and I knew he had to be tired. In my opinion, there are very few people who could operate on the amount of sleep Ross was getting, much less a three year old. When he did sleep, it was only for short periods of time and his sleep was constantly interrupted by periods of crying. He just never seemed to "give it up" and sleep.

Ross has always had a special connection with animals.

CHAPTER FIVE

Preschool Years

*Let your speech always be with grace, seasoned with salt,
that you may know how you ought to answer each one.*

COLOSSIANS 4:6 NKJV

Ross's Pre-K Characteristics

1. Counts things

2. Dominates conversations

3. Has difficulty waiting his turn

4. Talks a lot

5. Two volumes—loud and louder

6. Doesn't seem to listen well

7. Hyperactive

8. Demands a lot of attention

9. Ritualistic

10. Loves to draw

As Ross aged, he added more rituals to his daily routine. Playing "Pooh Bear Gets Stuck" was a ritual that he developed that he had to observe before eating each meal. He loved watching Winnie the Pooh and he latched on to this particular story segment, which is based on scenes from the movie, *Winnie the Pooh and the Honey Tree* (Disney, 1996). Ross would play the role of Pooh and I would play the role of Rabbit. The scene had to be played out in exact sequence. Forget about skipping a line to speed things up or you'll find yourself back at the beginning starting the role play over.

Pooh Bear (aka Ross):	"Is anybody at home?"
Rabbit (aka Me):	"No! You needn't shout so loud. I heard you quite well the first time."
Pooh Bear:	"Bother! Isn't there anybody here at all?"
Rabbit:	"Nobody."
Pooh Bear:	"Rabbit, isn't that you?"
Rabbit:	"No!"
Pooh Bear:	"Why, hello Rabbit."

Rabbit :	"Are you hungry Pooh Bear? Honey or condensed milk with your bread?"
Pooh Bear:	"Both."

At this point, Ross would eat his food. When he was finished, the game continued.

Rabbit:	"Are you sure you won't have any more?"
Pooh Bear:	"Is there any more?"
Rabbit:	"No."
Pooh Bear:	"Well I must be going."

Ross would walk over to the door and pretend he was stuck. He would yell out "I'm a Pooh Bear wedged in great tightness!" I would then have to go over and pretend I was pulling him out of the hole in which he was stuck. He would tell me to go get Christopher Robin.

The drill would continue with me pushing and pulling Ross to "unstick him from the hole." Finally, Ross would yell "Pop!" as if he were suddenly released, and the ritual was over.

This was a lot of work to do to get Ross to eat a peanut butter and jelly sandwich. Let me rephrase that. This was a lot of work to do to finish what was already a long and arduous process. Even making a

sandwich wasn't easy. The sandwich had to be made on a certain type of bread with a certain type of peanut butter and jelly, and had to be cut corner to corner. Heaven forbid you make the mistake of cutting the sandwich down the middle!

Every Kind of Dinosaur Imaginable

Ross developed an obsession with dinosaurs. He wanted dinosaur books, dinosaur figures, and dinosaur movies. He drew dinosaurs and literally talked hours every day about dinosaurs. He had an extensive vocabulary and used words that seemed strange coming from the mouth of a four-year-old.

Ross loved going to the video store and, as with most everything else, picked the same movies over and over. One of his favorites was *National Geographic's Really Wild Animals: Dinosaurs and Other Creature Features* (Grasshoff, 1996). The movie started with the words, "Featuring dinosaurs, maggots, cockroaches, komodo dragons and dung beetles. Those dinos were really, really wild." By rote memory, Ross would quote Paleontologist Robert Bakker:

T-rex, jaw wide open.

These teeth are not sharp, they are like railroad spikes. They are armor piercing teeth for crushing through the hide and bones of a triceratops and these jaws, no animal in the world has evolved

stronger jaws. Incredibly wide with muscles so strong that this T-rex could reach down and pick up a bull Indian Rhino and shake it like a rag doll. That's how it would kill... bite, penetrate, and shake the animal to death, then crush up its prey in chunks small enough to swallow.

Over and over, Ross repeated this phrase verbatim from the video. When he met new people, instead of engaging in a conversation, he would just recite this monologue over and over. People would look at me, and of course, I just smiled. I realize this really didn't sound like something a four-year-old would say.

Danny and the Dinosaur

Danny and the Dinosaur was a book that I read over and over to Ross. One night when Ross was about four years old, we sat down in the chair to read *Danny and the Dinosaur* yet again, but this time he wanted to read the book to me. Fifty-six pages of text he recited to me without missing a word! He couldn't read—he had memorized the book. I was amazed.

Rhett Is Born

I gave birth to my second child when Ross turned four. His name is Rhett Joseph Phillips. I will always consider Rhett a gift from God. Had God not intervened

and said I was having another child, I would not be blessed to have Rhett. I remember when I found out I was pregnant, I fell to my knees and wept. I said, "God, You say in Your Word You will never give us more than we can handle. In case You haven't noticed, I'm not doing that great of a job here. I'm an emotional wreck. I haven't had uninterrupted sleep in so long, I don't even know what it would be like. I have no help, no family that lives close, and I don't know how I am going to do this." I just began to pray every day that God would give me strength and a good-tempered baby who liked to sleep!

One of my biggest worries about having another baby concerned the time I would go to the hospital to give birth, which would mean leaving Ross alone at night with someone else. I know that sounds like a strange thing to worry about, but dealing with Ross at night was that intense an experience.

When Rhett was born, I noticed right away that he had a different temperament than Ross. He was much more relaxed and easier to console. He seemed happy. He actually slept! At this point, I was still getting up at night with Ross, more so than with the newborn baby.

Ross welcomed Rhett home and seemed to watch him intently. Ross was good to his little brother and loved feeding him his bottle. As Rhett got older, Rhett would wrestle in the floor with Ross, and Ross loved it.

Please, Not Wal-Mart

Trips to Wal-Mart were always entertaining. I can say they were entertaining now as I think back on them, but at the time these trips took place, they were stressful and embarrassing. Ross often spoke the first thing that popped into his head, so you can imagine the number of times I tried to intervene or steer him down a different aisle. If I saw anyone on an aisle with anything about them that seemed out of the ordinary, I tried to avoid them to curb Ross's questions. However, there were often too many people in the store to try to avoid. Ross would ask questions to satisfy his curious mind but those questions would leave me apologizing in their wake and feeling helpless.

One day as we were waiting for our food at the McDonald's counter inside Wal-Mart, along came a lady who was grossly overweight. I cut a look at Ross that said, *Don't...please don't.* As the lady approached the counter, Ross said, "Mom I'm not going to say a word about how big that lady is, but she looks like she weighs a ton." Yes, once again I was left apologizing, knowing my son had dashed someone's feelings on the rocks.

On yet another of our Wal-Mart adventures, we were walking down an aisle and a lady was coming toward us. She was extremely overweight to the point that her stomach was hanging down to her thighs. Ross turned to the lady and asked, "What is that hanging down there on your legs?" I smiled and apologized

profusely for my son's question. I talked to Ross repeatedly about not saying things that would hurt other people's feelings, even if his questions or observations were true and obvious. Please know that Ross never said things to intentionally hurt others. But we learned early on not to ever ask Ross a question if we didn't want an honest answer. He will not lie and will often tell you truths you would just as soon not hear.

Ross had an issue with wiping his own bottom. He absolutely refused to do it. This may seem like a big problem, but I had had such a problem getting him to go poopy in the potty in the first place that this didn't seem like that big of an issue. When Ross was being potty trained, he was able to master peeing in the potty, but the rest didn't go as well. He would hold his poopy for days. When he did try to go in the potty, the whole process literally freaked him out. He would cry and say, "No..no..no!" I had to eventually use suppositories to get him to go. So you can see, after clearing that hurdle, and trust me it took a long time, the wiping thing I could handle.

Anyway, back to Wal-Mart. One day I was standing in the check-out line with Rhett in his infant carrier and Ross standing beside me. About halfway through checkout, Ross announced, "I gotta poop!"

I said, "Wait just a minute."

"I can't wait, I gotta poop!" With Ross, waiting was never a virtue. I was standing right in front of the

restrooms in my check-out line, so I told him to go inside the bathroom and wait for me. Of all the times for my son to finish his business in a hurry, this was not one I would have chosen. Before I knew it, Ross came out of the bathroom with his pants around his ankles, saying "Come wipe me! Come wipe me!" The clerk just looked at me and I shook my head. All I wanted to do was get out of that store. I didn't pay attention nor would I have cared if she charged me fifty dollars more than my bill was supposed to be. I just wanted out of there.

One of Ross's favorite things has always been spending time with his Auntie and cousins. Pictured L to R: Ross Phillips, Connor Holiski, Holly Holiski (Ross's Auntie), Halle Holiski, and Rhett Phillips.

CHAPTER SIX

First Diagnosis: OCD

The LORD is close to the brokenhearted and saves those who are crushed in spirit.

PSALM 34:18

When Ross was four and a half years old, I was outside washing the window on the door to the kitchen when he had a meltdown and became hysterical. I thought he was going to break through the glass to get to me. He could clearly see me. It was just that the door was closed and he was separated from me. What he was experiencing was complete panic. He wasn't crying because he wasn't getting his way or because he needed something – it was because he couldn't get to me. I had known for some time that Ross was unique and that what I experienced with him wasn't typical, but what I didn't want to admit was that maybe underneath the "uniqueness" lay a real problem.

I knew I needed a professional to evaluate Ross to let me know how I could help my child, but to be honest, I didn't even know what kind of doctor to see. We had recently moved to Tulsa. I didn't know many people and didn't even really know the kinds of questions to ask to get me where I needed to go. I went through my days in a haze and all I really wanted was sleep and a little peace and quiet. By this time, I was so numb that I really didn't even cry that much anymore.

Ross's father and I took Ross to see a child psychologist in Tulsa. He spent some time with Ross and remarked that he is a very brilliant boy. Ross drew some pictures for him that were of Pooh Bear and Piglet. As the doctor asked him questions, Ross ran about as if he were on speed. He climbed on the furniture. He jumped from one chair to another and paid little attention to the doctor. The doctor tilted his head to the side and said, "Maybe you should consider the Tulsa University School for the Gifted."

While the doctor implied that there were indicators of ADHD, he didn't concretely diagnose anything. I thought to myself, *That's it? That's all you can tell me? I finally brought myself to seek help, and that's all you can say?*

We enrolled Ross in K-4 Preschool at Rejoice Christian School. Just the fact that the school had the word "Christian" in its name made me feel better. Ross was already five, but I didn't think he was behaviorally ready for kindergarten. I wanted him to go to preschool

more for the social aspects of school than the academic aspects. Academically Ross seemed to be fine, if not advanced, but socially, we were behind the curve. I wanted Ross to learn to interact with other children, to learn to wait his turn, and to learn when it is appropriate to talk and when it isn't.

Ross's preschool teacher was Ms. Shade. I communicated openly with her my concerns about Ross. I'm sure she could sense my nervousness about him starting school. He was a handful, and I knew it, but Ms. Shade seemed to handle him well. One day when I was inquiring about his progress, she said, "Dee, when we enter a room, he counts the ceiling tiles and the outlets in the room. Have you noticed this behavior at home?" I can't honestly say that I had observed that specific behavior, but the rigidity of his behavior had been prevalent since birth. This particular observation just added one more piece to the puzzle.

The school was hosting a free seminar about ADHD (attention deficit hyperactivity disorder). Since the child psychologist we consulted mentioned this as a possible diagnosis for Ross's condition, I decided to check it out. The speaker was Dr. Rick Walton. He lectured on the symptoms and problems associated with ADHD. Although some of the symptoms matched Ross's behavior, others didn't. I decided to book an appointment with Dr. Walton at his clinic and have him evaluate Ross.

March 2002

When Dr. Walton met with Ross, he performed a series of tests. He asked Ross questions directly and then directed questions toward me and Ross's father. He also had a questionnaire for Ross's teacher to complete.

Once Dr. Walton had completed his evaluation, we met with him and he asked us if we were familiar with OCD, or more formally, obsessive-compulsive disorder. For me, this diagnosis came out of the blue. I had already prepared myself for the ADHD diagnosis, but OCD? At the time, I didn't even know what OCD was. The only thing I really knew about OCD was that it often manifested itself in a propensity to be obsessed with washing your hands. That's pretty limited knowledge, I know. But once Dr. Walton presented us with this diagnosis, I went to work to find out as much about the condition as I could.

The American Psychiatric Association's *Diagnostic and Statistical Manual of Mental Disorders* (DSM), is used by mental health professionals to assist in the diagnosis of disorders. These diagnostic standards are established to ensure that people are appropriately diagnosed. I read through the DSM criteria for OCD and found that obsessions are defined by the following:

    🌀 Recurrent and persistent thoughts, impulses, or images that are experienced at some time during

the disturbance, as intrusive and inappropriate and that cause marked anxiety and distress.

⑤ The thoughts, impulses, or images are not simply excessive worries about real-life problems.

⑤ The person with these obsessions attempts to ignore or suppress such thoughts, impulses, or images, or to neutralize them with some other thought or action.

⑤ The person recognizes that the obsessional thoughts, impulses, or images are a product of his or her own mind (not imposed from without as in thought insertion).

With an understanding of the obsession portion of OCD, I now turned my attention to the compulsive issue. The DSM defined compulsions as:

⑤ Repetitive behaviors (e.g., hand washing, ordering, checking) or mental acts (e.g., praying, counting, repeating words silently) that the person feels driven to perform in response to an obsession, or according to rules that must be applied rigidly.

⑤ The behaviors or mental acts are aimed at preventing or reducing distress or preventing some dreaded event or situation; however, these behaviors or mental acts either are connected in a realistic way with what they are designed to neutralize or prevent or are clearly excessive.

The DSM went on to say that in OCD, the obsessions or compulsions cause the person with the disorder "marked distress, are time consuming (take more than 1 hour a day), or significantly interfere with the person's normal routine, occupational (or academic) functioning, or usual social activities or relationships." (American Psychiatric Association, *DSM-IV-TR,* 462-463.)

The further I went in my research, the more I saw that many of Ross's characteristics of behavior fit into the information I read, but there was an array of other issues that didn't seem to fit in the OCD mold. I didn't question the diagnosis, I just felt there was more to the problem. For instance, the major impairment in social interactions that Ross manifests didn't seem to be a prominent factor seen in an OCD diagnosis. But after much consideration, we elected to start Ross on medication to assist with OCD.

CHAPTER SEVEN

Second Diagnosis: ADHD

Therefore we also, since we are surrounded by so great a cloud of witnesses, let us lay aside every weight, and the sin which so easily ensnares us, and let us run with endurance the race that is set before us.

HEBREWS 12:1 NKJV

Throughout grade school, we continued to see Dr. Walton. Although we were making some progress, it was clear we still had other issues to address. After further testing, Dr. Walton diagnosed Ross with ADHD in addition to the OCD diagnosis.

I returned to the *American Psychiatric Association Diagnostic and Statistical Manual* (DSM) to review the criteria for ADHD. According to the DSM, for someone to be diagnosed with ADHD, they must exhibit six or more of the symptoms of inattention and six or more symptoms of hyperactivity or impulsivity for at least

six months, to a point that is inappropriate for the patient's development level.

The following is the list of possible symptoms of inattention, per the DSM:

- Often does not give close attention to details or makes careless mistakes in schoolwork, work, or other activities.

- Often has trouble keeping attention on tasks or play activities.

- Often does not seem to listen when spoken to directly.

- Often does not follow through on instructions and fails to finish schoolwork, chores, or duties in the workplace (not due to oppositional behavior or failure to understand instructions).

- Often has trouble organizing activities.

- Often avoids, dislikes, or doesn't want to do things that take a lot of mental effort for a long period of time (such as schoolwork or homework).

- Often loses things needed for tasks and activities (e.g., toys, school assignments, pencils, books, or tools).

- Is often easily distracted.

- Is often forgetful in daily activities.

The following is the list of possible symptoms for hyperactivity or impulsivity per the DSM:

- Often fidgets with hands or feet or squirms in seat when sitting still is expected.

- Often gets up from seat when remaining in seat is expected.

- Often excessively runs about or climbs when and where it is not appropriate (adolescents or adults feel very restless).

- Often has trouble playing or doing leisure activities quietly.

- Is often "on the go" or often acts as if "driven by a motor".

- Often talks excessively.

- Often blurts out answers before questions have been finished.

- Often has trouble waiting one's turn.

- Often interrupts or intrudes on others (e.g., butts into conversations or games).

(American Psychiatric Association, *DSM-IV-TR*, 92-93.)

As I reviewed the information I found during my research of ADHD, I saw that Ross definitely exhibited behaviors that were consistent with this diagnosis. He was hyper-verbal, impulsive, couldn't wait his turn and blurted out information. At this point, we added

another medication to address the ADHD to the OCD meds Ross was already taking.

Individual Education Program

Ross qualified for an IEP (Individual Education Program) at school. This acronym was something new to me. Up to this point, I didn't even know IEP's existed. I grew up in a small town and my exposure to kids who had disabilities was limited. I remember one particular boy from my kindergarten class who was put in a refrigerator box for interrupting other students and jumping from desk to desk during class. And then there was another unruly boy who was out of control and continually made fun of our elementary principal who had a prosthetic arm. That's about the sum total of my experience with kids who might have needed IEPs!

In my small town, any student who had a recognized learning disability was put in special ed classes. When I was now introduced to the IEP, I was clueless. I didn't have any idea what the function or purpose of such a thing might be. All I knew was that Ross was struggling in school, and I was willing to try anything to get him the help he needed.

In the United States, an Individual Education Program is mandated by the Individuals with Disabilities Education Act (IDEA). Once a child is determined to be eligible for services, an education plan is developed

based on the specific needs of that particular child. I came to realize that an IEP could be of great value to Ross. For more information on Individual Education Programs, I would refer you to http://idea.ed.gov.

No White Lies

Ross can't lie. Don't ask Ross a question if you don't want the honest answer because he does not know how to tell a "white" lie!

One day we were walking at the mall, school shopping. Of course this is NOT one of Ross's favorite things, but he is so picky about the clothes he wears that I thought it would be best if he helped pick them out. As we were walking along, he looked at me and said, "Mom, you know I will still love you even though you are losing it."

I said, "What do you mean, 'I'm losing it'?"

Ross said, "Well, you know you are starting to get those lines around your eyes and, well, you know, you don't look as good as you did in your 20's." He proceeded to tell the clerks at the Dillard's check-out counter how much better I used to look and then compared me to a poster hanging in the store, saying that's how my skin used to look! Of course the clerks were laughing at this point, but the funniest part was that Ross had no clue as to why the clerks thought what he said was so funny. He continued on in his

monologue format that is common to his manner of speaking. Ross couldn't care less if anyone converses, as long as he gets to tell his story.

So Volatile

On the way home from a doctor's appointment, Ross said he was really, really mad. I asked him what was wrong. He stated there were three things that were really making him mad. Of course, I asked what was bothering him and this was his response:

1. It wasn't going to rain. Earlier that day, the clouds had built and it looked like it was going to rain. It ended up not raining. Ross was mad and added, "You know how I love thunderstorms."

2. It was now 6:30 and the library was closed. Ross was interested in checking out a dinosaur book but now, it was too late to go to the library.

3. He had a lame pencil. It wasn't sharp enough to get his drawing just the way he wanted.

December 2006

Ross wrote a letter to Santa on December 11, 2006. He started the letter by saying he had been good and he asked Santa how he was doing and then he asked for the following things:

Have everyone in Hurricane Katrina
to have a good day.

Santa, you have a good Christmas.

Have everyone to get what they want.

Heal my dad's back on Christmas.

I also want everyone
to be happy on Christmas.

I want to have a good day on Christmas.

Santa, I want most of all
to have a snowy Christmas.

I want you to know that on the week of Christmas when we were visiting my father's house, they had a record snowfall with drifts as high as the roofs of the houses!

What stood out to me the most from Ross's list was that there was not one mention of a toy. It didn't contain a laundry list of material things he wanted, but he prayed instead to have peace and happiness, not only for himself, but for those around him. He has such an amazing heart.

Dear Santa,

I've been a very good boy this year. How are you doing? Send a note with that question and everything you want to say to me. Here below is everything I want you to give me for Christmas.

p.s. Have a good Christmas!

p.s.s.s. Have everyone in Hurricane Katrina to have a good day.

p.s.s. Have everyone get what they want.

Dear Santa,
I want dad back to be here on Christmas. I also want everyone to be happy on Christmas. I want to have a good day on Christmas. Santa I want most of all to have a snowy Christmas

By William Ross Phillips

2006

December 2006

CHAPTER EIGHT

My Son Has What?
Diagnosed with Asperger's Syndrome

*But those who wait on the LORD shall renew their strength;
they shall mount up with wings like eagles, they shall run
and not be weary, they shall walk and not faint.*

ISAIAH 40:31 NKJV

Ross's Characteristics at age 10

1. Moody and hard to please; argumentative; fractious

2. Did not enjoy many activities but loved to draw, loved movies, animals, planets, The Weather Channel and The Discovery Channel

3. Emotional; would have highs and lows in the same few minutes

4. Carried on one-sided conversations; garrulous

5. Did not recognize social cues

6. Easily overwhelmed; trouble organizing things

7. Suffered insomnia

8. Obsessive about certain things, liked order and sequence

9. Limited food choices

10. Preferred to be at home in his "happy place"

11. Very literal

12. Easily distracted and often had his head in the clouds

13. Put words and phrases together in peculiar ways. For instance, would say "maybe 10 or 8 or maybe 6 or 5," would always put the larger number first.

14. Still demanded a lot of attention and instruction, even on everyday tasks

By the time Ross turned 10, he shared some of the same interests any 10-year-old boy might have including Dragon Ball Z, sharks, and dinosaurs. He was also very interested in the weather, especially severe

weather like tornados, and he was interested in the universe and planets.

We continued to see Dr. Walton for a period of several years. Although he helped Ross, it seemed we were still missing a piece of the puzzle. Dr. Walton recommended that we seek the assistance of a developmental pediatrician. He referred us to a doctor who was regarded as one of the best in Tulsa.

During this time, I also met with the school counselor. She recommended we have more testing done in order to properly assess the problems we were facing. Ross was now in the third grade. He would frequently "melt down" in class. His third grade teacher described Ross as being extremely talkative, easily agitated and frustrated, cries easily, blurts out answers, has a hard time transitioning from one task to another, and as focusing entirely too much on menial details.

Ross had also started to develop tics. He would clear his throat over and over again, which was no doubt quite distracting to the other students sitting in class. He also would move his fingers as if he were clasping something in mid-air while he was talking. When I asked him about his finger clasping, he didn't even realize he was doing it. Furthermore, the more nervous he became, the more his tics intensified.

Ross's third grade year was a rough one for me, personally. Ross's father and I got divorced. Now, in addition to dealing with the trials of my child who was

struggling, I was struggling with issues of my own. I had so much pain in my life, there were days I found it physically difficult to breathe. I mustered up all the energy I had just to get through each day. My life was a mess.

After several months of waiting, the results of the tests the school had performed were in. The test results were sent to the new developmental pediatrician we were seeing. When we met with him, he diagnosed Ross with Asperger's Syndrome, an Autism Spectrum Disorder. I had never even heard of Asperger's Syndrome! OCD and ADHD I had heard of, but Asperger's? Our doctor went over the findings with us and reviewed the characteristic behaviors of a child with Asperger's. The described behaviors matched Ross very well. I hoped this diagnosis was the missing piece of the puzzle we were looking for.

These were a few of the characteristics the doctor listed of a child with Asperger's Syndrome:

- Often says the first thing that pops in their head
- Difficult time interacting with others
- Finds it hard to deal with changes in their environment
- Lengthy, one-sided conversations
- Asks the same thing over and over, and feels anxious if he has to stop

- Doesn't get social cues

- Rigidity in thought

- Has sensory issues

- Poor gross motor skills

- Has difficulty problem solving, analyzing, or synthesizing information

- Pedantic speech

- Has obsessive thoughts and rituals

- Egocentric

- Literal minded

- Easily upset with new routines or quick changes

- Often will interrupt

- Often perceived as rude and too straightforward

- Has a narrow range of interests

- Poor impulse control

- Difficulty with organizational skills

- Unable to read between the lines

Autism Spectrum Disorders

Once I began to research Ross's condition, I found that you don't have to look far to find headlines that show statistics relating to a surge in autism related

disorders. Whether we are seeing an actual dramatic increase in autism related disorders or if the increase in diagnoses is just a function of the change in the criteria and definitions used to diagnose the condition, it is clear that there is an increased awareness of the disorder. It is now speculated that about 36 out of every 10,000 people are diagnosed with Asperger's Syndrome, also called Asperger's Disorder. Asperger's Disorder affects four times as many males as females.

Asperger's is a neurological problem. It did not appear in the American Psychiatric Association's manual until 1994. The more I researched, looking for information, the more obvious it became that there are no clear cut answers to questions surrounding this disorder. Doctors and researchers still have little concrete information. They do not know what causes autism and although there are treatment suggestions, there is no cure. Imagine receiving this diagnosis—you have this problem, we don't know why you have this problem, it affects all people differently and to varying degrees, and there is no known cure.

My research led me again to the *American Psychiatric Association Diagnostic and Statistical Manual of Mental Disorders*. From Table 3.5, I found this information on Asperger's Syndrome, which had been adapted for young children. Asperger's Syndrome would be diagnosed if the child manifested at least two of the following behaviors:

ⓢ Poor eye contact; child doesn't naturally and consistently respond when you smile or frown at him; hard-to-read facial expressions; doesn't pick up on social cues.

ⓢ Hasn't made friends on his own from preschool or daycare; has difficulty engaging in give-and-take with peers his age; difficulty expanding play beyond his own interests.

ⓢ Doesn't spontaneously seek out peers to share enjoyment in his creations and projects to demonstrate interests.

ⓢ Just as happy playing by himself or next to a peer; seems indifferent to another child's interests and/or feelings.

Children with Asperger's would also manifest at least one of the following characteristics:

ⓢ Child is overly focused on a daily basis on one or two special interests or activities (e.g. dinosaurs/ space/ computer games/ replaying a video by rote).

ⓢ Repetitive rituals around things like eating, travel, bedtime, and bath.

ⓢ Finger flicking, spinning, hand flapping.

ⓢ Can get absorbed in an aspect of his special interest or object but not able to integrate it into the larger context (e.g. may have an interest in brand names of cars but no interest in

making up a story about the people who drive these cars).

(American Psychiatric Association, *DSM-IV-TR,* 84.)

Obviously, activities of this nature would make it hard for a child suffering from Asperger's to make friends or fit in with the other children around him. The information I found made it clear that children with Asperger's are not intellectually behind their peers—on the contrary, they often have IQs that are above average. I did find specific mention that children with Asperger's have difficulty with potty training. Validation at last for all I endured in training Ross to poopy in the potty!

Mozart and the Whale

I found the movie, *Mozart and the Whale* (Dimbort, 2005), at the movie store completely by accident. The movie title caught my eye because I had researched Mozart music as a way for Ross to focus and relax. The word "whale" in the title caught my attention because the whale is one of Ross's favorite animals. How surprised I was when I picked up the cover and read that the movie was about two adults with Asperger's Syndrome.

I loved watching the movie. I drew parallels between Ross's behavior and the behaviors the characters displayed in the movie. I thought to myself on several occasions, *That is so Ross.* Lines such as "I want

to have contact with people, I'm just pathetically clue-less," and "I can't sensor what I say, I just say what I think," hit home in a very real way as I thought about my son. I would recommend this movie to any parent who has a child with an Autistic Spectrum Disorder. It reminds you that you are not alone.

Age 9. Disorders are difficult to understand, because physically the child looks normal. Photo courtesy of Janet Hall.

Ross Phillips

I'm smart, funny, exst-
-rordinary, and good drawer.
I have a mom named See
Phillips and a dad named Phil
Phillips. I lover of God, my
family, and anommals.
   I feel sad, happy, and
jellesy. I need all dragon
boll v, and dragon boll books,
and all dragon boll v moives,
and a hundred feet fond, and
fifty feet wide flat screen
tu. I fer measles, hornets,
and bites. I'd like to be
at Yellowstown, and at
Barns and Nobles, and watch
mont stant Helens. I live in
Oklihoma.

CHAPTER NINE

Fifth Grade

Set your mind on things above, not on earthly things.

COLOSSIANS 3:2

On April 24, 2006, 9 years and 360 days since Ross was born, I decided to put pen to paper and share my experiences in raising a child with an Autistic Spectrum Disorder. It was and still is my hope that I can help someone who desperately needs validation or just give someone another person to relate to who has shared in something similar to what they're going through. There is comfort in knowing that someone else has experienced the same thing you are experiencing.

You might ask what was significant about April 24, 2006 that led me to my decision to record my experiences. This was the day the school called and told me that Ross was stuck in the bathroom and they couldn't get him out. On that day, the school was administering

standardized tests and they had locked the classrooms. They explained that they couldn't let Ross back in the classroom so I needed to come and get him. "What, he's in the bathroom?" I said. I didn't fully understand why they couldn't let him back in the classroom but with Ross, I had come to expect the unexpected. So I cancelled my meetings and headed for the school.

Though I didn't divulge to my colleagues why I had to cancel the meeting, all I could think about on the way to the school was *I can't believe I am cancelling a meeting because my son won't come out of the bathroom. How embarrassing.* That day was the proverbial straw that broke the camel's back. I don't know if I really thought I would end up writing a book, but I did know that all of my pent up frustration had to get out, so I sat down at my computer and allowed my feelings to flood the keyboard. It was such a release. Writing down my thoughts and feelings was, in a sense, therapy. It just made me feel better.

As Ross progressed from year to year, school became more difficult for him to manage. We knew that fifth grade was no doubt going to be a challenge. This year he started rotating classes. Instead of having one teacher, one desk, one room, he was now changing classes three times a day. For someone as disorganized as Ross, the more elements of change you enter into his day, the greater the risk of error and problems.

At fifth grade open house, I read an essay Ross had written in class describing himself. One of the things on

his list of descriptions was "Lover of God." Wow, Lover of God! My son was so open about his faith. At the tender age of 11, my son had found the one thing that is most precious in the world—love for God. It gave me comfort to know that despite all the challenges I faced with Ross, I had done something right. I had instilled in him the importance of a relationship with God.

Ross had an IEP in place, but when I met with his teachers to discuss problems we were having, I found that little or no modifications were being implemented. The teachers knew very little about his disorders. Knowledge is power. The fact that they knew so little about his disorders left them powerless and made it difficult for them to implement successful strategies.

As fifth grade progressed, so did the problems. I received regular emails from Ross's homeroom teacher. Here's just a sampling of the information she sent to me:

Email One

He's just a different guy from the first part of the year! He's constantly chewing his fingers and will say he knows to stop before it bleeds. He will blurt out a question and not even try to listen to the answer (shut-down mode). His pat response is, "I don't understand," to any type of explanation. It's like there's a thick wall between him and pretty much everything else. He is much more rigid (and I mean much) than he used to be. He slams to a halt if any little thing goes the

least bit differently. I can't really put my finger on anything else, but I am very sad to lose the Ross we had earlier. His OCD is REALLY bad right now. If I see anything else I'll let you know. In the meantime, I'll say a prayer. Several.

Email Two

I'm a little knocked off center at Ross's behavior. It's not bad, it's just very different. He is far less "flexible" than he has been in the past and he's having a harder time moving on to the next step in most assignments. He is far more likely to come to a screeching halt if some little thing gets in his way. Up to now he's been better about moving or bypassing something in favor of getting work done. I'm curious about why this is happening. It is creating friction between us, I think. Up to now, I have been able to get him over humps rather easily. Now it's like pulling teeth.

Email Three

I have noticed Ross doing some peculiar things lately. He actually smacked his head and face on his way to the computer to take a test. I have never seen him do that before. He's almost constantly chewing on his fingernails and cuticles (he's done that occasionally in the past, but it's constant now). He really gave the Spanish teacher a hard time, too. Every time she said

something in Spanish, he would frantically and repeatedly say, "What did you say? I don't understand! What did she say?" She handled him nicely, but I could tell it surprised her. I don't know if this is anything significant. I just think it's his anxieties trying to find an outlet.

Email Four

Ross can be happy-go-lucky one minute and the next minute, he's in meltdown mode and there's NOTHING I can do to get him out of it. He puts up that wall and there's no getting past it. It's very frustrating for me and for him. Also, he's been using his "condition" as an excuse for lots of things. He'll say, "But I don't want to do it! I won't do it because I've got (he'll use Asperger's or OCD here) and I shouldn't have to do it!" He does it quite a bit lately. Today, he's in a very good mood and I'm walking on eggshells hoping it'll stay that way. That WALL is a demon for me. I try all sorts of things to help him but he just flat can't hear me at that stage. Explaining is a waste of time because he can't hear it. It just makes things worse. But, if I don't at least attempt to explain, he will meltdown even more and will repeatedly say, "I don't get it..." and explode into tears. That's all I know right now.

Tics

Tics were also a problem. In addition to the tic of constantly clearing his throat, Ross developed a tic of clicking his teeth. He didn't even realize he was doing it. This tic was distracting in class. One of his teachers had little tolerance for this behavior and Ross would frequently get in trouble and have to miss recess as punishment for clicking his teeth. This created even more anxiety for him. Ross told me he wanted to give up. He didn't want to live anymore if this was how he had to live. These were words that would pierce any parent. It's so difficult to see a child struggle so hard.

Towards the end of the year, Ross was actually found in the classroom floor curled up in the fetal position, crying. His teacher had to call the counselor to come get him up. His anxiety had reached a point where he just couldn't handle it.

Amazingly, though Ross struggled, he never lost his sense of humor. As a class project, each student had to memorize and recite the Declaration of Independence in front of the class. Ross elected to do his presentation in a "goat boy" voice. The class stood up and cheered at the end of the presentation.

Accelerated Reading Goals

Accelerated Reading Goals, ugh!!! This became a "dirty" word at our house. I always knew a meltdown

was on the way when this was brought up. From what was explained to me about the Accelerated Reading program, according to the State of Oklahoma, there was a certain amount of reading and testing that had to be performed by each student. It wasn't the reading that was a problem, it was the kind of reading that was required that was the problem. Ross was a fact finder, a hardcore non-fiction reader. He saw no purpose in reading fiction. If a book wasn't packed with what he considered useful information, he wasn't interested in reading it. The problem was that much of the AR reading was fiction. This created a state of tension for us every night. Ross hated homework and AR reading. It wasn't just that he didn't want to do the homework, but that the homework created a great sense of anxiety for him, which meant a great sense of anxiety was also created for me. There are only so many battles you can fight in a day, and frankly I was worn out!

Bullies

Bullies! No matter where Ross went, bullies seemed to appear out of nowhere. Ross didn't really have any close friends, and maybe that is something bullies look for in a target. In Ross's terms, bullies "look for the one isolated from the herd." Ross's lack of appropriate social skills played into the hands of many bullies. He would do or say something that would leave him wide

open for ridicule. The most heartbreaking aspect was that Ross didn't recognize what that "something" was.

Don't Mess with My Legos

At our last visit with Ross's developmental pediatrician, we talked about Ross's numerous obsessions: weather, Dragon Ball Z, coin collecting, the invisible "fuzz" that he believes he must pick from his body, the splinters that no one else can see. "Ritualistic, querulous, habitual, rude, direct and to the point, no tact, state the obvious, demanding, self absorbed, isolated, prefers to play alone, in his own world," these are some of the words that had been used to describe Ross.

Ross, like most of us, is a creature of habit. However his routine was so habitual that if altered, it created a lot of stress for him. The end result was that Ross's stress caused a lot of stress for me, as well.

One of Ross's favorite activities in his late elementary years was playing with Legos. No matter where we went, the Legos went as well. He spent hours creating objects from Legos. Most items were things he created from his own mind, and not with the assistance of instructions. He had the amazing talent of being able to visualize an object and then create it in the real world using Legos.

Did Someone Say "Donuts"?

I swear, Ross could live on donuts and peanut butter and jelly. He was obsessed with donuts. I would actually plan my driving route to be sure I would not drive by a donut store because once Ross saw the donut store, the thought of donuts was imbedded in his mind. He would spend hours begging for donuts.

Barnes and Noble

Ross would rather go to Barnes and Noble than do most any other activity. For his 11th birthday, I asked him if he wanted to have a party or what he wanted to do. He said, "I just want to go to Barnes and Noble." But not just any Barnes and Noble would do, he wanted to go to the one we always went to. Remember, Ross likes predictability and routine. Once, Ross and his brother were invited to a birthday party at Incredible Pizza, a local pizza parlor that has an amazing collection of games and other activities for the patrons to enjoy. He said he didn't want to go to the party, but instead just wanted someone to take him to Barnes and Noble.

Ross watches the same movies over and over and has done that for as long as he's been alive. The problem is, he wants me to watch them with him. He will say, "Watch this Mom. Isn't this cool? Look at this part. Watch his face. Isn't that funny? Why aren't you

laughing?" Ross doesn't understand that after 10 times of watching the same segments, it's no longer that funny or amusing. (Though honestly, I didn't find it funny or appealing the first time I watched it anyway.)

One day we were in the car and Ross was giving me a play-by-play of the fight between Goku and Freeza (characters from the cartoon series Dragon Ball Z). This went on for about 15 minutes. No one else in the car was saying a word, we were all just trying to watch Ross's reenactment intensely. He had motions, facial expressions and the whole animated scene going. After I had maintained my attention for as long as I could, I interrupted and said "Honey, we're almost there. Hurry and finish your story."

Ross responded, "Ah Mom, can't we finish? I'm almost halfway through." He had no clue that everyone else had lost interest in his story after the first two minutes.

No Such Thing As a Small Detail

One day while Ross was in the fifth grade, I took the boys to meet the bus. We waited and waited but the bus never came. I decided to take the boys to school, so they wouldn't be tardy. When we reached the front of the subdivision we saw a plethora of emergency vehicles. Police car lights were flashing. There was an ambulance and at least three fire trucks. I pulled over and

asked a lady standing by the road what had happened and she said a child had had their foot ran over.

In my mind, the presence of all those emergency vehicles was a little excessive for an injured foot. But as we left the subdivision, Ross said, "This is the worst day ever." I told him we should focus on the positive and be glad that the child was going to be allright. He replied, "You don't know. A child could potentially lose a limb over this deal!" His mind seemed to migrate to the negative. Downplaying the event didn't seem to have much of an impact on him.

Social Skills Group (Summer 2008)

Between fifth and sixth grade, I decided to sign Ross up for a social skills class. Although I wasn't sure where the class would lead, I decided to give it a try. I was excited for the opportunity to meet other parents who were experiencing the same challenges that I faced and was interested in Ross being able to identify with other children as he would say, "of his own kind."

Before the first class, as we were waiting, in walked a boy and his mother. The boy walked in with his head down, playing a hand held video game. He wasn't interested in observing his surroundings and sat in a chair intently focused on his game.

I sat there studying each move the other Asperger's children made, trying to draw parallels in behavior

similar to Ross's. The need to constantly have something to occupy their time was evident. Not one child walked in and sat down without something in their hands.

On the third visit to social skills class, Ross forgot to wear shoes. I observed a conversation between three of the boys, which took place while all three boys were engaged in other activities. Ross was playing his hand held Yahtzee game. Another boy was playing his video game, and the third boy was drawing on a magnetic Magnadoodle. The conversation topic concerned the hand held Yahtzee game. Ross declared he was the "King of Yahtzee," to which the other boy replied, "No, I am the king of Yahtzee. Yahtzee is a game of chance and strategy, and at times, pure luck."

The boy playing the video game, while never looking up from his game, responded, "I've never played Yahtzee, but I am lucky. I had an accident and cut my leg, but it didn't cut it completely off." It was so interesting to listen and follow the train of thought of these three boys.

CHAPTER 10

Sixth Grade

Be on your guard; stand firm in the faith; be men of courage; be strong. Do everything in love.

I CORINTHIANS 16:13-14

After the struggles of fifth grade, I knew sixth grade was going to be a challenge. Fifth grade had been our hardest year so far. As other children grew and matured, it seemed like the gap between Ross and other children was widening. As a parent, it is hard to stand back and watch this process. I just wanted to fix whatever was wrong and make my son's difficulties go away! I was so frustrated! It's like the feeling you get when you know a snow storm is coming and there is no place to take shelter. You just stand there, waiting for the snow to fall. As the first snowflake falls, the anxiety builds, but there is nothing you can do to prevent the coming storm. I don't know how many times I've felt the gnawing in the pit of my stomach or

how many times my heart has ached. Seeing a child struggle, especially when it's your baby, is one of the hardest things a parent can go through. The helplessness I felt was overwhelming.

At the conclusion of fifth grade, there was a meeting at the sixth grade center to introduce parents to the protocol of the next year. The meeting was held in the gym of the sixth grade center. As parents hurried in from the May sunshine, I watched as many exchanged smiles with quick hand waves to their acquaintances. They looked as though they were comfortable in this setting and among friends. They looked like they belonged. Not me. As I sat there, I became painfully aware that I knew almost no one. After six years in the Owasso school system, I still felt as though it was my first year. I continued scanning the room for a familiar face. Finally, out of a gym filled with parents representing 600 new students, I found a familiar face—one I knew through my younger son.

Ms. Simons, the school counselor, began by saying, "Welcome to the Owasso Sixth Grade Center." I knew from previous experience that she and I would soon be up close and personal! That's just the way it seemed to go with me and school counselors. Ms. Simons gave out her direct phone number and I promptly wrote it down, knowing it would be a needed number for the future.

While other parents were chatting amongst themselves and discussing electives and whether their child would have first or second lunch, I sat there praying my

son could handle the change. It all sounded like so much to handle. Children of this age were expected to drastically increase their level of personal responsibility. They would attend seven different 45-minute classes, and have a 30-minute lunch. The day began with an assembly every morning at 7:45 a.m., followed by classes beginning at 8:00 a.m. I was stunned by the thought of the school day beginning 7:45 a.m.! How would I manage that? Ross had never been one to go to bed early and being up and ready to get on the bus at 7:00 a.m. seemed almost impossible. I reassured myself it would just be a matter of adjustment. But I knew all too well that adjustments were never an easy task.

When Ross was in fifth grade, I gave a letter to each of his teachers during a parent teacher conference, listing the problems that Ross faced in the classroom. It also outlined the typical Aspergerian traits. I welcomed communication from the teachers, as I knew from experience that open lines of communication seemed to be the most effective means to keeping Ross up to speed in class. They looked over the letter and asked questions that let me know quickly that they knew very little about Asperger's Syndrome. It seems to me that we put our children and the teachers in precarious situations when we ask them to teach children who have challenges the teachers know so little about. There must be a way to get this information to the teachers so they can be more effective in the classroom, which will lead to greater success for our students. Maybe this belief is rooted in my naivety or

a "save the world" personality, but I just think that increased knowledge could benefit both parties. It would benefit the other students in the classroom, too. It is no doubt that one child melting down in the classroom is a distraction to everyone. I can just see kids rolling their eyes and thinking, *Not him again!*

As Ross entered sixth grade, I again sent a letter to each of his teachers, similar to the letter I had provided his fifth grade teachers. I was determined to take a more proactive approach. I wanted to start the year off moving in the right direction. I wanted to build relationships that would foster an environment to help Ross be successful. The first week of school there was a "Meet the Teacher Night." Each teacher gave a 10-minute overview of classroom procedures and most included some personal information. I headed to the first class, wanting to make sure I introduced myself so the teacher could put a face to a name and establish the link of parent to child.

After the first session ended and the crowd had moved away from the teacher, I gave a smile as I extended my hand and said, "Hi, I'm Dee Phillips, Ross's mom." The teacher greeted me and then went on to say that a few of the kids from the class had made fun of Ross. She didn't say what for, but it didn't take much imagination for me to formulate a guess in my mind. She said she had asked Ross to leave the room, while she explained to the rest of the class that she wanted them to rally around Ross and help him. She

said she would not tolerate the students making fun of him and that they needed to be kind to special needs children. As odd as it may be, this is the first time anyone had called Ross "special needs" to my face. Although I knew it was true, hearing it said out loud pierced me in some way. My heart sank. Once again, I hated the fact that things that come easy to others take every bit of strength Ross can muster to accomplish. I hate that he feels left out and is always the underdog. My stomach churns every time he deals with yet another obsessive compulsive routine. I just want him to fit in. I don't want him to be miserable. Why does he have to struggle so hard?

What School Is Like, in Ross's Words

I asked Ross when he was in sixth grade to describe to me what school was like and how he felt. This is what he said:

> I feel like I'm in a race with school and me with OCD. And me as the turtle and my competitor is school, which is a cheetah. Make that a cheetah with a jet pack. I feel like I am two grades behind. I can advance my OCD and my control, but only as fast as a turtle can run. But the cheetah represented as the school and how fast school is going, by the time I'm in control of that semester, it's already another year. That's why it makes school so hard. I try even harder than last year to focus.

I feel that in school, people don't understand me that good, I'm misunderstood. As being a guy who's not regular, perhaps a medium amount of friends realize who I am really. I just have a disorder and I'm not that different. That's the reason I like them. A few people understand me and want to be around me. I'm glad to have friends like that. I just wish in the future that once in my lifetime I could be the turtle that beats the cheetah with the jetpack, just once! This year is harder because for some reason my OCD is harder to control. Teachers are not as understanding, some make it hard for me. It stacks up under pressure, even though I do half as much as most kids. It feels just as hard as doing all the homework of a normal kid. Conditions are different because there are a few teachers that are hard for me to keep up with, and it all stacks up and makes it harder for me. I'm just stacked up with the odds and it makes it hard with all the conditions I have.

Hitting Rock Bottom

In mid-November, I had the meeting with Ross's teachers that was described at the beginning of this book. That meeting left me knowing I had to do something. I had an appointment scheduled with Ross's developmental pediatrician the following week and I

assured the teachers I understood their frustration and concern and would keep them up to date regarding the doctor's visit and communicate any necessary changes.

The next week, we had our appointment with Dr. Bloom. As usual, Ross was first to talk to Dr. Bloom. In just a few minutes, Ross was back in the waiting room and Dr. Bloom motioned me to his office. He explained that Ross was quite oppositional and argumentative, which was not really anything new, but usually Dr. Bloom could transition him into some productive dialogue. But not today. Ross was completely off track with the conversation, talking about things that were of no relevance, other than to display exactly how bad Ross's condition was. I explained to Dr. Bloom about the meeting I had had with the teachers the previous week and explained their concerns. I told him about Ross's increasing paranoia. I asked him about options and what we should do next. He said he thought we might be looking at adding a mood disorder diagnosis to the mix.

We had started occupational and physical therapy a couple of months prior to this visit with Dr. Bloom. The OT specialist was working with Ross on his dysgraphia and the PT specialist was working on his core strength. The sessions seemed to be getting us nowhere. Ross cried through the occupational therapy and curled up in a fetal position while doing physical therapy. At this point, I didn't know what to do. I felt like I was being aggressive in finding treatment, but the results seemed

to be getting us nowhere. It all just served to give me a clearer picture of how bad things really were.

Since Ross's first breath, God has given me an abundance of patience and love for my child. For this, I thank Him every day. However, the frustration that I often feel can be overwhelming. Some days, every muscle in my body is tense from trying to keep myself together. There are times I want to lash out or scream or kick something or do all three. Until you have dealt with a child who is completely unreasonable, you probably don't understand how I feel. When Ross gets "stuck" there is no moving him! He can make the simplest task, a task you dread with all your might. He doesn't want to go to bed at night, and when he does, he can't sleep. Then he's tired so he doesn't want to get up in the morning. He has one speed, and that is slow. Rushing is not a talent of his. He doesn't want to take his medicine. He's picky about the kind of food he will eat. He only wants to wear certain clothes: jeans, a soft t-shirt, and Puma socks. If I don't help him gather up everything he needs for school, he'll leave his supplies at home. He won't eat at the cafeteria, he will just go without food. (The school actually called me and said they had to make him take a lunch, but he wouldn't eat any of it.) He doesn't want to do homework. He doesn't want to take a shower. He hates cleaning his room. Are you getting what I'm trying to communicate? There are no easy days!

CHAPTER ELEVEN

Seeing in Color

Dear friends, do not be surprised at the painful trial you are suffering, as though something strange were happening to you. But rejoice that you participate in the sufferings of Christ, so that you may be overjoyed when his glory is revealed.

1 PETER 4:12-13

The summer before Ross entered sixth grade, I read a book called *Change Your Brain, Change Your Life* by Dr. Daniel Amen. I was very intrigued by the book and shared some of the information with my sister. The book focused on the brain and showed photographs of SPECT scans that were done on people with a variety of disorders. It linked the problems of the brain to behavior issues. It discussed scans of people's brains who were faced with everything from head trauma to Alzheimer's. There was also some very valuable information about the chemicals that make the brain function normally

and the effects that manifest themselves if there is an imbalance in those chemicals.

One day my sister called me and said, "You're not going to believe this. You know the book you talked to me about, *Change Your Brain, Change Your Life?* My Director of Nursing has a relative who took her son to one of the Amen Clinics in California. She said since that visit, he is doing better. Do you want me to get the information?" The first thing I could think was, *Absolutely, absolutely, absolutely!*

I made a call to Jennifer, the mother of the boy my sister had mentioned, as soon as I got the information. She was sweet and very helpful. She explained that the doctor her son had visited who performed the SPECT scan was actually an old friend of hers. They had attended college together. She commented that he is a great guy and that she thought he was opening a clinic in Dallas, Texas.

Jennifer said her son was doing better now. She mentioned how empowering it was to see what was actually going on in her son's brain. She also said it was a relief to know that his behavior was linked to a malfunction of the brain. This removed the guilt she had been carrying, as she wondered if she was just a bad parent. You know people think that if you just spank your child, you can control their behavior. If that worked with Ross, the child would have been cured at age three. Parents of children with ADHD and

Asperger's know how frustrating it is that many times, discipline yields little to no result.

The name of the doctor Jennifer's son had seen was Dr. Todd Clements. I researched as much information as I could find about Dr. Clements. I was especially impressed with the fact that he was a Christian. In addition to having a list of impressive credentials in child psychiatry, he was also a youth pastor. Jennifer had given me Dr. Clements' email address. I emailed him and awaited a response.

Bright and early on Monday morning, I received a response. Dr. Clements confirmed that he had just opened a clinic in Dallas and said he would have his assistant give me a call and share some information with me. I was elated. There was something stirring inside of me. I knew that God was behind the scenes working things out for me. A renewed sense of hope filled my mind. At last I would see what was really going on with Ross. I would have something tangible. Not just speculation or a guess or an answer to appease me for a moment, but something I could see. I had spent twelve years wondering what was really going on inside his head, twelve years of blaming myself, twelve years of trying to hold it together while others dished out criticism and disgust. Now, I was finally going to get to see!

I received a phone call from Lynda at the Clements Clinic. She did an excellent job explaining the process and lending an ear as I vented in moments of frustration

and helplessness. She said I was going to need to fill out an evaluation form that was over twenty pages long. She also said that Ross was going to need to come off his medication before the scan and the consultation with the doctor. It took a moment for that to sink in...Ross, off his medication. Ross had been on meds since he was five. I wondered what he would be like without the medications. Part of me wondered if I was really up for the challenge. All I could think was *Sweet Jesus, You're going to have to help me on this one.* I was not at all interested in doing this one solo.

I scheduled the scan for the end of Christmas break so I could take Ross off his meds while he wasn't in school. Removing the meds from Ross's system had to be a gradual process. I just kept reminding myself that whatever we faced, it would be worth it in the end. I read positive affirmations over and over and quoted my favorite scriptures. I knew I was entering uncharted territory and a strong spirit and mind would be essential for a successful outcome! You may be thinking that I was a little dramatic about this whole thing. Let me assure you I was not. It was going to be an extremely difficult time.

My mom scheduled a flight and met me in Dallas. I was so grateful to have the support of a family member, but I'm not sure my mom really knew what she was signing up for. Simple words can't adequately describe Ross's behavior. Oh, my sweet mother of pearl. It was like a scene from the movie, *Tommy Boy,* when Tommy

and his partner are on a road trip to sell car parts to save the family company from collapse. On the way, they hit a deer in the road. They feel so bad for the deer, they pick it up and put it in the back seat of the car to take and dispose of it properly. As they travel down the road, Tommy looks in the review mirror only to see bright eyes and antlers starring back at him. The deer was not dead, but alive and now trapped in the back-seat of a car traveling down the highway. The trapped deer freaks out, completely destroying the car and its convertible top as he makes his exit. Ross was like the trapped deer—WILD!

I cannot articulate the degree to which Ross was out of control. He wasn't taking his sleep medication, and he literally went days with little or no sleep. At the Clements Clinic, he was beating his head against the wall. He put his head in the middle of a chair and was spinning around in a circle. He was opening and slamming the door into the clinic. I was literally following him around, trying to keep him from doing something he wasn't supposed to do. He would talk loudly and go on and on about a subject, even more than normal. As people in the clinic looked at me, I just smiled and apologized for his disruption. (I'm sure they were thinking it was a good idea I was seeking help!) I was somewhat embarrassed, although the degree of embarrassment wasn't nearly as severe as it was years ago. I guess I have grown thicker skin.

I tried taking Ross to see a movie, as watching movies has always been one of his favorite things, but he couldn't sit still long enough to watch. He was moving side to side in his chair, making noise, and kept asking me questions (not quietly, I might add). We ended up leaving early, and I was quite frustrated. *Can't you just sit still for a little while,* I thought. Ross wasn't just mildly irritated, he was in complete chaos.

The first day at the clinic, we answered a lot of questions and provided pages of information about Ross's behavior since birth. They asked extensive questions about Ross's father and me. Ross also received his first scan. While he was in a dimly lit room, the nurse put an IV in for a certain amount of time to allow Ross to get accustomed to his surroundings and relax a bit and then they performed the scan while he was resting. Even then, performing the scan was a challenge because Ross had great difficulty laying still. The technician repeatedly told him to lie still to ensure the greatest accuracy in reading the scans.

The second day at the clinic was more intense. Ross has a phobia about needles, so going back for the second IV was not going to happen without a fight. When we got up that morning, he informed me we were not going back for a second scan. He had rethought things and "he liked his uniqueness." I told him I liked his uniqueness too, but informed him that we WERE going to have a second scan unless there was some act of God or nature that prevented me from carrying him inside the clinic.

He didn't really like that answer. When it came time for the IV, he actually tried to escape out of the clinic. Not to worry, I was prepared and on heightened alert.

The second scan was performed when Ross was concentrating on the Connor's Continuous Performance Task, a 15-minute computerized test of attention. As soon as we finished the second scan, the first thing Ross asked for was his medicine. He stated, "I'm tired of being a raging maniac." It was only a couple of hours after taking his meds, that he settled down and was able to control himself more appropriately. This experience helped me realize that although we were still having severe problems, the medications that he was currently taking were more of an asset than I had realized!

Meeting with Dr. Clements

We met with Dr. Clements to discuss the results of the SPECT scans. Most of that meeting was a fog to me. Maybe this was because of my lack of sleep or maybe it was from the shock I felt when I saw Ross's brain scan compared to a scan of a normal brain of a child his age. The scans were color-coded making it easy to observe the differences. The color-coding related to the activity of the brain. White was the most active, followed by red, and then blue indicated the least activity. It only took one look to see that Ross's brain had a significantly greater amount of white and red areas than it was supposed to have.

Dr. Clements started our meeting by saying Ross is a very complex young man. This comment was starting to be universal among his doctors. He went over the findings of the scan. I didn't realize at the time, exactly what he was communicating. My mind seemed to be stuck on the image generated by the scan. In a sense, I was relieved—relieved that there was a physical reason for Ross's behavior. Another part of me mourned because of the challenges he would face the rest of his life. But I reminded myself that knowledge is power. The fact that we now had more information about Ross's disorders, made us more equipped to deal with the problems.

The SPECT scan showed what they called a "Ring of Fire" pattern in Ross's brain. When present, this pattern may be associated with mood issues, cognitive inflexibility, sensitivity to the environment, difficulty with transitions, anxiety and irritability. In some people, this pattern may be related to bipolar disorder, a diffuse inflammatory process, allergies that affect the brain, or some form of prior toxic exposure. Individuals with this finding often receive clinical diagnoses of ADHD, but tend to respond incompletely to ADHD meds. Symptoms associated with this pattern include mood dyscontrol, oppositional behavior, aggression, cognitive inflexibility, sensitivity to the environment, and difficulty with transitions.

Second, the SPECT scan showed evidence of increased tracer activity in the anterior cingulate

gyrus. Dr. Clements explained that this is often associated with problems shifting attention, which is manifested by a combination of symptoms such as cognitive inflexibility, obsessive thoughts, compulsive behaviors, excessive worrying, argumentativeness, and oppositional behavior of "getting stuck" on certain thoughts or actions. This is often seen in people with obsessive-compulsive disorders, oppositional defiant disorders, eating disorders, addictive disorders, anxiety disorders, Gilles de la Tourette's and chronic pain.

Third, the scan showed increased left and right parietal lobe tracer activity. This finding is often associated with hypersensitivity to light, noise, touch and other issues in the environment. This problem is also implicated in attentional issues.

The scan showed activity that would explain Ross's anxiety issues. It also showed activity that would explain his mood disorders, impulsivity, short attention span, distractibility and difficulties with organization and planning. Dr. Clements explained that the cerebellum is the most intensely active structure on the SPECT scan of a healthy individual. Ross's SPECT scan showed decreased activity in this area of his brain. There is growing literature describing behavioral disturbances associated with abnormalities of the cerebellar structure or function. The research seems to support the belief that the cerebellum is involved in coordinating higher-order processes such as planning and impulse control and other complex behaviors

because it is known to send projections to various regions of the cerebral cortex, especially the frontal and prefrontal cortices. The decreased activity in the cerebellar structure of Ross's brain would explain his inability to control himself and his moods.

Finally, the SPECT scan showed increased left and right temporal lobe tracer activity, especially on the scan when Ross was to be at rest.

Dr. Clements explained that this abnormality may be associated with several different symptoms including mood instability, irritability, memory problems, abnormal perceptions (auditory or visual illusions, periods of déjà vu), periods of anxiety and irritability with little provocation, periods of "spaciness" or confusion, and unexplained headaches or abdominal pain. Problems with the right temporal lobe have been associated with social withdrawal, social skills struggles and depression.

I remember Dr. Clements stating that physically, Ross was just not able to perform many of the daily tasks that were asked of him without great stress and anxiety. This was something he simply couldn't help. It was a relief to know that many of his behaviors were a function of brain development, and not a function of defiance. It has always been a battle for me to try to distinguish behaviors that he could control and those that he could not.

We ended the meeting with a list of things to do. We were going to change some of his prescription medications and we were going to introduce some vitamin and mineral supplements into his regimine. It was stressed that Ross needed regular physical activity, and that this activity would aid in his progress toward improvement. I left the meeting with a renewed sense of hope and a course to pursue from this point.

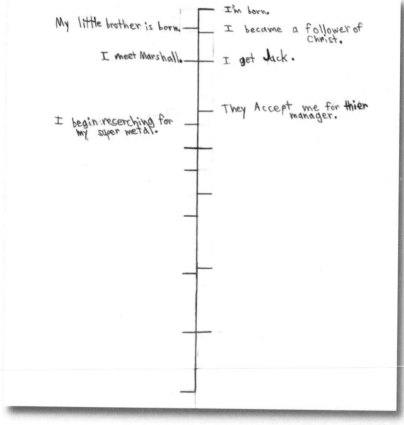

My little brother is born.

I meet Marshall.

I begin reserching for my super metal.

I'm born.

I became a follower of Christ.

I get Jack.

They Accept me for thier manager.

Ross made this timeline when he was age 11.
Even at a young age, he knew the value of following Christ!

WHEN I'M GROWN-UP

I will be honest.

Do grown-ups drive you crazy?
Well, you will be one yourself soon.
What will you be like then?

I hope I will be:

1. I hope I will be a dab with a lovely wife.
2. I hope I will be teaching my kids about the Lord.
3. I hope I go to heven.
4. I hope I will be hansom.
5. I hope I will be having a cute dog
6. I hope I will be funny.
7. I hope I will be helthy.

I hope I will not be:

1. I hope I will not be going to hell.
2. I hope I will not be a bad guy.
3. I hope I will not be a drug user.
4. I hope I will not have kids that uses drugs.
5. I hope I will not be suying
6. I hope I will not be evel.
7. I hope I will not be a couch petato.

Ross wrote this when he was in elementary school.
He outlines what he hopes for when he grows up.

CHAPTER TWELVE

Seventh Grade: A Turn Around

"Whoever humbles himself like this child is the greatest in the kingdom of heaven. And whoever welcomes a little child like this in my name welcomes me."

MATTHEW 18:4-5

Town and Country School (Fall 2009)

At the end of sixth grade, I knew we had to look into other schooling options for Ross. What we were doing was clearly not working, but what to do was always the daunting question. We had completed the SPECT scan, which clearly showed we had a problem. Since our meeting with Dr. Clements, we had seen improvement, but Ross was still so volatile. He could be happy one

minute and the next you would see his lip quiver as he fought back tears. He clearly was unhappy.

One day, close to the end of Ross's sixth grade year, I stopped by the school to take Ross a couple of gifts to give to his favorite teachers for Teacher Appreciation Day. He was sitting in the hall by the library, away from the noise of the cafeteria. With six hundred plus sixth graders at this school, the noise and the hustle and bustle of changing classes bothered me, so I can only imagine what it felt like to Ross. He was sitting on the floor away from the others, with his shoulders slumped forward and his head down. When I looked at him, he had tears streaming down his face. "Why can't I just fit in, Mom?" I encouraged him, as moms do, but deep inside I ached. To see a child struggle, puts a pit in your stomach. To see others be so cruel to my son, made me angry. I just wanted to take him and run away.

So we began looking into other options for schooling. Home schooling wasn't an option. Ross fought me so hard to complete one simple paper, crying for thirty minutes about a paper that would only take five minutes to complete, that the thought of fighting all day, every day, wasn't something I thought would be beneficial for either one of us.

Our research led us to a school that was primarily for children with ADD and Asperger's. It was located over thirty miles away from where we lived. There was a rather lengthy enrollment process, as they wanted to make sure that each student was a right fit for the

school. It was a private school, so therefore sending Ross there would require a rather substantial financial investment as well.

We went to an interview in June to meet with the director of the school. She interviewed Ross and asked several questions. As we walked through the school, I didn't note anything that was particularly special. The campus was composed of rather old buildings. However, those I talked to who had students who attended the school, seemed to give a rather majestic description of it. When we finished the interview, the director said she would review the information and let us know if Ross would be a good fit. Later that summer, we were contacted and welcomed to the new school. I was so hopeful this was an answer to prayer.

Starting a New School

The first few weeks at the new school didn't go so well. Ross refused to walk from building to building because of his paranoia of wasps. At times, it took three teachers to coax him to go outside. He refused to go outside during a fire drill, because he knew it was only a drill and he already knew how to exit the building. He stated, "What a complete waste of time."

He stood firm on his principle that schoolwork was a waste of time. He needed to complete his research in order to save the world!

Ms. Etier, the school principal, called me several times to discuss the problems Ross was having at school. During her fourth phone call to me, she said that she didn't know if the school was equipped to deal with a child whose condition was quite as severe as Ross's. She said that maybe the scope of his disorders were beyond what they could accommodate.

I felt so frustrated, felt such a deep mourning. The hurt was so bad. I had been so hopeful that this new school would help with the problems we were having. We had exhausted most of our resources, and had made a major time and financial commitment in the hope that this school would provide a solution.

To her credit, Ms. Etier did not give up on Ross. She quickly adjusted his schedule and provided solutions to help make his day more tolerable. This was a major difference from our experience with the public school system. She shorted his school hours to half a day. She provided Ross with a "wasp band" that he wore on his wrist to keep wasps away while he was at recess. She gave him permission to go to her office when he was feeling overwhelmed. She allowed him to call me if he felt it was necessary. In all of this, her goal was to keep him at school and engaged as long as possible. She spent time on the phone with me, discussing Ross's behaviors and listening to the feedback I gave her about past experiences. I felt like I was being heard!

I notified Ross's developmental pediatrician of the problems he was continuing to have at school. He

reviewed his file and the information from The Clements Clinic. He felt that based on Ross's behavior and the information from his SPECT scan, we needed to make some adjustments to Ross's medications.

Soon after the change in medication, Ross commented that he was able to go outside without his "wasp band" and was not afraid of wasps as much as he had been. He took our dog out for a walk by himself without his bracelet. He reported, "no tears at school." He did, however, say he got frustrated when he couldn't get the teeth correct on a dinosaur that he was drawing during free time. Overall, his stress level seemed much better. I talked to the principal about his progress. She said, "He is like a different child."

At home, Ross's behavior was improving as well. He seemed to have fewer meltdowns. He laughed more. He transitioned between tasks with greater ease. He had a greater use of his executive function and was thinking ahead more.

SPD (Sensory Processing Disorder)

I cannot stress enough how much the work of Ross's occupational therapist, Judy McCarter, contributed to his success. She provided a great deal of information to help us understand Asperger's Syndrome Disorder, especially in the area of sensory processing disorder.

According to Judy, Dr. Jean Ayres is a pioneer in the field of study of sensory processing disorders. Dr. Ayers defines sensory integration as the neurological process by which sensations are organized and become meaningful. The sensations come by way of auditory, visual, tactile, gustatory, olfactory, vestibular and proprioceptive input. Sensory integration dysfunction occurs when an individual has difficulty interpreting the sensations from the body. An example of this would be walking outside when it was cold but having your body not detect that the temperature was cold.

Sensory processing occurs when the nervous system interprets information from the sensory systems and is able to develop meaningful responses to that information. An example of proper sensory processing would be walking outside when it was cold, being able to process that feeling of being cold and then putting on a coat to warm yourself. Sensory regulation occurs when an individual is able to maintain a calm and focused state in the face of sensory processing.

The study of sensory processing disorders is personal for Judy McCarter, as this is something she admits she struggled with throughout her childhood. It is what drove her to become an occupational therapist, so that she could learn more about this disorder that can seem so subtle to the casual observer, but can be so debilitating to the one suffering from it, causing fear, uncertainty, decreased self-esteem and decreased self-confidence. On the outside, a person suffering from

sensory processing disorders might just appear to be clumsy, apathetic, unmotivated, sloppy, disorganized and not engaged with what is going on in the moment. But on the inside, SPD sufferers are actually fearful, anxious, apprehensive, uncertain and feel like their life is not predictable and that that they have little ability to control anything. These internal feelings are what causes SPD sufferers to react to things they way they do. For example, when something smells too strong or offensive, a SPD sufferer might flee the room and refuse to go back in. It is hard for people without SPD to understand these actions because they can't see, hear, smell or feel the sensations like someone with SPD does.

Think of this hypersensitivity like Superman's X-ray vision. Since individuals with SPD interpret sensory information differently, their perceptions of this sensory information might also be different. Just because we do not interpret things in the same way does not mean that we should not acknowledge that someone else's interpretation is just as real to them. The key is to embrace our differences and our different perspectives. Someone observing a person with a sensory processing disorder may think that they over-react or underreact to their environmental input. The reality is, many people with sensory processing disorders don't feel comfortable in their own skin. Their body feels a little bit "off".

For someone with SPD, their ability to process information can change multiple times within a given day, depending on how irritated their nervous system is from different types of sensory input, how much anxiety or anticipatory anxiety they are dealing with, or how many unpredictable changes have occurred in a given time period. Individuals with sensory processing disorder can improve through treatment and training in strategic compensation. This was the case with Ross. One day, Judy McCarter witnessed Ross standing under a covered picnic area at Town and Country School. He was spinning around, waving his arms and screeching, "Get away wasps!" Judy could tell that Ross wasn't scared—he was terrified. His sense of fear was strong and powerful and it was controlling his ability to function.

When Judy asked the principal about Ross's fears, she said that three teachers had to escort him between buildings to, as Ross put it, help protect him from the wasps. Judy suggested putting some kind of bug deterrent onto Ross to keep the wasps away, such as a sonic device that would emit sonic sounds. The principal purchased a bug band and put it on Ross. That allowed him to travel between buildings without fear.

Over time, Ross and Judy became fast friends and still share a certain kinship with being over responsive or under responsive to sensory stimuli. They both share compromised processing with their vestibular system, which can cause them to become dizzy or sick with

movement such as riding in a car. Ross has difficulty tolerating different textures, crowds and people being too close to him, and he doesn't like to be touched when he is not prepared for the touch. After all of their time together, Judy gave this description of Ross:

> *He is a funny, engaging, sympathetic and delightful young adult. Ross is extremely intuitive and sensitive and has a remarkable ability to produce visual arts and graphics. He continually amazes me with his insight into the way he processes sensory information. Ross is learning strategies to change his sensory regulation to provide tools for life which will help him understand the unique way he integrates his sensory information. It has been a blessing for me to have the opportunity to work with Ross. His individualistic perception is a gift that allows him to be his unique person with his special gifts and talents. It is a joy for me to work with a young man who can verbally articulate how his body is interpreting his sensory information. Ross is a teacher to me and helps me understand different ways that sensory information can be interpreted. He always looks forward to going to therapy or as he calls it "The Fun House."*

Meeting the Principal

Later in the school year, I set up a meeting with Ms. Etier, the Upper School Principal. I wanted to discuss

Ross's progress and learn more about the school. She began our meeting by emphasizing that no two students are alike at Town and Country School. This is actually one of her favorite things about the school. The students are all so unique and possess wonderfully great talents and abilities. Although two students may have the same diagnoses, how those behaviors are manifested differ for each child. She stated that with Asperger's Syndrome, OCD is the most common co-morbid disorder that she has experienced. She said a student will often focus or "obsess" about one thing.

In light of these facts, she said the school strives to make each student feel comfortable and to help students transition from one task to another. How each student responds is as different as the students themselves. Many need visual stimulation to help aid in the process. Teachers are trained on the principles of "Love and Logic."

Ms. Etier said one of the biggest frustrations in her job comes from parents. Some parents are truly wonderful and are realistic about situations, their children, and their abilities. However, that is not the general rule for all. Some parents enable their children, defending and rescuing when it isn't really necessary. The philosophy of Town and Country School is that children need to stand up and experience natural events and consequences and be left to navigate things on their own sometimes, even if they fail. They want their students to be free to learn certain lessons when there

is a safety net to catch them. To this end, the students are empowered to make choices for themselves. When you give them choices, it empowers them and usually the struggle diminishes. As to the success of Asperger's students, they have found that once they are engaged in a lesson, they are usually good students.

One of the most profound things Ms. Etier told me that day was that many teachers judge their success by their ability to control students. She stressed that what a teacher must realize is that controlling students is not the key to being a good teacher. The same principle can be applied to parenting. Just because you can't control your child, it doesn't mean you're not a good parent. If I've learned nothing else, I've learned that when you have a child who has disorders, all the planning and coaching in the world can't stop a meltdown.

Once Ms. Etier briefed me on the overall philosophy and organization of the school, the subject of our conversation then transitioned to Ross specifically. She stated Ross is the first student she has had at the school who is dealing with more than just Asperger's Syndrome or ADD. She said usually the students at the school struggle with the social side of school, like making friends or talking about a specific topic too much, but they don't have too many problems in the classroom.

With Ross's multiple diagnoses, Ms. Etier said she couldn't believe he made it through public school as long as he had. She said the number one complaint she hears most from parents who come to Town and

Country is that, in the public school system, children cannot get the specialized services they need, as all students are treated the same. The most rewarding part of her job is finding solutions for these children when before, others thought there was no hope.

In Ms. Etier's opinion, Ross's anxiety is the most debilitating of his illnesses. Transition is hard for him. With transition, comes anxiety. She witnessed Ross having cycling conversations in his head. He would tell himself he can't do it and would get himself all worked up before he even tried the new task. In his mind, he would convince himself that he can't do it and therefore, the anxiety is there before the new task even begins. She said this wasn't intentional, he just genuinely couldn't get a thought out of his head. When he gets stuck on a thought or an obsession, no amount of reasoning will change his mind!

She noticed that Ross also experiences more grandiose ideas and more of a "save the world" mentality than most of those with Asperger's. She stated she usually doesn't experience the "loss of reality" with most of her other students like she does with Ross.

Even with all of this, the meeting ended on a positive note. Despite all the issues Ross was facing, Ms. Etier said he was one of her most improved students since the beginning of year. I took comfort in the fact that we were seeing progress.

After I met with Ms. Etier, I thought back to our conversation many times. The two things Ms. Etier said that day that made the greatest impression on me were her confirmation that Ross really is a complex individual and her assertion that controlling students isn't the definition of a good teacher, nor is it the definition of a good parent. I'm not advocating doing away with discipline, but if you have a child like Ross and discipline doesn't seem to be a deterrent, it doesn't mean you are a failure as a parent.

I thought long and hard about the issue of control. Before I had Ross, I believed that a good parent was one who could control her children. She would "cut the look" or snap her fingers and the children would obey her requests.

What was revealed to me was that control of others is not a fruit of the Spirit. Nowhere in the Bible have I found that the fruitfulness of God's work in our lives is manifested in our ability to control others! No, we show our fruit by how we relate to our circumstances. Do we exhibit self-control, long suffering, peace and joy? These are evidence of the fruit of the Spirit. What a revelation this was! I cannot control the disorders my son has. I cannot control the reaction that he has to various situations. The only thing that I can control is me. Therefore my success as a parent and as a follower of God cannot be defined by my ability to control my son. What a relief!

14:31

Fourteen minutes and thirty-one seconds I spent on the phone listening to Ross clearly in "stress mode" over an inside recess at school. It was December and cold outside. The school was having an inside recess as opposed to going outside. Ross was upset for several reasons. First, he likes outside recess because he likes to swing. For him, this is a calming mechanism that helps him prepare for the rest of the day. Secondly, he had nothing to do while at inside recess. Just "hanging" with friends was a foreign concept. He needs to be engaged with an activity and idle time has never been a friend of his. Lastly, we had just returned from a vacation to see my family in New Mexico. The long ride in the car and disruption in routine, made him irritable and less flexible than normal. He wanted me to come and pick him up. He was sure a ride home with me and some time doing his favorite things would cheer him up.

The principal had given Ross the option to sit in her office during inside recess and draw or read books, since that's something he usually enjoys. But today, he was locked in a loop! No amount of reasoning was going to change his mind. So I listened patiently. Over and over he told me all the reasons why the principal's option would not work and how I needed to find another alternative for him. Ross was recalcitrant. I reinforced the principal's decision and stated that she was his authority figure and that he had to follow her

instructions. Ross replied, "You are my authority figure and I need you to fix this!" Again, I explained his options and said I would see him at two o'clock.

These sorts of conversations always have me swinging the pendulum in my mind as to the best way to handle Ross. I know how difficult school is for him. Interacting with others and the everyday routine demands are very taxing for him. He is literally drained by the time he gets home. He doesn't want to go anywhere or do much of anything. He likes to settle in on the History Channel, draw, or watch a movie he's seen numerous times. Expecting much more out of him will result in a letdown. He is spent! But the other part of me wants to teach him to problem solve. If he continually escapes his problems, running from the unpleasant feelings, then we will stall progress and his development. I stood firm on my decision to leave him at school. He was able to transition and finish the rest of the day.

Ross completed the year on a successful note. He made friends and, equally as important, he liked going to school. I talked to his teachers at the end of his school year and they all commented on his progress. I received an email from his math teacher the last week of school. Ross took a math test at the beginning of the year. He retook the same test in the spring. His math score almost doubled. Not only was he enjoying school more, he was progressing academically as well.

Keep Your Circle Open

At the end of the school year, we traveled to Texas and New Mexico to visit family. On the way home, I commented to Ross that he had good behavior and I was proud of him. He said he was trying to learn to keep his "circle open." I asked him what he meant by that. He said when your circle is closed, you are not willing to look at your options. If your circle is open, then you look at your options and are more willing to adapt. I liked this analogy. Better yet, I was impressed that he "got it." Now when I am feeling overwhelmed, I remind myself to "keep my circle open."

Ross is now 14 years old. When not at school, he fills his days researching ways to explore the universe. He transports mechanical pencils, a protractor, a ruler and paper most everywhere he goes. He still loves watching television. Science channels are his favorite.

> 10-27-09
>
> Ross P.
>
> Deadra owe Deadra.
> She's as sweet as candy
> and as lovible as a puppy.
> She's as beautiful as a
> flower. She's as cool as the
> North Pole and as hot as the
> Sun.

Ross wrote this poem for me when he was in seventh grade.

CHAPTER THIRTEEN

A Heart Reborn

Dear brothers, is your life full of difficulties and temptations? Then be happy, for when the way is rough, your patience has a chance to grow. So let it grow, and don't try to squirm out of your problems. For when your patience is in full bloom, then you will be ready for anything, strong in character, full and complete.

JAMES 1:2-5 TLB

Webster's New World Dictionary defines *change* as "to put or take a thing in place of something else; to make different." Sometimes we experience change in unlikely places. Sometimes change comes about through pain.

Because of what I have experienced in my life as I've raised my son, I am a changed person. I am a better person. I am so thankful that I have been given the opportunity to live deeper. I now have a compassionate

heart and a tender spirit. I have eyes that see others' pain. The growth I have experienced is not something you can buy. My shallow self and critical spirit are starting to vanish. I have a greater acceptance of others and respect for their differences. I now appreciate and can see that God has created us all, although not all the same. Consider these words God inspired Paul to write:

For I wish that all men were even as I myself. But each one has his own gift from God, one in this manner and another in that.

I CORINTHIANS 7:7 NKJV

Having then gifts differing according to the grace that is given to us, let us use them: if prophecy, let us prophesy in proportion to our faith.

ROMANS 12:6 NKJV

God clearly states in His Word that He has created us all different, so why is being different such a problem? I wish I could answer that question eloquently and with academic finesse, but I can't. However, the best way to approach these differences is what we, as parents, have to learn and teach our children.

I Am Not Skilled to Understand

One Sunday morning at church, the congregation sang a song that really made an impression on me. It went like this....

I am not skilled to understand
What God has willed, what God has planned
I only know at His right hand
Stands One who is my Savior...
(Aaron Shust, "My Savior, My God."
Copyright © 2006 by Bridge Building Music)

Those four lines spoke volumes to me. When we go through a crisis, we seek answers, looking for something to give us hope.

We have to decide to accept God's sovereignty.

I will never know the reasons why I face the challenges in my life that I face. I just know, there is a purpose.

No matter how much effort we put into trying to figure out why something has happened to us, there often is no clear answer. We search for hours wondering "why me" and asking how I can possibly be deserving of these circumstances. We may actually spend most of our lives regretting the choices we've made or simply complaining about our situation. We're frustrated that life isn't going the way we had it planned in our mind. We want immediate gratification and patience is a virtue we seem to overlook. We look for a quick fix or at least something that will make us feel better.

Reasoning doesn't provide us with answers, either. We look around at the proverbial "Neighbor" who looks to have it so much easier and better than we do. We

often fall into a pit of emotions, feeling helpless and exhausted. We become victims of our "unfair circumstances." We bathe in self-pity and excuses. Our "why me" attitude spills over to all areas of our life, leaving us dealing with problems in our personal relationships, careers and with ourselves.

When we go through a trial, it is in these times that we must challenge our present state of being and hopefully learn and grow from our experience. We may believe that we are the ones who need to help others, when in actuality, we may be the ones with the most to learn.

Learning Is a Process

I know how to be abased, and I know how to abound. Everywhere and in all things I have learned both to be full and to be hungry, both to abound and to suffer need.

PHILIPPIANS 4:12 NKJV

To learn... what does that mean? It means that whatever knowledge we have, we are not born with it. Only by experience and maturity do we learn. Learning is an action. In the same way, it's not our circumstances that determine our character, it's our response to those circumstances that defines us!

Paul, Peter and the other apostles learned the secret of developing an eternal perspective in the midst

of earthly problems. They were able to live above their circumstances and rejoice, even while being persecuted, because they had a firm grasp of who they were in Christ and where they were going.

What Ross Has Taught Me About Life

I've learned that life extends beyond "me." I need to be always looking for what I can do to help other people.

I've learned my patience can extend beyond what I thought was possible.

I've learned that no matter how difficult things are, we have to be persistent and not give up. We have to never quit pushing for progress.

I've learned to have a fresh perspective on life and to accept those different from myself.

I've learned that God is always working in my life, whether I see it or not.

I've learned that challenges make us stronger.

I've learned to be more flexible. Things don't always have to be done a certain way, and it's okay.

I've learned to be less critical. There may be circumstances beyond what the eye can see.

I've learned not to worry about the criticism of others, as long as I am true to my own convictions.

I've learned that true satisfaction in life comes from helping others.

I've learned that no matter how hard I try, I can never change someone else.

I've learned God doesn't operate on my timeline.

I have learned I will never be happy if I let circumstances dictate my happiness.

Most of all, I've learned how to feel the deepest love possible!

What I Love About Ross

I love laying on the bed with Ross and watching the movies he likes as he says, "Watch this part Mom, isn't it great?" like it's the first time I've ever seen it.

I love going to Barnes and Noble with Ross and watching him browse through books for hours.

I love listening to the honesty that rolls from Ross's lips and knowing where I stand with him. With him, there are no hidden agendas or false pretenses.

I love watching Ross interact with animals, seeing his gentleness and connection to them.

I love Ross's acceptance of others and his genuine nature.

I love watching Ross draw, seeing his brilliance come alive from the tip of a pencil.

I love how Ross admits his faults so openly.

I love Ross's sense of humor and at the same time, his cluelessness when it comes to jokes.

I love the way Ross lives "out of the box." It's so refreshing for a Type A personality.

I love Ross for who he is. I would never want him to be anything else.

In Conclusion...

Experience produces relative perceptions. Once you face something that is beyond your control, that you cannot fix no matter how hard you try, it is then that you develop humility. Your purpose in life shifts, or at least mine did. My experience has led to a desire to help others. I had always been performance driven until I gave birth to Ross. Through him, I learned I don't have to perform to be accepted. I am okay with being a mom and loving my child.

I have learned the full measure of what is contained in these three words: patience, endurance and faith. Isn't this what Christ asks of us? Even though we don't understand the obstacles of life, He asks that we be patient. And when the answer is not readily available, He asks us to endure and keep the faith as we face

whatever challenges are in our path. I've taken much solace in these words written by Paul:

> Because the foolishness of God is wiser than men, and the weakness of God is stronger than men. For you see your calling, brethren, that not many wise according to the flesh, not many mighty, not many noble, are called. But God has chosen the foolish things of the world to put to shame the wise, and God has chosen the weak things of the world to put to shame the things which are mighty; and the base things of the world and the things that are despised God has chosen, and the things which are not, to bring to nothing the things that are, that no flesh should glory in His presence.
>
> 1 Corinthians 25-29 NKJV

As you come to the close of this book, I wish I could be there to give you a hug. The expressions on our faces would testify to each other silently, without saying a word, the deep emotion that is part of raising a child with a disorder. I know you understand as I do, that the complete sorrow, frustration, and fear that we feel can be overwhelming. I hope that by sharing my story, I have touched a part of your soul, a part that can only be reached by someone with a similar experience.

I know you are exhausted. Maybe it's from holding your breath as you watch your child break every social rule known to man, or from trying to get your child to

stop talking as he engages once again in a monologue about the biggest dinosaur, with an adult who clearly has no interest in what your child has to say. Or maybe your exhaustion stems from the intense anguish you feel when you see other children walking away from your child, rolling their eyes and snickering as your child stands there broken. Maybe the exhaustion comes from frustration as you address the same issues over and over while seeing no improvement. Maybe the fatigue stems from jumping through every hurdle to keep the peace, only to realize there is no peace. Maybe it stems from listening to your child sob uncontrollably as they describe how they just want one friend. Maybe you're exhausted from watching your child melt down over a seemingly trivial issue in public in front of those "perfect parents" who give you "the eye" with laser speed (I know you know the look!), or say to you, "My child never behaves that way."

Maybe your exhaustion stems from listening as your child tells your best friend how dirty her bathroom is. Maybe the exhaustion is a result of the fear we feel when we hear the daunting news, "We don't know what causes your child's problems and, well, there is no cure."

Hope—isn't that all we really want? Hope that better days are ahead and that the struggles that our child faces will vanish and that one day, the overwhelming feelings will dissipate. We have given up on finding a miraculous cure and now hope is what keeps

us going. Sometimes all you need to find that hope is just someone to tell you it can and will get better.

Winning Endurance

You have to make up your mind! As a parent of a child with a disorder, you have to make up your mind to persevere. You have to have tenacity, because you will be tried over and over again. Take heart as you read these words from God written just for you.

He who earnestly seeks good finds favor.

PROVERBS 11:27 NKJV

Anxiety in the heart of man causes depression, but a good word makes it glad.

PROVERBS 12:25 NKJV

And do not be conformed to this world, but be transformed by the renewing of your mind, that you may prove what is that good and acceptable and perfect will of God.

ROMANS 12:2 NKJV

The things which you learned and received and heard and saw in me, these do, and the God of peace will be with you.

PHILIPPIANS 4:9 NKJV

CHAPTER FOURTEEN

Ross's Classics

As any parent knows, there are moments in your child's life that will remain in your memory forever. I wanted to share with you some of Ross's classic moments.

Age 5:

Ross had Ms. Shade in K-4. Ms. Shade must have been a very special teacher, as this was Ross's comment when he saw Ms. Shade: "When I see Ms. Shade, she makes my heart glow."

Age 9:

We had a red bird that kept flying into our window. Ross said, "You flying Red Bird of Death, quit hitting our window!"

Age 10:

Ross: "Grandma, will you cut up my cinnamon roll?"

Grandma: "Ross, I'm sure you can do it."

Ross: "But Grandma, I don't want to. It's a waste of time. I'm sure it will take me six or five minutes. I could be watching TV during that time."

Age 11:

The nurse at the pediatrician's office asked if Ross had had any major illnesses or surgeries, to which I replied "No." Ross said, "Excuse me, but I just was sick last week and it was torture to my buttocks." Later, when they checked his private area, he turned to me and said, "Oh, isn't this lovely."

One day, Ross said to me, "Mom, you look beautiful." I replied, "Why, thank you, Ross." Then he continued, "But, not so good when you wake up in the morning. But after you put your make-up on and do your hair and wear that one black shirt, then you look beautiful."

One day, Ross went off on his inability to ride a bike: "Why can't I ride a bike? It's not fair. Why can't I ride a bike? I've been doing this for ten or nine days and I still can't do this. Rhett can do it and he's four years younger than me. It's not fair." The truth is, Ross couldn't really care less if he rides a bike. He would rather be inside watching the Science Channel and building something with Legos. To him, sports are boring and a waste of time and he doesn't understand why anyone would want to exert that much energy!

Ross's reflection on getting old: "I don't want to get older because I don't want to get two chins."

Age 12:

This dialogue took place one day while Ross was at the table, eating.

Ross: *Burp*

Me: "Ross, don't burp like that. And say excuse me."

Ross: "Well, I had to burp; if I keep it in, it will turn to a fart."

Me: "Honey, don't say fart at the table."

Ross: "Why? What do you want me to say? A giant bubble coming out my behind?"

I tried to prepare and coach Ross before social situations in which I knew someone was going to be present with a situation or condition I did not want him to discuss. Ross lacked any sense of social decorum. In one instance, a friend and his girlfriend were coming over for dinner. The friend had lost his eye in an accident and had an artificial eye, which was very obvious. I explained to Ross that even though something is obvious, it doesn't mean it's acceptable to ask about it. Under normal circumstances, Ross would just ask question after question about how the eye had been lost. Something along the lines of, "Did it hurt? What were you doing? Did you call for help? You know you don't look so good? That fake eye makes you look weird." Ross agreed not to question our friend about his eye.

When the friend and his girlfriend arrived, Ross looked at him but didn't say anything about his eye. Later that night, Ross asked, "Are the two of you married?"

Our friend replied, "No."

"Are you going to be married?"

"Well, we're not for sure."

"Well, it could be that eye she's worried about."

In December 2007, we were in an ice storm and lost electricity for almost a week. While we were concerned about heat and the essentials, all Ross cared about was how many minutes it would be until his TV came back on. When we said our prayers that night, he told his brother to make sure and don't forget to pray for the cable.

Ross: "Mom?"

Me: "Yes, Ross."

Ross: "You know, I heard on the radio that people are getting electricity rage."

Me: "Really?"

Ross: "I think I'm getting that."

Me: "Why do you think that?"

Ross: "Because ever since I woke up this morning, I've been on my dark side."

I recently took Ross and his younger brother, Rhett, to play racquetball. Ross seemed to be interested in the sport and since he avoids all other physical activity like the plague, I thought we would give it a try. About halfway through our hour of court rental time, Ross decided he wanted a drink. I told him I had brought water and that it was in the gym bag. He told me the water wasn't cold enough so he didn't want it. I then told him there was money in the bag and he could go and get a Gatorade out of the vending machine. He came back crying, saying the vending machine took his money and didn't work. I told him as soon as I finished, which would be in about 10 minutes, that I would get him a drink.

As we were leaving, Rhett thanked me for bringing them to play and said he had had a good time. Ross then became upset again. He said, "I didn't have as much fun as I thought I would have. I was thirsty and wanted a drink."

I said, "If you were that thirsty, you could have walked down and got a drink out of the water fountain."

"What!" he said. "I didn't know they had water fountains. Stupid, stupid me! Ugh, that makes me so mad!" To most people, this seems like a trivial issue—just go and get a drink. But for the Asperger's child, the old adage of making a mountain out of a molehill applies. The rigidity of their thought process seems to overrule any amount of logic you try to convey.

Ross's comments on his memory: "I don't know why I can't remember things. My brain just kicks it out. I can't get everything in my head like I want it to be. I like for things to fit right in that place in my mind."

Ross on the importance of his dog: "Jackie (our Shihtzu dog) is the most important to me besides family. My life would be ruined if Jackie died. I would never smile again."

Ross on breath: "I don't like the smell of breath. Not of anyone. Not even after they brush their teeth. I hold my breath as long as I can. I don't like people close to me."

Ross: "Mom?"

Me: "Yes, Ross."

Ross: "I like it when the wind blows."

Me: "You do, why is that?"

Ross: "Because the trees talk."

Ross's comments on my work schedule (I worked two jobs): "Why do you work two jobs? For Pete's sake, you are a working woman of madness."

Ross, on familiarity: "I like using the same things over and over. I like sitting in the same place. I don't feel comfortable sitting in another desk or place from where I sit."

Ross, on dressing for church: "I don't like church shirts...feel too fancy."

Age 13:

Ross's explanation of how it feels for someone with OCD to be stuck on a thought: "I can't help it. It's like bobbing itself out—like the biggest star in the sky."

One day Ross asked me a question, to which I gave him my honest answer. He said, "Thanks, Mom," in a sarcastic voice, to which I replied, "You asked me to tell you the truth." Ross said, "No, I meant, I wanted the positive truth!"

One day Ross was disrespectful to me. I called him on his behavior. His reply was, "I'm sorry. I'm nothing better than a two-faced jackal."

Ross had to complete a project for school in which he had to read a book about a character and do a book report. In the report, he was asked to pick out ten key items in the story and answer the following question: "If you could meet your character today, do you think you would be friends? Why or why not?"

This was Ross's response:

The reason I think Abraham Lincoln and I would get along is because we're both smart. We also love to read. The book says that he read a book every chance he had. I love to read non-fiction books with lots of good pictures and a lot of information and data.

We're both kind and gentle natured. Although I have the tendency to be a little self-centered, I

have a great heart and I love my family members, friends, God, and Jesus.

We both had obstacles to overcome when we were children. For instance, when I was a child, I had only two friends, and he had a family death crisis to overcome. But look at us now. I have a lot of outstanding friends and Lincoln became the president.

We're both interested in the government and other people. We also like to help others in need. As president, he influenced many people and I intend to help a lot of people when I grow up too.

Ross had a recurring episode with the flu, which included diarrhea, which he absolutely hates. After about three trips to the restroom, he turned to me and said, "I'm not going to take this anymore." Later on that day, he told me how bad his bottom was hurting. I responded with, "Bless your heart." He said, "No Mom, it's not my heart that hurts, it's my bottom."

Ross had a severe fear of wasps. One day there was a wasp near us and I killed it. Ross said,"Are you sure you killed it? Are you sure you pierced the exoskeleton?"

Ross told me recently that if he ever had to move away from me, that he would starve. I asked what he meant. He said, "I get scared of the dark and it paralyzes me. I'm afraid I would never leave my room and be able to walk to the kitchen in the dark. It doesn't

even have to be dark inside. If the sun is down, there is no safe territory."

Ross on "getting stuck": "When I get stuck and I really want to do something and I can't, it's like a blood sucking leech glued to my head—no, hot glued to my head...it's painful. It's like friction on top of my brain when I want something. It's like pushing down right on top of my head."

Ross: "Mom?"

Me: "Yes, Ross."

Ross: "Look at the sun. It's like a mystical orb hovering in the sky."

In the Spring of 2010, when Ross was 14, we had to make a trip to the doctor. Ross was sick and we thought he had strep throat. I have a hard time convincing him to go to the doctor because of his fear of shots. He made me promise, triple swear, and then promise again that he would only get a shot if it was a life or death situation. Once we got to the doctor's office, there were masks available on the counter if someone had a fear of germs or spreading germs. Of course, we both wore one at Ross's request.

When the doctor took a look at Ross's throat, she said we needed to test for strep. This involved swabbing the back of his throat. Now, based on what has been discussed in this book, exactly how easy do you think it's going to be to stick a Q-tip on Ross's tonsil?

You are exactly right! First he was trying to convince the nurse that he could cough in his hand, and they could test the bacteria in his hand. When that didn't work, he said he thought he would throw up. So here I was, holding a trashcan up to Ross's mouth, trying to convince him that this is the only way for them to get what they need for the strep test. Every time he would open his mouth and stick his tongue out, the very minute the nurse got the Q-tip in his mouth, down went his jaw muscles. This image is quite amusing if you're reading about it in a book, but if you're living this moment, it's not so funny!

Ross: "The stupid curiosity of the cat did get it killed."

Ross: "Even when you think you have me figured out, you still haven't."

One day school was cancelled because of inclement weather. On this day, the wind was blowing hard. Ross commented, "Beefiness does have its advantages."

Ross had another school day that was cancelled because of bad weather. We had already left the house for school when we heard about the cancellation so Ross asked if we could go to McDonald's. As we entered the parking lot, he started talking about the smell of McDonald's and how good the smell was. As we pulled up to the drive-through window, he said, "Wow, I'm getting a little too pumped up over a cinnamon melt."

CHAPTER FIFTEEN

Family Sentiments

Raising a child with special needs affects everyone in the family. Here are the insights of two other members of the family who have loved Ross and persevered with him through the years.

My First Grandchild
(Judy Little, Ross's Grandma)

Ross was my first grandchild. Dee had some trouble with the pregnancy and we prayed fervently for this child. My, what a blessing he has been. I was the first one to hold Ross because they took Dee for some minor surgery after he was born. Ross was a fussy baby and we just thought he had colic. He was inconsolable and nursing him seemed the only way to calm him down. Dee had very little sleep during those early days and we had no clue as to what was ahead.

As Ross became older, he would line up all his animals in a row and if one was ever switched, he would notice it immediately. He became obsessed with dinosaurs. He knew every kind, how much they weighed, and what they ate. He has drawn some very excellent pictures of them. He has a photographic memory and can draw something he has seen on television.

Ross has always loved to come to our house in the summer. Since he had separation anxiety when he was away from his mother, we felt honored that he felt comfortable with us. He has always been close to his Pepaw, Lonnie, my husband. Lonnie would get in the floor and play with Ross for hours. The last time we visited, Ross said, "Pepaw, I love you." Dee said that doesn't happen very often.

When Ross was about seven, he asked my mom, "What are those lines on your face?" She said that when you get older, you get wrinkles. He said, "How old are you anyway?" Ross has trouble knowing what could hurt someone's feelings. He is just brutally honest.

Nothing is ever easy with Ross, but now that we better understand his disability, it is easier to cope with. I met Dee and Ross in Dallas and took him to Dr. Clements. He had to be off of his medications for several days so they could test his brain. In the motel room, he would run and jump on the bed then he would get in the swivel chair and go round and round. He was jumping off the sofa when the phone rang and the front desk said the people under us were complaining about

the noise. He was out of control. The next day at the doctor's office, he was sitting backward in the chair, banging his head on the wall! Some people have been critical of the decision to put Ross on medicine, but I think the medication has been a God-send.

At Dr. Clements' office, they had to put in an IV so the medicine would show what was going on in Ross's brain. What an ordeal! Like I said, nothing is ever easy with Ross. Now I don't mean to paint a bleak picture. Ross is unique and wonderful. He has kept Dee and I laughing at the funny things he says. Like the time when Dee and Ross were at the cosmetics counter and the sales lady said to Ross, "You are so handsome, would you like to be my boyfriend?" He looked at her and said, "You do realize there is an age difference here!"

I do want to applaud my daughter. She has been very proactive in finding help for Ross. She has read countless books and taken him to the best doctors she could find. She has been so patient and loving to Ross. He thinks the sun and moon rise just for her. Ross is extremely intelligent and I think his dream of saving the world will come true.

Sibling Rivalry
(Rhett Phillips, Ross's 10-year-old brother)

Being Ross's brother is hard. He is frustrating and expects me to do things for him. He won't look for

things on his own. I have to be the flexible one. I review his countless drawings and play the games he wants to play. But when it's my turn to play a game I want, he says he is too tired. He wants people to do things for him, but he's not so good at giving back to others. He talks a lot. He goes on and on about a topic. Sometimes it's hard to get my turn to talk. I feel like Ross gets attention because he is more difficult. He makes me so mad sometimes. I just want him to be fair.

Although he is difficult, I love him a ton. I love him. I love him. I love him. I enjoy hanging around him. I appreciate his efforts to do stuff. I like it when he wrestles with me. I have liked it for as long as I can remember. Mom has pictures of us wrestling when I was real little. He can be generous. He gave me a cell phone. He will give me money if he has it, to buy whatever I want.

I have learned a lot about science and animals, like dinosaurs, Big Foot and The Loch Ness Monster. Ross knows so much about that stuff. It is hard for me to deal with him when he is not reasonable. I have learned to be more patient. I will stand up for kids that are being bullied. I have learned to eat the food while it's there, cause Ross will suck it up like a vacuum.

My mom helps me out with Ross. She gives me a lot of attention and snuggles with me when we watch football and our favorite movies. She is always there for me when I need her. She will take time for me. I like little things she does for me the most. I like it when all of our

family does things together. It's the smallest things I like the best.

§

If you suspect your child has a disorder, the following is a list of items that can assist you in confirming your suspicions and following through on getting your child the help they need. I often wondered why someone didn't give me a list that said, "If you have a child with Asperger's or ADHD, do the following...." I searched for information and found valuable tools in different information and books, but I often wondered why someone hadn't developed something comprehensive.

Not all items on this checklist will be relevant to all children. My goal is to provide you with a list of items to investigate to determine the items that best suit your situation. I've often felt like a turtle in the road, laying on my back and struggling with all my might to turn over and find the right path. I will say this sternly—*you are the best advocate for your child.* No one wants the best for your child more than you do. There isn't going to be anyone who will pay attention to the details like you will. When you have a child with a special need, that is exactly what it is—a special need. Many teachers and educators have limited knowledge, at best, concerning the challenges your child faces. You have to be the one who interfaces for your child. Some may label this as the "squeaky wheel syndrome," in other words, the one who makes the

most noise is the one who gets the attention. It must be clear to educators, doctors, therapists, counselors, and everyone else involved that you are interested in your child's success and that you are holding them accountable for their part.

1. See a Developmental Pediatrician.

2. Consult an Occupational Therapist to help identify sensory issues.

3. Consult an allergist.

4. Consider physical therapy.

5. Enlist the assistance of a Speech Pathologist.

6. Consider securing a SPECT Scan.

7. Ask your doctor about supplements such as Omega 3.

8. Research, research, research. Remember, knowledge is power.

9. Determine if your child qualifies for an IEP (Individual Education Program). For more information, visit http://idea.ed.gov.

10. Develop a relationship with your child's school counselor.

11. Meet with your child's teachers and develop relationships.

12. Educate your child's teachers on the best methods to use with your child.

13. Determine if your child qualifies for classroom support.

14. Research schools that specialize in serving kids with Asperger's Syndrome and ADHD.

15. Explore Music Therapy.

16. Encourage exercise.

17. Pay attention to your child's diet and nutrition.

18. Join a Social Skills Group.

19. Lava Lamps, weighted blankets, and swings can be very soothing.

20. Consider brushing and massage therapy.

21. Formulate your own list of calming procedures before bed.

22. Give your child positive reinforcement.

23. Formulate written routines.

24. Remove clutter from your home to maintain organization.

25. Learn to prepare your child for upcoming situations.

26. Surround yourself with positive affirmations.

27. Pick your battles.

28. Learn to relax.

29. Find humor in everyday life.

30. Look for the brilliant characteristics of your child.

31. Provide unconditional love.

32. Set boundaries and let your child know what you expect.

33. Remember that God has given this child to you for a reason. Seize the opportunity.

William Ross Phillips's Birthday Condition Wish List

There must be that white cake I love so much.

It must be at Mazzios.

We must invite all my class mates.

There must be balloons.

There must be all my presents at the party.

Everyone has to have a great time.

There must be 14 candles on the cake.

I also want Mazzios customers to sing me the happy birthday song.

Ross created this list for me in preparation for celebrating his 14th birthday.

Ross and Rhett Phillips. June 2011.
Courtesy of TG Photography. www.tgphotographybytrisha.com

Ross with his father, Phil Phillips.

Ross was obsessed with going to dig for diamonds
even though it was brutally hot. We succumbed to his wishes,
only to have him declare it was a "death trap."

Ross has always had a fascination with aliens. This picture was
taken in 2007 in Roswell, NM at the International UFO Museum.

Dear President Obama,

I have a plan to see if there's life out in our universe. I
know I have the technology to do it. But I don't have the
money, but my plan I mentioned about earlier. My plan is a
way to make a lot of money for the program. I'm William
Ross Phillips. But everyone just calls me Ross. I'm thirteen
years old. I live in Owasso, Oklahoma in Timber Gate. My
address is 18894 East 80th St North. Here's my plan. First,
we'll set up funding programs. Since two thirds of the
world believes in aliens, we'll get enough money in a year
or two. Second, we'll build my design. Next, we'll check
for flaws in my design. Then, we'll fix my flaws in my
design. After that, we'll test my design. Finally, we'll shoot
into space and come back in a month or two. Send back a
letter and say if you accept my plan or not. If you accept, in
your letter, tell where we will discus my plan If you accept
my letter, I'll tell you a way to make pure energy with no
waste deposits. A.K.A: A way to make pure energy with no
waste. I'll trough in that information for free, If you accept
my letter.

By William Ross Phillips

This letter is a great example of the way Ross's mind works.
Ross assumes everyone is as fascinated with aliens as he is.

All that my mom does that I'm thankful for

: = I'm thankful...

: that my mom is there every day to protect me.

: that she puts up with me for most of her life.

: that my mom has the largest heart, besides God and Jesus.

: that my mom makes me food for my hungry belly.

: that she loves me.

: that she is there when I need her the most, and when I just need something small.

: that she pays attention to me.

: that she makes me sweets.

: that she will be there for a long time.

: that she is beautiful and cute.

: that she also teaches me about Christianity.

William Ross Phillips

Ross gave this to me for Mother's Day this year.
This was one of my best gifts ever!

The Light Paradox   *2-13-11*   **By William Ross Phillips**

Mass is how big an object is in relationship to its **Weight**. So, that means, in simpler terms, that the larger an object, the bigger it's **Mass**. **Density** involves some. That means **Light** shouldn't exist, because, it's **Massless**. Is **Light** a **Paradox**?

A **Paradox** is an apparent contradiction in physical descriptions of the **Universe**. in other words, if you went back in time, in a time machine, and killed your grandfather; how could have you been born, and therefore, traveled back in time to kill him? The time machine just wouldn't work. The **Universe** just finds ways to prevents **Paradoxes**, every time. Then again, maybe not.

What if **Light's a Paradox**? If it was a **Paradox**, which being **Massless** should make you a **Paradox**, then why does **Light** exist? Does this mean that **Paradoxes** can exist, thus proving the **Multiverse Theory**? Probably. Here below is the new science info on the **Universe**.

- Light is a Paradox
- The Multiverse Theory should be true

Ross is regularly forming theories and attempts to explain them to me.
I listen, although I'm embarrassed to say, it really doesn't register.

ABOUT THE AUTHOR

In addition to being a mom to her two sons, Dee Phillips-Goodnight teaches high school at Tulsa's East Central High School, where she is passionate about educating her students. She also sells Real Estate for Chinowth and Cohen Realtors.

Dee knows that it is only through the strength of Christ that she has the ability to do what she does. She has a compassionate and caring spirit that is a direct result of the adversity she has faced in life.

Ross continues to go to school at Town and Country School in Tulsa. He hopes to graduate and go to college to study aerospace engineering. He says he will never give up on his dream to "Save the World." He has a deep desire to contribute to making the world a better place. Every day is a challenge for him, but he is diligent in his efforts. He hopes to someday be able to help other children who face the same struggles he faces.

www.mysilentscream.org